MW01278095

PASSION BEACH

Passion Beach

Carol Anderson

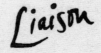

First published in Great Britain in 1998
by HEADLINE BOOK PUBLISHING

A HEADLINE LIAISON paperback

10 9 8 7 6 5 4 3 2 1

ISBN 0 7472 6037 0

Typeset by CBS, Felixstowe, Suffolk

Printed and bound in Great Britain by
Mackays of Chatham plc, Chatham, Kent

HEADLINE BOOK PUBLISHING
A division of Hodder Headline PLC
338 Euston Road
London NW1 3BH

Passion Beach

Chapter 1

Belle O'Malley glanced around the luxurious interior of the wooden cabin before closing the door. Outside, swinging in the hammock on the veranda, Eva grinned. 'So, what time is she arriving?'

'After dark. You remember what I told you?'

Eva waved her anxiety away. 'Oh, come on, Belle, we all know it by heart. Keep our clothes on in public, no screwing clients in the foyer. Give us a break – we're not stupid.'

Belle, not really listening, sighed. 'I wonder if I should have met Laura in Sydney after all.'

Eva shrugged. 'Too late now, darling. She's already on her way here. Are you sure you'll be able to keep business under wraps?'

'I can't see why not. Leo is going to take her out and about. I thought we might go down to Cairns for a few days – sail out to the Barrier Reef, take a trip into the outback. All the usual tourist places. It'll be just fine. And she's only here for a month.'

'You don't sound very convinced.' Eva glanced down at her Cartier watch. 'Gotta go, Zac Sherman is booked in for a little late afternoon pleasure. See you later.'

Lazily, she uncurled herself from the hammock. Nearly six feet tall, Eva had a face that would have inspired the Old Masters – and a body to match. Unselfconsciously, she straightened her tiny white silk chemise. Pulled down it still barely covered her shapely, sun-tanned thighs. She twisted her thick blonde hair up into a knot and padded barefoot across the boardwalk towards the main hotel.

Belle O'Malley watched her go; hips swaying provocatively from side to side, Eva was one of her best

1

girls, on a year's sabbatical between her degree and her PhD. Eva exuded sexual promise from every pore. It might not be as easy as Belle hoped to keep the true nature of O'Malley's Hotel from her niece, Laura, but she intended to try.

Laura Carter glanced back over her shoulder. Leo's truck was parked up against the verge, headlights full on, insects dancing a tango in the yellow beams. The long drive up from Cairns in the truck's air-conditioned cab hadn't prepared her for the humidity in the rainforest.

She pushed a strand of hair back from her face; it felt as if she had been travelling forever. The thin cotton dress she was wearing clung to her like an eager lover, beads of sweat trickling into the valley between her small, pert breasts. Leo waved her on to a path cut amongst the trees.

Just a few yards from the road the glow from the headlights was cut off by the dense foliage. The darkness was so intense it seemed almost alive. Grateful that Leo had a torch, Laura glanced up and caught a glimpse of the Southern Cross between the leaves of rainforest canopy. Despite the heat, she shivered, feeling far from home under unfamiliar stars.

The noise of the rainforest – the tree frogs and insects – was so loud that she couldn't hear her own footfalls on the metalled path. Leo, holding the torch, turned towards her, pointing out a railed viewing-point.

'Thought you'd like to take a look. This is Bayman's Lookout; they bring all the tourists up here. You can see the hotel.' With a flick of a switch they were plunged into darkness.

As her eyes adjusted Laura could see, far below them on the rocky promontory, a string of twinkling lights reflected in the rolling ocean beyond. The night was so dark and clear that it seemed as if she could lean forward and touch them.

Leo, close by but invisible in the gloom, whispered. 'Amazing, isn't it? What a view. O'Malley's was built by some of the first people to settle up here. Christ, the times we've had in that place.'

2

Laura nodded dumbly. She was exhausted, her whole body ached after the long flight from Heathrow. The last thirty-odd hours of her life felt as if they had been rearranged into a series of fragmented, unrelated slides.

She forced a smile. 'It's wonderful. Look, I'm really tired, Leo. Will it be much longer before we get there?'

Leo flicked the torch back on. 'Not far now.'

Laura smiled philosophically; it had taken them four hours so far, driving out across sugar cane fields on the great flood plain around Cairns, past the holiday resorts strung out along the Cook Highway, crossing the Daintree River on the ferry and then slowly making the long and treacherous journey up through the Alexander Ranges. The narrow road was bounded on either side by an unbroken expanse of tropical rainforest. It seemed that 'not far' was as much in the eye of the beholder as beauty.

Leo was good company though. She wondered why it was he'd tied himself so tight to her aunt, Belle O'Malley. Belle must be over fifty, while Leo could be no more than thirty with lean, muscular sun-tanned limbs, his vigour emphasised by faded denim shorts, heavy walking boots and a white tee shirt. Under a weather-beaten bush hat his face was framed by dark hair pulled back into a pony-tail.

It would be very easy to imagine herself folded into those strong brown arms, easy to imagine the heat of his body as he drove his cock deep inside her. The snippet of fantasy took Laura completely by surprise. She shook her head to clear it and hastily turned away.

Leo grinned and she wondered if he had seen the flash of desire in her eyes. He indicated the path, shepherding Laura back out through the velvety night.

Climbing into the truck Laura snapped on her seat belt, relieved to be back on the road. Leo slid into the driving seat and pulled out a bottle of water from a cooler box under the dashboard. After taking a hefty swig, he wiped the top and handed it over. Thirstily, Laura took a long pull.

'Get into the habit,' he said, gunning the engine into life. 'Around here everyone carries water – you can dehydrate quicker 'n hell. You need water, insect repellent, sun block

3

and a hat.' He laughed as the truck pulled back onto the road. 'Welcome to Australia.'

Laura smiled and let silence embrace them. Coming to Australia was the dream of a lifetime. She'd worked like crazy to get the money together for the trip, alongside taking a course in business management that would give her a new career when she went home. Her visit to Belle's hotel was a rite of passage. It had taken her three years working at nights to raise the airfare.

Ahead of them the road snaked back and forth; the treescape was relentless.

'How far is it now?'

Leo shrugged. 'Not far. Why? Not pining for company already, are you?'

Laura laughed, settling herself back into the seat. She already felt comfortable with Leo. 'No, not really. I was thinking more about finally meeting Belle after all these years – and a soft bed, a hot meal and a cold shower.'

'Not missing your man?'

Laura stared out into the darkness. Her boyfriend, Gareth, was twelve thousand miles away. She glanced at her watch. He would still be having his lunch, straightening his tie, carefully folding a serviette into a smaller and smaller triangle while deciding whether he could allow himself a slice of cheese cake. It had never seriously crossed her mind to invite him along on the trip.

'He's not really the adventurous type,' she said flatly. 'And he would have had trouble getting time off work.'

'Right. So what are you, married, engaged, living together?' Leo glanced across at her.

She could see something dark and sensual in his eyes and hastily looked away. 'No.' She stopped, gathering her thoughts. 'It's hard to explain. I've been going out with him for years but . . . the words dried in her throat as they swung round a sharp left-hand bend. In the distance, set against the oily silk of the Coral Sea and a star-kissed black sky was the row of bobbing lights.

'There you go,' said Leo triumphantly, 'told you it wasn't far, didn't I?' He grinned. 'So about this man of yours –

maybe you aren't ready to settle down yet?'

If only it was that simple. Before she could reply, the truck lumped down heavily into a pothole, throwing Laura towards Leo. As if orchestrated he caught her, arm tight around her shoulders. She gasped. He smelt of sun and sweat, mingled with aftershave.

'Whoa,' he said, though she noticed he hadn't let go of her. 'Sorry about that, this track is a complete bastard. During the wet season the floods wash the surface away. A couple of days' rain and the ballast they repair it with shifts.'

It didn't really matter what he was saying, she wasn't listening. She was so close she could hear his heart beating through his tee shirt. As she shifted back into her seat he kept his arm around her and she didn't resist or move it, instead she let her body relax, relishing the sensation of physical closeness.

He kissed the top of her head, lips brushing her hair. 'Not feeling lonely already are you?'

Laura shivered, feeling a pulse of sexual tension arc between them. She chose not to answer; it was as if Leo had read her thoughts.

'Come on, Belle's waiting.'

A minute or two later the truck pulled up outside the main entrance to the hotel. Laura climbed stiffly out of the passenger seat and looked up in astonishment.

Constructed from native wood, the hotel and restaurant clung to the very fringes of the beach. It was built on great balks of timber, lifting it up above the coral sand. Laura smiled. O'Malley's looked, for all the world, like a wedding cake, trimmed with a decorative web of balconies, fretwork and intricate wrought-iron balustrades. Beautifully lit, it seemed an incongruous outpost of European civilisation in a tropical wilderness.

The smell of a barbecue, carried on the sea breeze, made Laura's mouth water. Leo took her arm and guided her up the steps to the main entrance.

Inside, chandeliers hung in the vaulted ceilings alongside the overhead fans. The blades chopped the tropical night into hot damp breaths, each rotation making the crystals around the lights ripple and tinkle.

The foyer was boarded out with dark, shiny red wood, the parameters of the large room marked by the reception desk ahead of her, and double doors on each of the remaining sides. Chesterfield sofas, carver chairs and tables formed conversational groups, and a sprinkling of guests carried on with their conversation as Laura and Leo crossed the room.

Beside the reception desk a wide open-tread staircase led to the upper floors, its details masked in shadow. Out beyond the windows and the fly screens the night was already as black as Whitby jet.

Before they had chance to ring the bell, Belle O'Malley appeared from behind the reception area, her expression one of sheer joy. Laura would have known her anywhere; her handsome face was an older version of her own.

Belle grinned and stepped forward with her arms open.

'Laura! At last! Belle's arms folded round her, and Laura felt relief flood through her; the tension and anxiety of the long, long journey draining away.

'Oh, Belle, it's so lovely to see you.'

After a second or two Belle held her at arm's length, examining her face. Her eyes were bright with emotion. 'You look so much like your mother. How is she? I've got you a room all ready. Oh God, there's so much I want to ask you – how was the journey?'

Grabbing her suitcase from Leo, Belle – talking nineteen to the dozen – led Laura out to a wooden cabin joined to the main building by a covered walkway. They left Leo at the bar, cradling a cool beer.

'You know,' said Belle dropping her bags at the end of the bed. 'I can't believe you're really here. Help yourself to whatever you need: towels, cold drinks in the fridge, just make yourself at home. I thought you'd be better out here – it's far more private, less noise.'

Laura smiled. 'Maybe I could give you a hand while I'm here. Earn my keep?'

Bella laughed and waved the offer away. 'Don't be silly. You're on holiday. If you can't find what you need pick up the phone. I've lit a mozzie coil, the little blighters love new

6

blood.' She indicated a wisp of smoke coming up from what looked like a giant spiral joss stick in a flat tin on the floor. 'And I've hung a mosquito net. Oh, and I've organised one of the jeeps for you.'

Laura smiled, touched by her generosity. 'Thank you so much, I really appreciate this.'

Belle reddened. 'Don't be ridiculous. You're family. It's just so good to see you. Look, I'll let you get settled in, grab a shower, unpack, and then we'll catch up.' She hesitated in the doorway for a few seconds, eyes moist with tears; the silence broken only by the whirr of the overhead fan. 'I'm so glad you came. Dinner will be ready in about an hour. All right? My chef, Tom, cooks the best Barra Mundi and prawns on the Barbary Coast. Have you ever eaten Barra Mundi?'

Laura shook her head.

Belle grinned. 'Time you did then.'

As soon as Belle closed the door Laura slumped down on the bed, exhaustion creeping over her like a warm blanket. It was tempting just to lay down and sleep, instead she pulled a wash bag out of her holdall and headed off to the shower.

Closing the bathroom door, she discarded her clothes onto the cool white tiles and stepped under the torrent of icy water; it was bliss. She ran her hand over her body, relishing the sensation of the water as it coursed down over her. Every bone, every muscle in her body ached.

The memory of Leo's arm around her shoulders, the feeling of his body close to hers replayed in her mind. She smiled, soaping her breasts, teasing her taut pink nipples until they stiffened under her finger tips. Maybe when she got to know him a little better she might take him up on his unspoken invitation. To her surprise the idea took flight.

She imagined Leo's lean sun-tanned body pressing against her, his muscular frame a sharp contrast to her own slim body. He would lean forward and kiss her furiously, tongue seeking entry, lips working against hers, hands gliding down over her narrow waist and broad hips, pulling her close to him.

She could almost feel her breasts pressing against the

7

soft covering of curls on his chest. Slowly, he would sink to the floor, kissing her nipples, her ribs, her belly, his tongue outlining the contours of her navel.

Laura shivered, fingers tracing Leo's imaginary journey. As she parted the soft contours of her sex she was stunned to discover how wet she was, her body ready for the attentions of her fantasy lover. One finger glided inside, whilst with her other hand she circled the engorged ridge of her clitoris. The first brush against its sensitive hood sent a lightning bolt of pleasure through her body. Her sex tightened instinctively around her exploring finger, drawing her in deeper. She began to stroke rhythmically at her pleasure bud, oblivious to the water now, her mind suffused with images of Leo's tongue and fingers working their magic on her body. She thrust forward, milking the sensation as her mind and body were consumed by a white hot cascade of pleasure.

Gasping she slumped forward, head resting against the wet tiles while she caught her breath. The raw sensual hunger in her belly surprised her. In all the years she had known him her boyfriend, Gareth, had never made her feel like this.

Later wrapped in a towel she took a can of beer from the fridge and headed out onto the veranda at the back of the cabin; it looked out over a beach and she could make out the white ribbon of the water's edge lapping at the coral. It took her breath away.

Leaning against the handrail, Laura tried to take stock of what was happening to her. She glanced around, as if someone might be able to see her or sense her need. The tropical heat had already lifted a sheen of sweat on her shoulders and face, igniting a pulse in her stomach as wild and uninhibited as the landscape.

She took a long pull on the beer and the alcohol moved mischievously through her bloodstream. She was hungry and the beer made her more so.

Around her the noises of the forest beat out a steady counterpoint to the rhythm of her heart. Staring out towards the ocean she felt desperately alone.

In a secluded corner of the hotel gardens, Leo stepped up onto another veranda, his handsome features caught in sharp relief.

A girl, idling in the shadows, looked up and met his gaze.

He smiled and lifted a can of beer in salute. 'Great view. I thought you might like a little company.'

Eva grinned. The air crackled with expectation. 'Done baby-sitting? You must be a mind reader. I was just feeling a long way from home. Care to join me?'

The next few seconds seemed to take an eternity, both of them frozen like statues, eyes locked in an electric gaze before without a word, they stepped into each others' arms. An instant later Eva's lips were on his. Beneath his palms, Leo could feel the smooth, tight muscles of her back. She pressed against him; he could feel the heat of her body and the frantic beat of her heart. Her kisses were tender but insistent, her tongue begging entry as his arms encircled her. He groaned, feeling her whole body respond to his touch.

His tongue eased between her open lips, his hands slid up under her chemise. She was naked beneath. Leo murmured his approval as she wriggled closer. Working down over her shoulders and throat, his kisses patchworked over her glowing flesh.

As his hands moved over her body, his cock, hard and hungry begged for attention. He gasped as Eva instinctively reached for his belt, tugging at the buckle, eager to free him. He moaned, moving under her touch as she struggled with his zip. His lips circled the hardening peaks of her nipples, picked out under the thin fabric, fuelling the beacon fires in her belly.

'Please,' she gasped frantically as his hands slid down to encircle her hips. 'Please . . .' the words oozed out on a hot breath rather than being spoken and he didn't care whether she was begging him to stop or was begging him to carry on.

'My God, you're so beautiful,' he murmured, easing her up against the handrail of the veranda as his cock finally sprung free.

Her fingers closed round it. The foreskin was as soft as spun silk, a stunning contrast to the ram-rod hardness that it sheathed. In response he slid a hand between her thighs. Groaning with delight he slipped his fingers into the wet confines of her sex, easing her thighs apart to explore the fragrant folds, slick and engorged with desire.

She tipped her face towards him; her eyes were closed, her features a mask of sheer delight. He shuddered, teeth gritted, and pulled her legs up around him, encouraging her to guide his throbbing cock deep inside her.

She gasped as he breached her, writhing with sheer pleasure as his shaft slowly worked deep inside her. Thrusting his hips up to meet hers, he felt her body open eagerly to receive him.

Hands under her buttocks he pulled her further onto him, oblivious to her weight. Each thrust of their bodies pulsed through the heavy night air, echoing the beat of their hearts. Now when she looked up at him her eyes were open, dark with desire, drinking him in.

'So Belle's niece turned you on, huh?' she said with a sly grin.

Leo groaned and pushed deeper. Eva didn't know how close she was to the truth, but now really wasn't the moment to tell her. 'I've been thinking about you all afternoon,' he said thickly.

Eva snorted. 'Oh, you liar.'

She pulled him closer. He pressed his mouth to hers, aware of the salty taste of her lips and the soft invitation of her tongue against his. For a moment his rogue imagination wondered what it would be like to kiss Laura.

There was a moment's stillness and then they began to move in earnest. It was as if at some mutual unspoken signal any final restraint was cast aside. Mewling with pleasure, Eva wrapped her legs tight around him, drawing him in still deeper.

Leo gasped and then, unbridled, they began to ride each other, clawing and writhing like wild animals. In his belly the pleasure that had been building threatened to engulf him.

Finally, as he felt himself losing control, Eva shuddered, instinct taking over. Matching him stroke for stroke, the stunning blonde threw back her head and roared with sheer pleasure as they crashed on towards oblivion.

That this moment was, in Leo's imagination at least, meant for Laura, was lost in the flames of orgasm.

It took a few minutes for the intense after-shocks of pleasure to abate. Finally, Eva extricated herself from his arms, his cock sliding, spent and exhausted from her sex. She stooped down to pick up a towel from the floor. Leo watched her every move.

'Been swimming?' he said in a throaty voice, catching hold of the towel and wrapping it around her neck.

She nodded. 'Nothing better than the sensation of the sea on naked skin. Shame you weren't here earlier, you could have come in with me.'

He pulled her close and kissed her full on the lips. Taking her hand he led her back into the cabin, and gently guided her down onto the bed. Laying back amongst the crisp white sheets she watched as he began to strip off his clothes.

'And what exactly do you think you're doing?' she teased.

'Keeping you company,' he said with a wry grin. 'It's my new job, didn't Belle tell you?'

His body was as lean as a race horse. He threw his tee shirt onto the bedside chair. Unselfconsciously, he padded over to the fridge to grab a couple of beers. He moved with a fluid grace, not an ounce of spare flesh on his body. When he returned he slithered under the sheet, handed her the ice-cold beer and then pulled the mosquito net down around them.

'Belle's welcome dinner is in an hour,' Eva said.

Leo flicked off the bedside lamp. 'There's an awful lot we can do in an hour.'

'Shouldn't you go check up on your little friend? Perhaps she'd like a little *company*?'

He shook his head. Maybe later, when he knew Laura better. What he needed now was the warm body of a compliant woman curled against him.

'She'll be just fine.' he said. 'Drink your beer.'

11

Chapter 2

An hour or so later a waiter served supper on the covered
terrace outside the bar. They ate by the light of candles, the
soft, dancing flames sheltered from the sea breeze inside
glass lanterns. The same breeze tugged mischievously at
Laura's hair. At last she felt cool and relaxed, the tension
and excitement of the journey fading.

She guided another forkful of prawn into her mouth; it
was the best she had ever tasted.

Belle poured a glass of wine, a heady Australian white,
and lifted it in salute. 'Here's to family and friends.'

Laura felt her eyes fill with tears as she, Leo, and Belle
touched glasses.

Before Laura could let the emotion take hold, Belle
grinned. 'So what do you think of Barra Mundi?'

Under a lime and avocado sauce it fell into moist
succulent flakes when Laura drew a knife through it. She
took another bite and groaned appreciatively.

'Amazing. It's like this whole place – I can't quite believe
any of it's quite real.'

Across the table Leo laughed. 'Oh, don't be fooled. It's
real all right. Mosquitoes, alligators, sand flies an' all.' His
gaze lingered on her body for a second or two longer than
was comfortable, drinking her in. Laura reddened under
his undisguised interest.

'In a funny kind of way,' he said. 'I feel as if I've known
you for years.'

Belle poked him. 'Take no notice, Laura, he's talking
about your letters.'

'Sorry?'

'Didn't you know?' Leo said, pushing himself away from

13

the table, eyes bright with mischief. 'Belle reads all your letters to me.'

Laura's colour deepened. 'Are you serious?'

She had been writing to Belle since she was a little girl, ever since she found out she had a relative in Australia. Over nearly fifteen years of correspondence they had become real friends – and if what Leo said was true another thought struck her.

'You know all about Gareth, then. Were all those questions in the truck a joke?'

Leo shrugged. 'If you mean that he's a tight-arsed English banker, boring as a grey wool suit, who doesn't know a good thing when he sees it, won't make a commitment, irons his socks, doesn't turn you on and is slowly driving you mad, then yeah, I reckon I know all about him.'

Laura groaned with a mixture of embarrassment and amusement. 'Belle *how could you?*'

Belle laughed and took a long pull on her wine. 'Sorry, darling, they were just too good to keep to myself. I devour every word, every last one, every P.S., every quick note, every birthday card.'

Belle topped up Laura's wine glass. Her niece moved with a quiet self-confidence and exuded an air of subdued sensuality, an erotic innocence that she knew men found irresistible. Belle stared at Laura's face. Her eyes were bright with wine and unshed tears. In lots of ways Laura reminded Belle of herself twenty-five years earlier when she had first arrived in Australia clutching a secretarial diploma and very little else.

An awful lot had happened since then. The thoughts and memories surfaced unbidden as she rolled the wine glass around in her long fingers.

Caught in the candlelight, Laura could have been the twin of the girl Belle had once been. Dressed in a little black cocktail dress that emphasised her pale skin, dark hair caught up into a loose bun, Laura was quite stunning. Belle reached into her handbag and took out a jewellery case. She had been looking for the proper moment to give Laura this gift. With her mind tangled up in memories of the past it seemed like the ideal time. Belle slid the battered velvet box across the table cloth.

'Laura,' she said, 'I'd really like you to have these.'

Laura glanced down. 'Oh no, I couldn't,' she said hastily, reddening with embarrassment.

Belle waved her protests away. 'Don't be ridiculous. At least look at them. They were given to me when I was twenty-one and they need to be worn – consider them a late coming-of-age present. If you hadn't decided to come and visit us, I'd have had to post them.'

Laura unsnapped the box. Inside was a single row of pearls and pair of matching pearl and diamond-chip earrings. Laura stared at her. 'Oh Belle, they're lovely – but I really can't accept them.'

'Don't be silly, of course you can. They've been in the family for years. They should go to the oldest daughter and as I haven't got any children you should think of them as something you're looking after for the next generation. Leo, help Laura put them on.'

Leo dropped the beads around the girl's throat. Belle couldn't help noticing the way his fingers lingered on Laura's spine; he was completely incorrigible.

The pearls went perfectly with Laura's dress and seeing them against her niece's smooth creamy skin did very little to help Belle's state of mind. As Laura thanked her, Belle tried to shake the impression that she was somehow looking back into a mirror onto her own past.

'How did you end up at the Cape?' Laura asked casually, helping herself to another glass of wine.

Belle stiffened. It was almost as if Laura had picked up on her thoughts.

'Almost by accident,' she said slowly. 'Originally I came up to Cairns to work for a cane farmer as his secretary.'

Laura nodded her encouragement, while Belle struggled to recall the sanitised version of her autobiography she had sent to Laura over the years.

'And you married him?'

'That's right. Eventually. We used to spend weekends up here, and holidays. In those days the roads over the ranges were no more than dirt tracks. Impassable in the rainy season. We often sailed up the coast rather than try and get over the hills.'

Laura smiled. Belle had her undivided attention.

'Abel O'Malley was quite a lot older than me,' Belle continued. 'And when he retired we spent more and more of the year up there. After he died I moved up here permanently. He'd often said this place would make a good hotel and the tourist trade was just beginning to develop . . .'

Belle's voice faded as the waiter arrived to clear the table and Leo moved the conversation onto local tourist spots – but Belle found it hard to shift the images that filled her head. And the more she looked at Laura the more difficult it seemed.

She had been nearly twenty-two – the same age as Laura – when Abel O'Malley had picked her up from the railhead at Cairns. She had been in Australia six weeks and the position on the cane farm was her first proper job. She had travelled to Cairns, in comfort, at her new employer's expense.

Half an hour before the train pulled into the station she had changed her clothes from jeans and a cotton shirt to a smart suit more becoming of a secretary. She remembered vividly clipping on the pearl necklace and the little earrings – a tangible link that had started off this chain of thought.

Standing on the platform her new employer had seemed to epitomise everything Belle had ever seen or read about Australians – tall, bronzed, wearing a cream bush hat, opened-necked shirt and tailored shorts, Abel O'Malley was a giant of a man. She had been so overawed by his good looks and sheer physical stature that she hadn't noticed then the way he looked at her.

Abel pumped her hand, smiling a welcome. She remembered how hot the stiff, unforgiving skirt and jacket had felt in the tropical sunshine, but Belle considered the outfit gave the right impression; smart, efficient, a girl who was not to be trifled with. How wrong she had been!

As Abel O'Malley slung her luggage into the back of his truck she remembered the way he had looked at her. His eyes moving over her body as if she were a possession, as much his as the horses he rode and the land he farmed.

They had driven away from the city. He seemed quiet and gentle, told her he was a widower – a lay preacher, well thought of and deeply respectable – and as the miles rolled by he told her about his wife and the farm they had built up together.

Tired, lulled by the sound of his low voice she had relaxed, finally feeling safe and glad to have found a place to stay at last. Mentally she began to compose a letter home.

It didn't take her very long to appreciate that appearances could be deceptive. She had found out the first night what Abel O'Malley saw as her true role on the farm – miles from anywhere, a stranger in a strange land – he had come into her room when she was asleep and dragged her out of bed.

Terrified, she had pulled away from him and fled into the house, with him in hot pursuit. As she threw open the front door he had caught hold of her and kissed her fiercely, work-roughened hands working up under her night dress. She had gasped – almost too shocked to fight him off, stunned by his brutality and at the same time strangely excited. Pushing her to the ground he had unbuckled his belt. She knew then what was to follow. He knelt over her and kissed her again.

'Don't be afraid,' he had murmured, voice thick with desire. 'It's been so long, so very long. I won't hurt you. I need you.' Pushing up her nightdress he had parted her thighs, moaning softly as his eyes moved over her pale, naked flesh.

She was trembling, too terrified to move. His fingers worked eagerly over her breasts and the mound of her sex, seeking out the hidden places as if he had found the holy grail. She could see the raw hunger in his eyes – completely at odds with his earlier gentle manner – and knew there was no way she could resist him. She had two choices – to give him what he wanted or to let him take it.

It had taken an instant to make up her mind. Slowly she had reached out to him, hands trembling with a mixture of

17

fear and expectancy. She unbuttoned his shirt and undid his zip, all the time trying to control the frantic beat of her heart.

He roared like a caged animal as she freed his cock, gasping as she closed her fingers around it and pulled him down onto her.

Under his roof everything belonged to him to do with as he pleased. There was no question in his mind that she was his to possess. That night Abel O'Malley had broken her in, staking a claim over her body that was to last until the day he died . . .

'Are you feeling okay? You're very quiet.' Laura's voice made Belle jump. She realised with horror that she hadn't heard a word her niece or Leo had said.

'I'm so sorry,' she said quickly, regaining her composure. 'I was miles away. Thinking about the old days.' Belle smiled. 'Now, do you reckon you can manage a dessert? Coffee? My chef, Tom, does this thing with meringue, fresh pineapple and chocolate sauce that you've got to taste to believe.' She paused for a second or two. 'I'm really so pleased you came. All those photos of you growing up – seems like I missed out on a real good thing.'

Laura laughed.

But Belle still couldn't quite shake off the images of Abel O'Malley, they lingered like ghosts.

'Thank you so much for the present,' said Laura, running her fingers along the string of pearls. 'I'll take really good care of them.'

Belle nodded, and waved the waiter over to bring them coffee. The diamond chips in Laura's earrings reflected the candlelight and Belle looked away, realising that even now there was part of her that still missed the sensation of Abel's body curled tight around hers.

Aware that Laura was still watching her closely, Belle smiled, pushing the memories back into the far reaches of her mind.

'Don't look so concerned. I'm just feeling sentimental. Now what about that dessert?'

'I'll go and organise it with Tom,' Leo said. As he stood

Belle was aware of his gaze moving appreciatively over Laura's slender frame. The simple, sleeveless black mini-dress did nothing to hide her curves and his expression flickered with desire.

He grinned as he looked away and realised Belle had been watching him. 'Won't be a minute.'

Belle nodded and then dropped her napkin onto the table with an air of finality. 'Excuse me, Laura, I just need to check up on a few things before we close up the restaurant for the night. Won't take me more than a minute.'

Inside, Belle caught hold of Leo's arm as he strode towards the kitchen. 'She's strictly out of bounds, Leo, don't forget that. And I thought Eva said she was coming too? Have you seen her tonight?'

Leo shrugged. 'Maybe she didn't want to gatecrash the family reunion.' He paused, eyes twinkling. 'Or maybe she was just too tired.'

Belle snorted. 'I've told you before about handling the merchandise, Leo. Where is she now?'

Leo pulled a small notebook out of his shirt pocket. 'Tim Haroldson is in cabin three with Nona and Jackie, Maria Mortimer is—'

Belle held up a hand to silence him. 'I do know what's going on in my own house. I'm disappointed that Eva couldn't make dinner. Tonight was special for me.'

Leo's expression softened. 'I know, Belle. But maybe it wasn't such a bad idea her skipping off. Eva's a bright spark and good company, but one look at her and your little niece would be left in absolutely no doubt what sort of place you were running here. Eva is sex on a stick.'

Belle reddened. 'Don't be so ridiculous, Eva can go anywhere – she's the soul of discretion.'

Leo snorted. 'You're looking with the eyes of a brothel-keeper, babe.'

'Excuse me?' A low voice cut across Leo's sentence.

Both Leo and Belle swung round; Laura was standing no more than a foot away. She smiled. 'Would you mind very much if I gave dessert a miss? I'm really sorry, but I'm absolutely shattered.'

'Not at all,' said Belle quickly, shooting Leo a warning glance. 'If you're sure.'

Laura, suppressing a yawn, nodded. 'Really, I'm all in.' She leant forward and brushed her lips against Belle's cheek. 'Thank you so much for letting me stay here with you – I've dreamt about this for years.' She touched the pearls at her throat. 'And I'll treasure these. Thank you.'

'Not at all.' Belle reddened. 'We'll get Tom to cook us up his special another time. Night-night, baby, sweet dreams.'

Laura lifted a hand in a gesture of thanks and headed back out into the night.

'Do you think she heard?' Belle snapped as the doors closed behind Laura.

Leo shrugged. 'Who knows? Besides she's a big girl now.'

'We'll just have to be more careful.'

'That didn't seem such a bad idea before she arrived but she's not stupid, Belle. You can't make her wear blinkers. There are clients crawling all over O'Malley's – it'd be much easier just to tell her the truth.'

'And what do you suggest I say, Leo? Nice of you to come see us, Laura. By the way I thought I ought to mention O'Malley's is a high class whore-house?'

Leo helped himself to a brandy from behind the bar and handed one to Belle. 'You could save yourself a whole load of trouble. She's bound to find out sooner or later.'

Belle took a hefty slug from the brandy balloon, keeping her thoughts to herself.

Leo leant forward and kissed her gently. His tongue insinuated itself between her lips. As he pulled away, he whispered. 'Belle O'Malley, you run the sweetest little whore-house on the whole of Barbary Coast. Clean. Wholesome, good old-fashioned fun. I reckon you're underestimating Laura, she looks like a chip off the old block to me – pleasure is in her blood.'

Belle downed the rest of her brandy. 'Well, let's try and make sure she doesn't get the chance to find out, shall we?

Laura, exhaustion seeping through every bone, went back to her cabin and slipped off her clothes. Laying down on the bed she dropped the mosquito net, while the overhead fan softly stirred the warm, fragrant air. In the middle of the night, she woke, wondering where on earth she was. The answer followed an instant later, followed by a tiny glimmer of panic. She was so far away from home and from the people who knew her.

Through the fly screens Laura could just see the first golden light of a tropical dawn cracking the rich darkness, and hear the sounds of the sea and the rainforest. Lulled by the peaceful rhythm of the waves, she pulled the sheet up over her shoulders and was about to close her eyes when she heard a peculiar sound that made every hair on her head stand on end – a shriek, throaty and nervous.

Picking up a robe, she slipped out of bed and tiptoed out onto the veranda. Looking round she realised that there were several other cabins dotted around amongst the trees. She heard the noise again and then caught a flash of someone running down towards the beach.

A dark-haired woman dressed in a little black, silky camisole top and matching bikini pants, cut high so her legs seemed to go on forever, hurtled down onto the sand, panting hard. Behind a man dressed in a towelling robe, was hot on her heels. As he caught up to her the woman swung round.

'What the hell are you doing?' she snapped.

'I thought you looked a little lonely – maybe wanted a bit of company,' the man said, eyes dark with desire. The woman backed away, as if she was afraid of him, but before she chanced to make good her escape he made a grab for her. With the reflexes of a cat she sprung out of his way. He let out a little hiss of frustration as she headed further along the sand, with him no more than a pace behind. She zigzagged left and right, twisting back and forth to escape his clutches.

'Bitch,' he snorted, after another fruitless lunge.

As they drew level with Laura, the woman rounded on her pursuer, fists clenched, knees bent, her whole body sprung and ready to fight him off.

He laughed and moved closer. 'Think you can stop me,

21

do you?' he said in an undertone.

'C'mon you, bastard,' she hissed, eyes flaring with a mixture of excitement and anger as she beckoned him nearer.

The two figures, eyes locked, circled each other on the white coral sand.

Laura wondered what she should do, perhaps she ought to get Leo or Belle. Then as she looked again she realised that the woman was enjoying herself; the pursuit was part of some private erotic game. It was compelling to watch. The man was heavily set and muscular. He moved slowly with careful deliberation, while the woman was lithe and quick, letting instinct guide her. Their obvious physical differences, oddly, made them remarkably evenly matched.

The woman slipped time and again from her hunter's fingers – though all the while Laura sensed she was egging him on, teasing him almost beyond endurance.

Finally he made a wild lunge forward, intent on capture. The woman laughed and jerked away, but not quite quickly enough – her pursuer was in earnest. Grabbing her shoulders he caught hold of the straps of her camisole top and with a violent grunt ripped the thin fabric apart. She shrieked, tumbling backwards into the sand and then scrambled away from him on all fours, breasts jiggling, butt up in the air.

Triumphantly he leapt forward again and caught hold of her round her waist, flicking her over onto her back he pinned her down.

Crouched amongst a tumble of vines Laura struggled to breathe. She found it impossible to tear her eyes away from the couple and prayed they wouldn't turn round and see her. Her whole body tingled with expectation.

On the sand the woman was still struggling furiously, and managed to disentangle herself from her captor. Laura could sense the subtle mixture of play acting and real tension. Their desire was obvious in every movement.

Her own excitement had rekindled, tiredness fading away as the vivid images took hold. She licked her lips, attention firmly fixed on the couple on the sand.

Pulling the robe from his belt the man grabbed the woman's wrists and deftly looped the fabric around them, jerking it tight. The dark-haired woman yelled in frustration. He looked down at his prize and then started to kiss her furiously, running his hands over her prone body.

She was panting, her nipples like coffee beans, hard and upright in the morning air. When he kissed her again, Laura saw the woman open her mouth, letting the man lick at it, treating it like her sex.

Laura stifled a moan of pleasure, feeling the heat stir in her belly as she imagined the eager touch of his tongue and lips – it was almost more than she could bear.

The man dipped into the woman's mouth, licking around her lips, trailing his tongue down over her chin and her throat. As he moved down over her body he slid a knee between her thighs, levering her legs open, forcing them wide apart. Her quim, held tight inside tiny panties seemed to thrust upwards.

Pulling off his robe, he bundled it up under her hips so that she was tipped up towards him. Laura was so close to the lovers that she could see the woman was trembling with excitement, her skin flushed pink.

The man grabbed hold of the sides of her knickers and pulled them down a little way – just far enough so that he could get his hand inside followed an instant later by his tongue. He cupped the woman's sex in his fingers, opening her, moaning with delight as he found his goal.

She was so wet that her juices had dampened the front of her panties, soaking them with a glossy slick patch. Pulling her up towards him, he ran his tongue over the lips of her sex, dipping inside her with his fingers, smearing the silky, gossamer strands all over her thighs and up over her breasts so that everywhere he touched, everywhere he kissed, Laura knew that all he would smell was the woman's musky excitement.

As he started to work on her clitoris, lapping round and gently sucking on the swollen bud, the woman started to groan – forcing herself up, encouraging him on. Stunned by the power of their passion, Laura could feel the energy

23

arcing deep inside her own belly, her body hungry for satisfaction.

Roughly, making a mockery of her submission, the man dragged the woman's knickers off, so the material cut into her skin leaving tiny red weals. It seemed he just couldn't wait any longer. There was a look of ecstasy on his face as he rubbed her body against his and for an instant Laura imagined the sensation of his torso rubbing across her breasts, her thighs, her sex – and she shivered.

The woman lifted up again, silently begging the man to take her. Kneeling between her long, milky white thighs, he answered her unspoken invitation and plunged his cock deep inside her.

Laura gasped. The woman started to move, little rippling thrusts designed to take them both out to the brink. She eased herself up to meet him again and again. Sweat trickled down over her breasts in glittering little crystals. Her mouth was open, eyes closed.

Her lover started to grind into her, long slow strokes that echoed the rhythm of the ocean waves that rolled in just a few feet from their writhing bodies. Another thrust, and Laura knew that he was sharing the woman's white hot journey out towards release, and was horrified to find that she was being drawn into the spiral with them.

They were struggling to hold on, and then suddenly the woman started to gasp and mewl like a kitten, hands clenching into fists.

Laura was transfixed; she had never seen anything so erotic in her entire life. Her boyfriend, Gareth, liked to make love in the dark, brief unfulfilling couplings that always left her cold – and hungry for something more.

As she watched them tumbling into the abyss, down and down, Laura closed her eyes, the expression on the woman's face already fixed in her mind. Without so much as a caress she felt the tremors echo deep in her belly. The sensation of orgasm could have been no more intense if she had been lying naked on the beach, her sex pulsating hungrily around a lover's throbbing cock. Finally, she turned away, swallowing hard, wiping a trickle of sweat off her top lip.

'You like to watch, also?' said a heavily accented male voice.

Laura jumped in horror. Her eyes snapped open in complete astonishment and embarrassment. At her shoulder a tall man, dressed in cream slacks and polo shirt, grinned lazily down at her.

Before she could speak, the man continued, 'You're new here, aren't you? I know what Maria likes, she likes it best when she feels as if the man has conquered her. Billy, he is very good?'

Laura looked up into dark brown eyes set in a handsome, olive-skinned face. Her unexpected companion extended his hand as if they were being formally introduced at a party.

'Giuseppe Blanco, but all my friends call me Joe.' Every languid rolling syllable revealed his Italian origins. Struggling to compose herself Laura took his hand and shook it with something she hoped resembled a normal handshake.

Joe indicated the beach. 'They are better if they know they have an audience. Perhaps you like to come join them?'

To Laura's total horror Joe immediately stepped out from behind the bushes and clapped loudly. 'Bravo, bravo, *bellissimo*! You were magnificent.' He kissed his finger tips in a display of approval.

On the beach the two figures sat up, grinning. 'You wanna join us?' said the man patting the sand.

Joe held up his hands in a gesture of regret.

The woman laughed. 'Oh, come on, Joey. You know it's much more fun if you get your feet wet, better than just sitting on the side.' Her eyes narrowed mischievously. 'I promise to be very gentle with you.'

The man beside the dark-haired woman laughed. 'Feet, huh?'

Joe looked back over his shoulder to where Laura was still hiding. 'You want to come play? They really won't mind – and then we can swim?'

Laura, who had been rooted to the spot during their exchange, took a deep breath and shook her head firmly. Before he could say anything else she took to her heels and ran back towards the cabin, heart beating out a frantic rhythm in her chest. Without looking back she slammed the door shut and leant against it, trying to get a grip on her thoughts.

Her mind was still reeling from the events on the beach, intense erotic images overlaying each other in a collage of passion. Part of her couldn't quite believe what she had seen or been invited to join. She ought to say something to Belle – but what?

Laura glanced at the bed, the sheets tangled into a heap, recording how disturbed her sleep had been. Perhaps she could convince herself it had been a dream. Between her legs Laura could still feel an unfulfilled ache; she had almost been tempted to take Joe up on his offer. The realisation was a revelation.

She took another deep breath, wondering if Belle had any idea what her guests were up to.

Chapter 3

'So, what do you want to do today? Belle asked, handing Laura a glass of freshly squeezed fruit juice. It was breakfast time and Laura and Belle had been talking for almost an hour, catching up on family news.

Safe under the veranda outside the hotel, Laura began to wonder if perhaps the events on the beach had been just a dream. Every time there was a lull in the conversation she found her mind drifting away, replaying the images and sounds of passion. Dream or not, the impression the scene on the beach had left her was uncomfortably vivid.

Around their table things looked so normal. Waiters serving the hotel guests. Couples sharing a breakfast of tropical fruit and toast. The smell of freshly brewed coffee made Laura's mouth water.

Under the eaves a tiny sun bird was weaving a nest out of dried grass, while brightly coloured parrots waited in the trees for scraps. Although the veranda was in shadow, bright morning sunshine picked out the pink and yellow flowers of creepers that grew close by. The scent, the sounds and the colours were overwhelming. Out on the coral sand a horse and rider trotted silently along the water's edge.

'I've got a friend with a boat who takes tourists out onto the Reef – you can go diving or snorkelling,' Belle said, breaking into her thoughts.

Laura jumped, realising that her mind had been wandering. All she could think about was the woman on the sand, arching upwards with pleasure as her lover drove deep inside her.

She reddened, mumbling an apology as Belle continued, 'I told him you were coming to stay. It's a really fantastic day out. Leo could take you down to the pick-up point. Would you like me to give them a ring?'

Laura shook her head, quickly gathering her thoughts together. 'If it's all right with you I'd really like a day or two to get the feel of the place and settle in. Maybe explore the beach.'

'Sure, I'll have Leo bring the jeep round for you.'

Laura stared out at the ocean; she planned to begin exploring much closer to home.

As if on cue, Leo padded across to their table. He looked gorgeous in a blue cotton shirt and off-white chinos. Turning a chair round, he pulled it up to their table, and casually swung a leg over it.

After greeting Belle he turned his attention to Laura. 'Morning, kiddo, sleep well?'

She glanced at up him, wondering if he knew what she had seen earlier. 'Not bad. I'm just not used to the heat.'

He took a sliver of papaya from the platter in the centre of the table and dropped it into his open mouth. 'Takes a while. Looks like you're dressed for the tropics though.'

She felt his eyes moving appreciatively over her crisp white blouse and tailored cream trousers. A heavy leather belt emphasised her narrow waist and she guessed that Leo had already taken in every detail.

'So, what's on the agenda for today then? The reef? The rainforest? Your wish is my command.' He poured himself a coffee. 'I suppose you know Belle's appointed me your official tour guide. So, am I chauffeuring you down to the boat or what?'

'There's really no need for you both to go to all this trouble,' Laura protested.

Belle lifted a hand to silence her. 'It's all right, Leo knows everything there is to know about local sights. I just feel guilty that I can't entertain you myself but I've got to stay here – it's one of our busiest times of the year.'

'I don't mind,' Laura said.

Leo's voice dropped to a conspiratorial purr. 'I'll be pleased to show you whatever you want.'

Laura caught Belle shooting Leo a warning glance and

wondered how she could convince them that she really didn't need a minder. What she wanted was to explore alone.

'Would you mind very much if I stayed here today?'

Leo pulled a face of mock disappointment. 'Are you serious? Means Belle'll get me working.'

Belle snorted. 'Some chance. Take no notice of him, Laura. Do what you want, darling. We can arrange trips when you've settled in.' She glanced at her watch. 'Got to be off. Leo, if you've not nothing better to do, can you sort out the spa pool once you've brought the jeep round?'

An hour later, with her swimsuit wrapped in a towel, Laura was walking along the coral sand watching the sea break in foam-fringed fingers on the beach. A few hundred yards away from the hotel frontage the beach was deserted. Palm trees above the high water mark offered secluded shady places to sit or read, while overhead the sky was crystal blue and cloudless – the perfect place for a swim. Laura found a sheltered spot to change and began to unbutton her shirt. She tugged her blouse out of her trousers and was about to slip it off her shoulders when something caught her eye.

'Joe? Is that you?' she whispered in an undertone, hardly believing that she was calling to a total stranger. She had to be mistaken, surely?

From a few yards away the good-looking Italian she had met earlier slipped furtively from behind a palm tree. He blushed crimson.

'You followed me?' she said in disbelief.

He shrugged, looking uncomfortable. 'It was too good a chance to miss. I saw you having breakfast with Belle and then I watched you come back with your swimming things. I always have the cabin by the sea.' His eyes brightened as he pointed back along the beach. 'You can see everything from there. I thought that you might . . .' his voice faded and the look of discomfort returned. 'Well, you know,' he said weakly.

Laura smiled. Far from feeling threatened some part of her was amused and quite flattered. 'You thought you might get to see me undress?'

Joe shifted from foot to foot, for all the world looking like a naughty school boy. 'You're very beautiful,' he offered. 'And you ran away so fast this morning. We didn't get a chance to talk. I don't want to touch you, I only want to look. I like to look – honest.'

Laura felt a peculiar sense of mischief trickle through her veins.

'Really?' she said, undoing another button and sliding her blouse off her shoulders. Underneath, because she had intended to change into her swim suit, she was naked. She held the fabric between her fingers like a shawl so that all Joe could see was the curve of her shoulders and the plane of pale brown skin above her breasts.

Joe swallowed hard. She had his undivided attention. It gave her an odd sense of power.

'And what was it exactly that you thought you might see, Joe?'

He struggled to compose himself. 'You know – your breasts, your long, long legs, your . . . his colour deepened as his gaze dropped below her leather belt. 'All of you,' he added hastily.

Laura reddened. In England, with Gareth, she would never have considered being so uninhibited or so provocative, but here, twelve thousand miles from home, who would know or care what she did? The idea caught hold.

She turned away from him, letting her blouse slip a little lower so that he could see more and more of her naked back. She felt hot, nervous excitement mingling with the sense of mischief.

'Oh yes,' Joe murmured in an undertone. His words gave her the push she needed. Stepping well away from him she unfastened her belt and pushed the zip of her trousers undone.

He moaned again, swallowing hard as if he was salivating. 'You really shouldn't have run away this morning,' he said. 'You should have joined them. I would have loved to see you.'

Laura shivered, afraid to acknowledge that some part of her had been tempted. She began to move, Joe's eyes following her as if they were fixed to her body by glue. The flurry of pleasure grew and her pulse quickened. There was something deliciously wanton about posing for the handsome Italian's approval.

Gently she let the shirt drop to the sand, still with her back towards him, and then turned her attention to guiding the thin cotton trousers down over her rounded hips. Behind her she heard him gasp with delight. Gracefully, aware of the image she must present in Joe's mind, she stepped out of them, standing naked except for a tiny pair of white cotton knickers.

She slowly turned, posing provocatively for him – and herself – aware of his heavy breathing and the way his eyes explored every inch of her body. It was strangely exhilarating. She moved again, letting her hands work a solitary dance of pleasure over her shoulders, her arms, her breasts and belly.

Joe, eyes alight, watched her open mouthed.

'Is this what you had in mind?' she said, teasing her nipples with a finger tip.

Joe, unable to find the words, nodded. He indicated her panties with another nod of his head.

'And those too, please,' he muttered when he finally managed to find a voice. 'Take them off. I'd like to see the rest.'

There was no going back now. She had already chosen to take part in this little charade of her own free will. Trembling with excitement she hooked her thumbs into either side of her knickers and began to ease them down over her hips.

As the tension arced between them a white hot flare of excitement rippled through her. She had never felt so uninhibited or so reckless. Joe had already warned her that he didn't want to touch and she wondered what she could do with the terrible sense of need that was rapidly growing deep inside her.

Her knickers dropped silently to the ground. Her sex was trimmed with a corona of raven black hair. She bent her knees slightly, letting Joe get a glimpse of the moist pink folds within, feeling incredibly brazen and yet at the same time incredibly free.

Joe moaned. 'My God,' he murmured, 'you are exquisite, just so lovely. Come here, let me look at you.'

Stepping closer so that she was no more than a yard away from him, she posed for his approval. Laura blushed as his eyes, as intimate as a lover's caress, moved slowly down over her body, drinking her in. For an instant he turned away, as if fixing the image in his subconscious, and then continued his intimate appraisal of her nakedness.

Despite her growing excitement, part of her was screaming out in frustration, wanting him to reach forward and run a hand over her trembling body.

It felt as if making love was the only thing that would earth her, that would feed her, instead Joe's eyes just moved slowly on. It was sweet torture – almost more than she could bear.

Casting off any lingering shreds of restraint she began to move her hips, an invitation she was sure he would find impossible to resist. Almost without thinking, as the need grew, her hand crept down over her belly to explore the soft, moist contours that held Joe rapt. It felt so good – an instant later she began to circle the throbbing pleasure bud that nestled within.

She didn't need Joe to tell her that he approved, his expression gave him away, encouraging her on.

She began to move in earnest, a single finger working its way into the slick warm depths of her quim, while another worked on her clitoris. Even as the waves of passion rose up to engulf her and the image of Joe's dark eyes were fixed forever on her soul, she would have given anything for him to join her in the ancient dance towards release. Anything to have him pull her down into the sand and plunge his shaft deep into her hungry body.

It was almost impossible to believe that all he truly wanted was to watch – or that he would be able to resist her. Gasping for breath she staggered forward, knees buckling, as orgasm closed over her like a raging sea.

As gentle as a priest, Joe caught hold of her shoulders

and held her tight as the after shocks of pleasure rolled through her. Finally he leant forward and kissed each of her nipples in turn and then planted a chaste, dry kiss on her lips. She reddened, amazed by the way she had behaved.

'You are truly magnificent,' he murmured thickly. 'But I think that what you need is a man.' To her relief there was no disdain in his manner, just tenderness and appreciation.

Laughing in spite of herself, Laura nodded. 'You're right. Do you think you can help me find one?'

He picked up her towel and unrolled it onto the sand. 'Maybe. If you want. Would you let me watch?'

Laura let him guide her down into the sand and didn't resist as he wrapped her shirt around her shoulders. 'You really are the limit, Joe,' she murmured.

He shrugged and then dropped onto the sand beside her. 'Oh no, not the limit.' He looked hurt.

There was something strangely comforting about his physical presence, and without thinking she leant against him. 'Okay, so maybe not the limit. But close to it.' She looked up into his big brown eyes. 'I don't understand how that can't turn you on – why you don't . . .?'

She stopped again, wondering how to frame her question. What was it that held him back?

'Is it something to do with me?' She already knew the answer. Joe had declined to join the couple on the beach too.

Joe kissed the top of her head. 'No, I think you are very, very beautiful but I don't need to touch to get pleasure.

Still bemused Laura picked up her bathing costume. 'I really came down here to have a swim. Care to join me?'

Joe grinned. 'I don't swim either.' He pulled a dog-eared paperback out of his back pocket. 'But you go ahead and then maybe later we go for lunch? I know a great place.' His face folded into a mask of amusement. 'Lots of nice men.'

Laura groaned and put on her swim suit.

At midday, Belle got up from her desk and poured herself a coffee. There was an air of barely contained chaos about the little office. Every surface was covered with piles of papers and invoices. A better whore-monger than an accountant she thought ruefully, rubbing her eyes.

It hadn't always been like that. Abel O'Malley had employed her as a book-keeper: within a matter of months of arriving at his farm she had taken over his accounts and the management of all his financial affairs. As time went on he had come to trust her more than anyone else and had grown to need her more than either of them could ever have imagined – and at night she learnt to indulge his bizarre fantasies.

For the first few weeks she had lived in fear of him. He was insatiable and she sensed that if she tried to deny him he would take what it was he wanted. One night, when she threatened to leave, he had carried her out to the barn and beaten her with a horse whip before handing her over to his men. Even then, when they had done with her, he carried her back to the house and made love to her – if making love was indeed the word for it.

She began to realise she was a fool to fight him. He was physically stronger and she was doomed to lose. Belle knew she had to find another way to defeat him, and as he forced his way into her, his body reeking of horses and sweat she understood that in a strange way it was she who held the power. He wasn't a bad man or a cruel man. Her body, her sex was like a magnetic force that drew him.

Every day he hunted her down, eyes alight with raw animal desire. And as the weeks and months unfolded she began to use her sexuality, like a carrot, to lead him in any particular way she fancied. She would give him whatever he desired, but at a price. It was a bargain that he was only too happy to go along with.

At weekends they sailed up to the Cape, off to the retreat where he could indulge his passions. Later, as the years had gone on his friends often joined them and Belle recruited other girls to join their hedonistic house parties. But Belle ensured no other woman ever had to endure the fear she had.

By the time she and Abel retired up to the house in the rainforest there was a clique of well-connected businessmen and dignitaries who regularly visited the isolated beach house, safe in the knowledge that they could indulge their darkest dreams – normally so carefully hidden behind the week-in-week-out facade of church-going respectability.

Belle had married Abel O'Malley a few months before he died, by which time she knew exactly what she would do once he was gone. He left her a very wealthy woman, but in the years since his death Belle had more than doubled his fortune. She could still see his face if she closed her eyes . . .

Outside the office window, Belle noticed Laura was deep in conversation with Joe Blanco. She smiled, letting Abel's ghost free. Joe was the soul of discretion, really in some ways he would make the ideal holiday companion for Laura, and – she thought with a wry grin – he would be far less trouble than Leo.

A few minutes later Laura, smiling broadly, appeared through the office door. 'Hi, I hope I'm not disturbing you. I thought I'd better come and tell you, Joe and I are going to lunch at somewhere called Home Cove. Is that okay?'

She glanced around the chaotic room. 'You ought to let me give you a hand with some of this. I'm great at arranging things. I specialised in information management. I could have this lot filed away in no time.'

Belle waved her away. 'Kind offer, darling, but I know where most things are. It looks worse than it is. Besides, you're on holiday. Here—' She took a set of keys from the desk board behind her. 'Take the little blue jeep, it's all gassed up and ready to roll. Have a nice time. By the way, how was the swim?'

Laura grinned. 'Wonderful. I don't know how long we're going to be, Joe said something about a wild-life sanctuary?'

Belle nodded, wondering why it hadn't occurred to her to ask Joe to chaperone Laura before.

As Laura climbed into the driver's seat Joe began hastily doing up the jeep windows. She stared at him. 'What? You don't like fresh air either?'

Joe grinned. 'You're hot, right?'

Laura nodded. Despite the sea breeze the midday air was humid and oppressive.

He leant forward and turned a switch on the dashboard. 'Then start her up, close the windows, sit back and enjoy the air conditioning.' He mimed a whip crack with one hand. 'Wagon's roll. C'mon, all this sea air is making me hungry.'

Laura laughed as she gunned the engine into life. 'Okay. Are you going to tell me what you're doing up here in the back of beyond? Or is it just so you can accost defenceless women on the beach?'

Joe settled himself into the comfortable bucket seat. 'You think that's not a good enough reason?' He winked at her and continued, 'Belle rents me the cabin on a more or less permanent basis. It's the closest thing I've got to a home. Actually, I'm a writer.'

Laura stared at him, embarrassment growing. 'A writer? Oh, my God. What do you write about?'

Joe seemed keener to get their journey underway than to answer her questions. 'Turn left out of the gates,' he said, pointing furiously. He glanced across at her, still grinning. 'Don't look so worried. I write mostly travel articles, ecologically sound adventures, diving, sailing. Relax, you aren't going to turn up in "sights worth seeing".' He paused, and then laughed. 'Although I have to say, in my opinion you would be well worth a mention.'

Laura reddened, feeling self-conscious. 'I've never ever done anything like that before.'

Joe lifted his hands in an expansive Latin gesture. 'What's to worry about? Hey, this is the tropics, it brings out the animal in us all.'

Laura turned her attention back to negotiating the jeep along the narrow winding road. The steamy climate might be Joe's explanation for her behaviour but she wasn't so sure. It was as if, on the beach, under his hungry gaze she caught a glimpse of some part of her nature that she never knew existed.

Beside her Joe pulled a hat out of the briefcase he was carrying, dropped it over his face then crossed his arms over his chest, giving every impression he intended to sleep.

36

'Aren't you going to help me navigate?' she asked in surprise.

Lazily he opened one eye. 'You can't miss it, it's the first place you come to on the left.'

And he was right; three-quarters of an hour later Laura took a left hand turning marked 'Home Cove Resort' and followed the obviously new, winding road down towards the coast.

Home Cove was a stark contrast to O'Malley's olde worlde colonial charm. The main building was like an enormous log cabin. Built from natural red timber, up on stilts, it reminded Laura of a tree house she had had as a child.

Enormous arched windows graced the front elevation, giving Laura an uninterrupted view of the ocean beyond. A winding wooden bridge over a man-made stream led to the main foyer. Framed by royal palms, the resort was quite beautiful. Its elegant native design whispered wealth and luxury on a discreet outward breath.

As Laura killed the engine, Joe snuffled his way back to consciousness.

'Are we there yet?' he said from under his hat.

'I think so. You might have warned me we were going somewhere so posh. I'd have worn something smarter.'

Joe, still half asleep, laughed. 'You should have left your ideas about class alongside your inhibitions. This is Australia – if you can pay you can stay. Get a look at the dress code over the bar.'

Laura still wasn't sure. As she clambered out of the jeep she wondered if she wouldn't have been better giving Home Cove a miss until she'd got her high heels on.

Inside, through the huge windows, she could see uniformed staff discreetly serving lunch to the guests. The whole atmosphere was one of understated luxury – plush armchairs and elegant tables were arranged in groups around a central waterfall and pool.

Pushing open the heavy plate glass door she felt distinctly under-dressed; a state of mind not helped by the arrival of a middle-aged uniformed waiter.

To her surprise when he spotted Joe, the man grinned. 'Hiya Joe, how's it going mate? he said warmly. 'Usual table?'

Joe shook his proffered hand and introduced Laura as a friend from the old country.

'Think we'll have a drink first, Barry,' Joe said pleasantly as the waiter handed them both a menu.

The man nodded. 'No worries. I'll set you up by the window when you're ready. Just give me the nod.'

Joe guided Laura to the bar and then pointed to a sign above it. It read, 'Patrons are respectfully requested to wear shoes.'

Joe grinned. 'Australian dress code. What do you want to drink?'

Relaxing a little, Laura ordered a glass of wine.

Joe picked up his beer. 'Will you be all right on your own for a minute or two? I have to have a word with the manager, I'm doing a promo article for him for one of the New York glossies.'

Laura nodded and settled herself down on a stool to take in the details of her surroundings. Overhead the ceiling was made up of intricate arched beams, spiralling away into the ether. She didn't notice the barman coming back. He slid a handful of coins across the bar.

'Sorry,' he said with a grin. 'Didn't realise you were staff. You should have said something.'

Laura swung round. 'Staff?'

The man nodded. 'Yeah, you're working over at O'Malley's, right? Barry on the desk told me.'

Before she could contradict him, the man continued. 'I was going to ring Belle this afternoon. We've got a party of Americans in, they're real high rollers looking for a little light entertainment. I was wondering whether she could organise a take-way for them tonight?'

Laura frowned, not quite understanding the question. 'A take-away?'

The man nodded. 'Yeah, three girls – at least one blonde. Around eight o'clock. Okay?'

Comprehension was slowly dawning. Cautiously, Laura nodded. 'I'll pass the message on,' she said.

'Great. You're new, right? Don't suppose you're working today? Only we've got a guy in from—'

Before he could complete the sentence Joe reappeared with a handful of brochures. The barman touched the side of his nose in a gesture of conspiracy. 'Sorry. You won't forget to tell Belle, will you?'

Laura shook her head. 'No.'

'Do you want to eat now?' said Joe, indicating a table in the window.

Laura nodded. It was very tempting to ask him about Belle's take-away service and the rest of the goings on at O'Malley's, but she decided to wait. Maybe if she played her cards right she could find out the answers for herself.

Chapter 4

After lunch Joe took Laura to see the wildlife sanctuary but it was difficult to concentrate on habits of fruit bats and wild birds when her mind was replaying the barman's intriguing request.

Halfway through the guided tour, Joe caught hold of her arm. 'Are you okay?'

She nodded.

'You look real tired. Jet lag maybe? Do you want to go back to the hotel?'

Laura smiled; back to O'Malley's to tell her aunt that some man in a bar wanted a take-away that involved three girls, one of whom had to be a blonde. She wondered what Belle would say and what her expression might give away.

'Would you mind?'

Joe shook his head. 'No. Not at all. I'll drive back if you like.'

Belle was sitting in her office when Laura arrived.

'Did you have a nice time?' she said closing the ledger on her desk.

Laura nodded. 'Wonderful. The food was great.'

Belle got to her feet. 'Good. I'm ready for a break. I reckon we're just in time for afternoon tea.'

Laura couldn't help notice that Belle was gently but firmly guiding her away from the desk where a sheaf of papers and an appointment book lay open.

'Sounds fine. Oh, and I've got a message for you from the barman at Home Cove.'

Belle looked a little uncomfortable. 'That'll be Murray, he's their trainee manager. What did he want?'

'He said he'd like a take-away for tonight.'

Belle reddened momentarily. 'Right,' she said briskly. 'Did he mention exactly what it was he wanted?'

Laura, face impassive, shook her head. 'Not really, for three I think – sorry. I should have asked him for more details.'

Belle, appearing to regain her composure, smiled. 'Don't worry, it doesn't matter. I'll ring him later. We'll see what Tom's got on the dessert trolley. How was the wildlife sanctuary? Did Joe tell you he'd written a book about it?'

Laura sensed that her aunt was guiding the conversation away from Home Cove as skilfully as she had led her away from her desk. She suppressed a smile. Although Belle didn't realise it, her secret was safe, in fact far from it upsetting her, it sparked off a whole new series of possibilities in Laura's imagination.

As they got to the dining room Laura said, in a casual throwaway voice, 'Oh and Joe said that maybe we could go out tonight – drive along by the coast – if you don't mind. I didn't know if you had any other plans?'

Belle shook her head. 'Sounds like a great idea. I just wish I could come with you. Maybe we'll be able to organise something for next week. There's a great back-packers' bar up at the Cape, live music, fantastic atmosphere, get Joe to take you up there to round the drive off – you'll love it.'

After they had shared a pot of tea, Laura hurried over to Joe's cabin to sound him out about their evening trip. Her plan – which had evolved as she had been talking to Belle – was to follow the Home Cove take-away to its destination and see for herself what was going on.

Joe Blanco didn't take much persuading.

At just before seven Laura re-emerged from her cabin dressed in a tight fitting blue silk column dress and matching sandals, her long dark hair caught up into a loose bun. She checked her reflection in the window before heading towards the main hotel building. The result made her smile; she looked good.

As she crossed the covered boardwalk she heard a low whistle of appreciation and looked up to see who was watching. She could hardly believe that Joe was still following her. From the shadows of the hotel veranda Leo appeared cradling a beer.

'You look good,' he said, eyes moving unashamedly over her body. 'Going somewhere special?'

She grinned and dipped a mock curtsey. 'Well, thank you. Actually, I'm going out with one of the guests. Joe? You know, Joe Blanco?'

Leo pulled a face. 'I have to warn you, if you're looking for a little holiday romance you're wasting your time there.'

Laura guessed that Leo knew all about Joe's tastes when it came to pleasure, but decided to play dumb. 'Really? Why? Is he spoken for. Gay?'

Leo took a long pull on his beer. 'Worse. Much worse.'

Behind them the dining room doors opened and a group of guests took their seats for dinner on the veranda. Leo moved closer; Laura could sense the desire in his expression and instinctively took a step back.

'Don't run away. I don't bite. You'd be better off letting me take you out on the reef. Joe's a nice guy but he can't give you what you want.'

Laura felt desire trickle down her spine like iced water. Ignoring the hubbub around them she tipped her head on one side so that she looked at him coquettishly from under her dark lashes.

'Oh really, and what is it that you think I want, Leo?'

He reached out and stroked a fingertip over her cheek. His caress lit a beacon fire in her belly so intense it was painful.

'Oh, I don't think, Laura, I know,' he purred. 'I know.'

She pulled away as if he had bitten her. Glancing down at her watch she said hastily. 'I've got to go, Joe will be waiting.'

Leo grinned. 'Whatever.' He lifted a hand in salute as she scurried away.

Outside the main hotel entrance Joe was standing by the steps smoking a cigarette.

'All ready? You look great,' he said as she approached

43

him. 'Are you sure you want to go back to Home Cove, if you wanted we could—'

Before he could finish his sentence, three girls appeared from one of the cabins and headed towards them. They were dressed to kill. Laura waved Joe into silence, a new plan rapidly evolving. Amongst the girls was a statuesque blonde.

Laura took a deep breath and with a confidence she didn't feel, said, 'Hi, you're the take-away for the Americans at Home Cove, right?'

The tall blonde girl, dressed in a sleeveless cream mini dress that fitted like a second skin, looked at her suspiciously. 'Yes.'

Laura nodded and pointed towards the jeep she had been loaned by Belle. 'Better climb aboard then. Belle asked me to drive you over there.'

Beside her, Joe began to protest. Laura swung round and glared at him. 'Maybe you'll get the chance to watch, okay?' she whispered. His reply was a conspiratorial wink.

He lifted an arm. 'This way, ladies. All aboard.'

The blonde eyed Laura up and down. 'I don't understand, we usually drive ourselves or Leo comes with us. Maybe I ought to go over and have a word with Belle.'

Laura rolled her eyes heavenwards in what she hoped was a display of impatience. 'Come on, I took the order myself from Murray this afternoon. Get in. We're going to be late as it is.'

The two brunettes, both dressed in red, were already inside, buckling up their seat belts, but still the blonde hung back. 'What's going on? You aren't supposed to know anything about Belle's business,' she said flatly.

Laura waved Joe round towards the driver's seat. 'Things change. Let's get going. Either get in or stay behind. Up to you.'

Reluctantly the blonde clambered in alongside her two companions. As she took her seat she looked long and hard at Laura.

'You know, you're just like Belle,' she said after a second or two.

Laura grinned. The bluff had worked; she was just relieved

that the statuesque blonde couldn't see that her hands were shaking.

'My name's Laura,' she said over her shoulder as Joe guided the jeep out of the hotel grounds and onto the main road.

The blonde grinned. 'We already know who you are. My name's Eva, this is Martine and Felicity.'

Laura was curious to ask them about Belle's business but to her surprise, before she had chance, Joe slipped a cassette into the music consul and they drove down toward Home Cove to the sounds of Eric Clapton picking his way through bluesy rock classics, the sweet melodies killing any chance of real conversation.

At Home Cove, Murray was waiting for the girls in the foyer and with hardly a word shepherded them away to meet their clients in a private room. Joe, eyes alight with anticipation followed close behind. Laura glanced round the main room – it was almost empty. Perhaps she would have a drink first before following her charges upstairs – Dutch courage.

Laura settled herself by the bar. Outside on the wooden deck a chef was preparing an al fresco supper. The smell made her realise how hungry she was. Keen to get to Home Cove, she had completely forgotten about dinner.

'Smells good, doesn't it?' said a low deep voice.

Laura swung round and looked straight into a pair of bright blue eyes, smiling at her from further along the bar. Sitting on the stool, their owner was in his late twenties, his skin tanned to the colour of golden toffee. In places his short curly blonde hair was sunbleached almost white. He lifted his glass.

'Maybe you'd like to join me for supper? Seems like all the guests are set for the night.' He was dressed in a dark green polo shirt and tailored shorts. Embroidered above his breast pocket was a discreet logo.

'You work here?'

'No, I'm a tour guide. You don't mind if I join you, do you?' He grinned and extended his hand. 'Danny Collins.'

His handshake was firm and friendly but his fingers

lingered a little too long in hers for the greeting to be purely formal.

'Laura,' she said, 'Laura Carter.'

He nodded towards the door. 'I saw you arriving earlier with Joe and the girls – you work over at Belle's, too?'

Wasn't there anyone locally who hadn't heard of O'Malley's?

Laura looked at him; he was good looking, the web of lines around his eyes recording his outdoor life. His gaze held hers, expression alight with mischief and flirtation.

She took a long pull on her glass. 'Not really' she said, quelling the nervous tremor that rose inside her stomach. 'I just drove them over for the evening.'

Danny nodded. 'I know, I asked Murray to book them. Seems a shame to be all alone while they're working.' He indicated the barbecue. 'Maybe we could have a little dinner and keep each other company? Waiting around, time drags.'

Although the words were innocent enough Laura sensed that there was more on offer than just dinner. As he spoke he moved almost imperceptibly closer.

She was unable to suppress a tremor as his fingers casually traced a slow circle on her shoulder.

'New, huh? What are you? A student? Belle always gets the best; brains and great bodies, what more could a guy want?'

Laura reddened, feeling as if she was rooted to the spot. Part of her wanted to run, but there was also a terrible compunction to stay. She took another sip of wine, wondering what she ought to say. A single word would send Danny away, but she couldn't bring herself to say no to him.

She realised, staring into his dark blue eyes that her body ached to be touched. She thought about the frustration she had felt on the beach with Joe. She needed a man almost as much as she needed to eat. The sensation, raw and unexpected, took her by surprise.

She looked away, wondering if he could sense both her apprehension and her need.

Danny waved the waiter closer. 'Let me top that up.' He

took the glass from her fingers, moving closer still. When he spoke again his voice was no more than a whisper.

'First time? It's got to be real tough to lay it on the line. You needn't worry, I'll break you in real easy.'

Laura shivered, desire rippling up through her body like an earth tremor.

'Why don't we eat first?' he said. 'And then if you like I could show you my cabin. It's got a great view out over the ocean.'

Laura took a deep breath – letting Danny take the lead absolved of her of the responsibility, but was that what she really wanted? The desire was as much hers as his.

She took another sip of wine. 'Do you make a habit of picking up women in bars?'

He grinned. 'Who doesn't? Nice work if you can get it.'

Laura glanced out at the night sky, clearing her mind, trying to still the sexual hunger in her stomach.

Eventually she smiled. 'Have you got a table in this cabin of yours?' she said, struggling to make her tone sound normal.

Danny nodded. 'Yeah, right out under the stars. Hang on, I'm with you – sounds a great idea. We'll eat down there, yeah? I've got wine, beer, maybe even some champagne in the cooler. Fancy a little supper out under the stars?'

Laura suppressed a smile. On an empty stomach the wine had already found its way into her bloodstream, making her feel light headed. 'Okay.'

He got to his feet and took her hand. 'You're shivering,' he said with surprise. 'Are you nervous?'

Laura forced herself not to snatch her hand away, afraid to say anything in case her apprehension turned to panic. Danny slipped his arm around her waist.

'Just relax, it'll be all right – I'll be real gentle.'

Wordlessly, Laura let him guide her out through the glass doors onto the deck. She barely noticed him collecting the tray of food for them. Her mind was elsewhere, drinking in the details of his lithe muscular body and unhurried, almost feline movements. And alongside her observations was a little nagging voice of doubt; what exactly was she doing?

47

Danny's invitation was explicit. If she went to the cabin with him he expected her to make love – the idea glowed and smouldered somewhere low in her belly.

Away from the main building, a row of twinkling lights marked their route towards a row of cabins.

'You've gone very quiet,' he said softly, indicating that she should follow him off the beaten track away from the guest rooms.

Laura's heart was already racing. The further they got away from the bar and the other guests the tighter the knot in her stomach was growing. Fleetingly she wondered if it was too late to change her mind and go back and find Joe.

'I've never done anything like this before,' she said in a low voice.

Beside her in the growing gloom she heard Danny laugh softly. 'I've already told you, just relax. Why don't you tell me about yourself, what do you do when you're not whoring over at O'Malley's.'

The word flashed like a neon light inside her head. Was that what she was doing? She struggled to tell him something about her life in England, asked him what he did. It was hard to make normal conversation; the promise of what might follow hung in her mind like the stars of the Southern Cross above them.

Danny's cabin faced the sea, a canvas awning slung outside to give a little shelter from the elements. He set the tray down on the table and then turned towards her. Her mind absorbed the setting in an instant; the sounds of the wind as it rippled through the canvas, the palm trees and the give of the sand beneath her feet as he moved closer.

Before she had time to say anything his hands slid up over her thighs, pushing her dress up as he went, making her gasp in surprise.

'Oh yes, very nice.' He purred, hands resting on her hips. 'You feel real good. You're going to be in big demand when you loosen up. Why don't you just take these off.' His fingers eased under the sides of her white lace knickers. 'A man likes the opportunity to examine the merchandise.'

Laura swallowed hard; if she had expected some sort of

prelude, some gentle introduction it was obvious Danny had other plans. She had completely misjudged him. His eyes glinted in the darkness.

'Or would you prefer me to do it for you?'

Before she had time to reply he tugged them lower. 'Most of the whores I know don't bother to wear them – they just get in the way.'

She shivered. 'I thought you said you were going to be gentle.'

Danny laughed. 'Oh I am, I really am. Why don't you help me?'

Laura stepped away from him, and then slowly pushed the thin fabric down, her heart rate increasing with every passing second.

Danny leant against the table, eyes fixed on the gathered folds of her dress. She reddened: earlier in the day Joe's interest had been non-threatening – the desire and the hunger not his but hers. With Danny it was different. Danny Collins had the eyes of a predator.

'Lift your skirt higher,' he said softly, gesturing with his fingers. 'Good, very good. You're going to make a great little whore.'

Laura's eyes filled up with tears; the reaction took her by surprise. Whatever Danny had said in the bar, he wasn't interested in her at all – watching her, he had reduced her to her sexual essence. He wanted her body, nothing more.

As her panties dropped onto the sand, he stepped forward and slid a hand between her thighs, fingers eagerly seeking out the soft moist folds of her sex. She gasped. In spite of her fears she knew she was wet, hungry – her need as raw as any bitch on heat.

His fingers brushed her clitoris making her moan with pleasure.

Inches from her face, his eyes glittered. 'Maybe not quite so sweet and innocent as you like to pretend. You like that, huh?' he whispered.

Dumbly Laura nodded, whatever her mind thought, her body seemed to have other ideas. He dipped into her; she could already feel her juices trickling out onto her thighs, easing his way, like a river guiding him home. This time it was Danny that moaned.

'My God, you're so wet – you've been thinking about this all night, haven't you? Since you delivered the rest of the girls,' he murmured, as his fingers worked deeper. 'Thinking about what they're getting and what you'd be missing. Good job I came along.'

She didn't want or need to answer him, instinctively her body began to move against his. The desire that had been building steadily during the last forty-eight hours seemed to have gathered momentum and rose up like a tidal wave inside her, driving away all reason.

Danny turned her round so that she faced the table, pulling her dress up over her hips as he did so. She leant forward taking her weight on her hands, imagining what he could see; her legs open, accentuating the ripe curves of her backside, glittering droplets of excitement clinging to the dark hair around her sex. The image fuelled her desire.

She sensed him moving closer, running a hand over her smooth, slim buttocks, and then his fingers moved lower, dipping again and again into the pool of pleasure that lay between her legs. She began to tremble, her whole body suffused by a low, earthy hum. The sensation was as primeval and ancient as the ocean.

She mewled as he parted the engorged folds of her quim. Before she had time to think, or to protest, he pushed her down over the table, one hand undoing the zip at the back of her dress so that it slithered off her shoulders, exposing her breasts.

As he pressed her forward his hands seemed to be everywhere, fondling and cupping her breasts, teasing at her nipples, rolling them into pulsating peaks, while all the while, behind her she could feel the hard press of his cock begging entry.

She thrust back into his belly, offering herself up – an animal unleashed and baying for satisfaction. He snorted and then she heard the soft growl of his zip. An instant later she felt his cock, hard and hungry, nuzzling against her, looking for a way in.

Caught up in an abstract need to feel a man deep inside her, she slipped a hand between her legs and wrapping her fingers around his slick shaft guided him home. As he breached her she closed her eyes, concentrating on the sensation of his cock easing smoothly home into her body.

Her whole consciousness seemed to be centred on that hot wet junction. He began to move, slowly at first, and she moved with him, finding a natural rhythm.

Danny moaned as if he too was savouring the heat and the wetness. And then, once he was sure of her compliance, he began to move more quickly, aggressively, forcing her down onto the rough boards.

She shrieked as he powered into her, her body matching his stroke for stroke as he drove towards oblivion.

At the very point of release he pulled her back into an arc against him, her body flexing like a bow to take his arrow. His fingers nipped cruelly at her breasts, while his other hand snaked down over her belly brushing the glittering bud that nestled in the depths of her quim. She gasped, struggling to breath, struggling to retain some shred of control but it was impossible.

Their climax exploded like a lightning strike, making her thrust back again and again, drowning in a sea of white-hot pleasure, relishing the sensation of her body closing around him, sucking him dry.

There seemed to be an instant of stillness, a moment of total silence and then Laura was aware of Danny's weight, aware of his frantic breathing and the rough boards against her breasts.

Slowly he eased out of her, his spent cock trickling his seed and her juices out onto her thighs. The sea breeze cooled them instantly, leaving a trail of glistening kisses on her glowing skin.

Without speaking he pulled out a chair and sat down. She looked across at him, her body still trembling.

To her surprise he grinned. 'You'd better eat something,' he said breathlessly. 'It's going to be a long night.' He dragged the tray closer and lifted the cover off. There were no sweet

51

words, no thanks, nothing – Laura felt her embarrassment returning.

He glanced towards the open cabin door. 'I'm all in. I've gotta be up at dawn to take those guys out on the reef. You know your way back to the hotel, don't you?'

Laura was stunned by his apparent indifference. As he spoke he got unsteadily to his feet and put his hand into his pocket. From inside he produced a wallet and pulled out a few crumpled notes.

'Not bad for a beginner,' he said, dropping them onto the table beside her. 'Maybe we can get together again some time when I'm out this way.'

Laura stared at him. 'I thought . . .' she began, pulling her dress back up over her shoulders, 'that maybe we could talk, eat – you know – I . . .' she stopped, feeling terribly self-conscious.

Danny smiled, the predatory glint had returned to his eyes as he indicated the money on the table. 'Maybe another time. I'm not one of those guys who pays a woman to talk dirty. You better get used to the idea that this is purely business, babe, I would have thought Belle would have told you that.'

Without another word he walked towards the cabin. Before she could think of anything to say he closed the door.

Laura looked down at the money – payment for services rendered. She bit her lip. She felt used and yet at the same time strangely elated; sex for sex sake, as pure and clean and exciting as anything she had ever experienced. Ignoring the food she picked up the money and dropped it into her handbag – she'd eat in the main hotel while she waited for Joe and the others to return.

Chapter 5

Belle O'Malley yawned and stood the empty brandy balloon down beside her supper tray.

'I thought you were taking Eva and the girls over to Home Cove tonight?' she said to Leo, who was sitting on the far side of her desk, legs out-stretched, feet up, resting amongst a stack of papers.

He shook his head. 'No. They wanted to drive themselves. Eva said she didn't know what time they'd be getting back.'

He had no intention of telling Belle that the last time he had seen her precious three girl take-away it was in a jeep being driven by Laura and Joe Blanco.

Belle stared out of the open window. 'Do you think Laura will be okay?'

Leo wondered for a moment whether Belle had read his mind.

'She's with Joe, isn't she?' he asked, careful to keep his tone as neutral as his expression.

Belle nodded. 'Yes. She said they were driving up to the Cape along the coast road.'

Leo relaxed. 'Joe's a good driver, they'll be fine. You worry too much.'

Belle stretched. 'You're right. We'd better get into the bar. I was thinking that maybe next week I could arrange a few days off, take Laura out. Do you think you could manage here on your own?'

Leo grinned and unfolded himself from the chair. 'Not a problem. Your trouble is you think you're indispensable. It'll be fine. Who have we got booked in tonight?'

It was the early hours of the morning before Laura finally

got back to her cabin. The other girls had fallen asleep on the way home. Laura didn't have to ask Joe how his evening had gone; the delighted look in his eyes gave him away.

Conversation was subdued on the way home. Laura felt no desire to share her exploits with Danny Collins with the good-looking Italian voyeur and Eva and the other girls were asleep within minutes of the jeep pulling away from Home Cove.

Looking out at the dense rainforest trees picked out in the truck's headlights, Laura found it hard to believe that she had willingly sold her body to a total stranger.

Beside her, Joe turned the radio on low.

'Did you have a good night?' he said softly. 'I kept thinking you must be bored down there all on your own – I wondered whether you might come up and join us. It was a very good night.'

Laura laughed. 'I thought you might have seen enough of me for one day.'

'Never,' he said with good humour. 'But then again maybe you don't like to . . .' He reddened, tripping over his own embarrassment. 'You know – do the business.'

It was such a coy expression that Laura couldn't help smiling. 'No,' she said evenly. 'I really quite like the business.'

Joe nodded. 'Then you should have come upstairs with us. Lots going on up there – you could have taken your pick.'

She could hear the satisfaction in his voice.

'Maybe you're right,' she said casually as she settled herself back in the comfortable bucket seat and closed her eyes. The memory of Danny Collin's features filled her tired mind, the sounds of his breath and sensation of his cock throbbing deep inside her suffusing her senses. If only Joe knew.

When she woke again the jeep was pulling to a halt outside O'Malley's. With barely a word the three girls in the back slipped out into the darkness. Joe dropped the jeep into first and crept up over the lawn until he drew level with Laura's cabin. Leaning across he kissed her on the cheek.

'Don't worry. Laura, I promise you that next time we go

out we'll find you a man,' he said.

Laura smiled. 'Night, Joe,' she said and clambered out into the tropical night. Around her the tree frogs and cicadas chirruped out a pre-dawn chorus. Joe lifted a hand in farewell and then drove off slowly down towards his beach house.

Laura pulled the key out of her bag to unlock the cabin door. The fold of notes Danny had given her were still tucked alongside her purse. She turned them over thoughtfully in her fingers – weren't they all the proof she needed that O'Malley's wasn't just a hotel? But what did they tell her about herself?

She shivered and headed for the bathroom; the smell of Danny's body clung to her like an exotic perfume. A few minutes later, still damp from the shower she slipped into bed and dropped the mosquito net. In her dreams she imagined Danny's hawkish eyes and the perfunctory touch of his hands on her body as he forced her down over the table, taking her again and again.

It was mid-morning when Laura woke again and as she surfaced into consciousness a horrible thought struck her. What if Eva or one of the other girls let slip to Belle that she and Joe had driven them over to Home Cove?

As the idea caught hold she clambered out of bed and pulled a thin cotton dress out of the wardrobe.

Better if she talked to Belle herself.

Five minutes later she was hurrying towards the main hotel. The sunshine was already hot and bright. Taking a deep breath, not exactly certain what she was going to say, Laura knocked on the office door and opened it without waiting for a reply.

Before her eyes had adjusted to the gloom she pulled the bundle of notes out of her handbag and dropped them onto the desk.

'I think we really have to talk – I went to Home Cove last night,' she began and then realised that the figure on the other side of the desk was not Belle, but Leo.

He grinned and dropped a pen amongst the papers he had been reading. 'I already know all about it.'

Laura blushed crimson. 'I thought . . . Where's Belle?'

Her voice faded as Leo looked her up and down. His expression was impassive but his eyes glittered. It was the same look of predatory interest she had seen on Danny's face.

'She's gone down to the ferry to pick up supplies,' he replied, eyes still moving over her body.

Laura turned to leave but Leo was already on his feet. 'Whoa – hang on – what's your problem? I'm not going to bite you. Besides I've already heard about your little adventure. Danny Collins rang me first thing this morning.' He paused. 'Fortunately Belle had already left.'

Laura stared at him. 'Danny rang here?'

Leo grinned. 'He most certainly did. He reckoned you were pretty good for a beginner.'

Laura's colour deepened, as Leo continued, 'Your first satisfied customer. I knew I'd got you pegged from the moment I laid eyes on you ...'

'What do you mean?' she said unsteadily.

'I told Belle you were a natural.' He moved round behind her, so close that she could feel his breath on her skin. 'So what are your plans for today? The reef? The rainforest – or, now that you've had a little taste of what O'Malley's has got to offer, perhaps you fancy combining business with pleasure? We've got a couple of lonely company executives booked in at lunch time – maybe you'd like to team up with one of the other girls and make it into a working holiday?'

Laura swallowed hard. 'A working holiday?' she repeated.

Before she had time to compose her thoughts Leo stepped up close and ran his hands over her breasts and belly. She stiffened, feeling the unnerving flare of desire returning.

'Why not?' he whispered, kissing the sensitive skin in the curve of her neck. 'I know you'd enjoy it, and besides, didn't you suggest to Belle that you'd like to do something to earn your keep?'

Laura swung round. 'Are you serious?' she hissed. They were so close that their faces were practically touching.

Leo grinned, fingers straying to outline the hardening peaks of her nipples. 'Oh, I think so,' he said. 'What about you?'

Laura, mind racing, stepped away from him. Her body had started to respond instantly to his masculinity; the desire already growing stronger, unbidden, in her belly.

'I don't think . . .' she began haltingly.

He smiled, eyes alight. 'Oh, this isn't about thinking, Laura, it's about feeling. And I already know what you're feeling. I can see the look in your eyes. I've seen it a thousand times before. You want to say yes, don't you?'

Without waiting for her reply he jerked her closer, lips closing on hers, tongue forcing its way into her mouth. She gasped, struggling to stay in control. Part of her screamed out in astonishment while her lips opened, a rush of adrenaline coursing through her veins.

'Leo,' she gasped in surprise, pushing him away. 'Don't. I can't, please.'

But while her logical mind said one thing her body said quite another. She didn't resist as he pulled her back towards him, drinking in his kisses, relishing the heat and the sensation of his strong muscular arms around her. Her whole body ached for his touch. His fingers were already on the fastenings of her dress. She had dressed quickly, eager to get to Belle's office and under the thin cotton shift she was naked.

As the zip gave way the little dress offered no resistance. Sliding down over her body like a whisper it dropped to the floor and pooled around her feet.

Leo pulled back, holding her at arm's length, eyes working over her nakedness in detached professional appraisal.

'Joe and Danny were right,' he said. 'Great body, but you know that Joe only likes to look, not touch. Bet that drove you wild – no wonder you went hunting for a little companionship last night.'

Hurriedly, Laura bent down to pick her dress up and cover herself.

'Don't,' snapped Leo, pushing the door closed with his foot. In what seemed like a single well-oiled gesture he turned the key in the lock and handed it to her.

'Belle will be gone until late afternoon. Plenty of time for me to show you what you need to know. Or,' he indicated the key in her hand. 'If you like, you can go now and I won't mention it again and I'll make sure Belle never finds out about your little escapade over at Home Cove. Your choice.'

Laura hesitated; the metal key felt cool against her warm flesh. She looked up at Leo, afraid and excited by turns.

'I don't know,' she said after a second or two. It surprised her that she was even considering his offer.

He grinned and stepped closer, gently easing the cotton dress out of her fingers. 'Oh, but I think you do, Laura,' he said, and guided her down onto the office floor. 'I really think you do.'

With a certain detachment he began to explore her body, opening her legs, watching her all the time with his glittering cool eyes. His fingers circled the peaks of her breasts, teasing the nipples making her tremble with excitement. She swallowed hard; his touch was electric. Every molecule seemed to reach up to absorb his caresses.

Slowly he worked his way down over her belly, watching her reactions. Finally, he skirted the sensitive hairs around her sex and without thinking she thrust up to meet him. He grinned, and slowly slid a finger down between the hot, wet lips of her quim. She whimpered as he brushed the hood of her clitoris.

'You know,' he said in a voice barely above a whisper. 'Your trouble is that you've been going out with that boyfriend of yours too long. Sex shouldn't be something you have done to you, it's something you share – in Belle's case something you sell. A bargain – you give, they take, you can both share the pleasure. It's alive, a living thing, not passive. And I know you need it, baby – just look at you.'

He rubbed the little bud again; she bit her lip, relishing the tiny flickers of intense pleasure that his touch gave her.

'If you're going to be a whore, Laura, you've got to learn to relax, to go with what you feel, drink it in like a great wine.'

She stared up at him, desperately aware of her nakedness and vulnerability and yet at the same time incredibly excited and eager for more.

'Will you help me?' she said, struggling to find a voice as

he trailed his finger over the junction of her outer lips.

He grinned. 'If that's what you want. But I need to be sure.'

Laura glanced down at the key, still clenched in her fist. Slowly she uncurled her fingers and handed it back to him.

'I'm sure,' she said in a tiny voice.

Leo held out his hand and helped her to her feet. 'Then we'll start your first lesson. Put your dress back on.' He picked it up and threw it at her.

Still naked she stared at him. 'But I thought . . .' she began, glancing down at the floor where seconds earlier she was convinced he was going to make love to her.

He shook his head. 'Oh no, that comes later. You've got to second guess what it is I want, turn me on, give me the thing I am paying for – guys arrive real nervous sometimes. You're the professional here, you've got to help me.'

Laura reddened. 'Help you?'

He sat down at the desk and put his feet up. 'That's right.'

'But how?'

Leo laughed. 'Come on – don't play coy with me. It's no great mystery. How did you pick Danny up?'

'But I didn't,' she protested, dragging the dress on over her head.

Leo snorted. 'Oh come on, don't be so modest. He knew just what you were, took one look and just knew. A whore on the make, looking for a little company to pass the time.'

Laura's colour deepened. Hadn't she arrived at Home Cove thinking about sex, imagining what Eva and the girls would be doing upstairs – and in her belly there had been a fierce hunger. She stared at Leo as revelation dawned. That was what Danny had seen and recognised.

She turned away, reluctant to let Leo see the comprehension in her eyes.

'Come on,' he purred. 'What were you thinking? Show me.'

Laura glanced at the desk, nestling among the papers was the key that Leo had discarded. The key to a bargain – hadn't she already made her choice? When she looked at Leo again he grinned.

'Oh yes,' he murmured. 'That's it. Tell me what you're thinking.'

Laura swallowed hard, struggling to find a voice. 'How much I wanted you to make love to me on the floor just now, how I thought you were going to make me feel,' she stumbled over the words. 'When you touched me, slipped your fingers inside me. I imagined what it would be like to feel your cock inside me, feel you skin against mine, I . . .' Her voice failed her.

Leo's expression hadn't changed. 'That's good, feel it, go with it. Imagine what it would be like to feel me fucking you, taking you, making you cry out for more, fingers raking down my back, as you thrust that tight little cunt up against me. Feel it.'

Laura felt the heat rising up inside her, sweat forming in crystal beads on her skin.

'You need to hold onto that feeling,' he said softly, beckoning her closer. 'Every guy who ever comes here wants that, that desire, that hunger – they may want to do some things a little different, some special little game that they played over and over in their minds a thousand times, and you are there to give it to them, but at the end of it all there is only pleasure – that's what they have come looking for. And you are there to help them find it.'

Laura approached the desk, pulse racing.

'Lift up your skirt,' he said softly. 'Up around your waist. Let me look at you.'

Wordlessly Laura complied. His words echoed those of Danny's the night before. Leo, like Danny, only wanted her body. He ran his hands over her thighs, parting them roughly. She gasped as his fingers found their goal. He seemed satisfied and patted the desk in front of him. 'Now get up here.'

Slowly she climbed onto the desk so that she sat facing him, her knees demurely closed.

Leo grinned. 'Don't lose it now, baby, open up for me. Feet up here on the desk too. I want all of you.'

Blushing furiously she did as she was told. Totally exposed now she closed her eyes tight, as he began to explore her quim which opened like a scarlet flower under his fingertips.

She felt something brush her inner thighs and then an instant later let out a little gasp of sheer delight as she felt his tongue ease its way into the hot shimmering depths.

He groaned appreciatively as his fingers followed close behind his tongue, holding her wide open for his explorations. Sliding deep inside her he began to lap and suck hungrily at her clitoris.

His tongue seemed to touch her with a strange erotic magic. As his tongue circled round and round it felt as if her body was melting. Lifting herself up towards him she mewled with ecstasy. To her delight he murmured his approval and began to stroke the sensitive bridge of flesh between her sex and the tight puckering of her backside.

A single finger teased around the dark closure, the caress as delicate as a feather. No man had ever touched her there before, and for a few seconds she thought she would faint from sheer intensity of the sensation. Meanwhile all the time his tongue worked its spell over her throbbing pleasure bud.

'Give yourself to me. Come on,' Leo murmured. 'I want all of you – don't hold back. Hold yourself open for me.'

Without hesitation she slid her hands down over her belly, eager to comply, and opened the lips of her sex for his mouth, lips and wicked tongue. The juices that lubricated her fingers were as warm and compelling as liquid silk.

Feeling the hot wet folds of her body mingling with the soft press of Leo's tongue and fingers was the final straw. She gasped and lay back amongst the piles of papers, lifting her hips and pelvis in time with his glorious ministrations. Her body seemed to be spinning away into oblivion, absorbed in a web of pleasure. Thrusting up again and again she screamed with delight as the waves of excitement exploded deep inside her.

Gasping she looked at Leo. His lips were wet, his eyes dark with desire, and as she struggled to sit up she could see the rigid outline of his cock, desperate for attention, forced up against the cotton drill of his cream chinos. He leaned back a little.

'Now it's my turn,' he said in a thick voice. 'Come here and give me what I want.'

Without hesitation Laura slithered off the desk, legs still trembling with the after-shocks of orgasm. Kneeling on the floor beside him she undid his zip and freed the great curving phallus that was imprisoned within.

Without thinking she guided him into her mouth, sucking him deep, hand closing around the length of his shaft, fingers and mouth working in tandem. He instantly thrust up towards her. She could taste the robust saltiness of his excitement and eased her hands lower so that she could cup the heavy, pendulous bulk of his balls.

Artfully she ran her tongue around the ridged head of his cock, nibbling and sucking as she slid his foreskin back and forth. He gasped and thrust again, moaning breathlessly as she brought him closer and closer to the edge.

Beneath her fingertips she felt a sharp contraction, a compelling erotic pulse – he was seconds away from the moment of no return.

Scrambling to her feet, keeping his cock in her mouth until the very last second, she lifted her skirt and straddled his waist, guiding him deep inside her in a single unbroken movement.

As he drove his cock home her sex closed around him like a silken fist. With that first thrust she felt her own pleasure re-ignite and pressed down hard against him, brushing her sex up against his belly.

He gasped. She thrust again, taking the lead, setting the pace, and with this he joined her in a wild dance out towards the edge of madness. Frantically she ground her body against his, and then suddenly she felt his cock throb deep inside her, the surging, furious pulse echoing through her again and again.

Laura tightened her muscles, taking him with her, on and on and on, until she couldn't distinguish where his orgasm stopped and hers began.

Finally, laughing and gasping for air, Leo pushed her off. 'Sweet Jesus,' he snorted appreciatively. 'You really are good. No wonder Danny Collins wanted to see you again.'

'Shared pleasure?'

He nodded, tidying his clothes. 'What was it you trained to do in England?'

Laura pulled her dress straight and gathered her hair up into a knot. 'Office management.'

Leo shook his head in disbelief. 'What a waste. I think it's time you saw the other side of O'Malley's.'

'Now?' Laura asked in surprise.

Leo shook his head. 'No, the action doesn't really start until the sun goes down.' He gazed thoughtfully out of the office window. 'And we've got to make sure Belle doesn't get wind of what we're up to. Don't worry. I'll organise it before tonight.'

Chapter 6

Rain began to fall as Laura walked back to her cabin. Her body and mind ached. For the first time since her arrival the air was cool. Out beyond the shelter of the covered boardwalk the rain fell in a continuous sheet, vertically, like water from a celestial tap. Where the huge droplets exploded onto the palm fronds and vines, the leaves glowed like emeralds.

The sound of the water falling was unbelievably loud – raindrops beating on the leaves, rushing down over corrugated iron roofs, bouncing off the metalled pathways – a whole orchestra of sounds that astonished Laura and, for a little while at least, stilled the thoughts that had filled her mind.

She stared out at the hotel gardens. Over the ocean lightning flashed as an electrical storm illuminated the rapidly darkening sky. It was awe-inspiring and yet in a strange way seemed to reflect her mood perfectly. She sat down on the veranda and stared out at the weather, caged, it seemed, behind a curtain of tumbling water.

It was late afternoon when Belle, her face almost obscured by a large raffia sun hat, stepped up onto Laura's veranda. 'Hiya, darling,' she said, slipping off her waterproof and shaking it. 'Leo said I'd find you out here. Are you sure you're not bored rigid hanging round the hotel?'

Laura, who had been dozing, closed the book on her lap. She was having a siesta, mesmerised by the hypnotic throb of the falling rain. Curled up on a rattan sofa outside her cabin, covered up by a rug, her mind had replayed her encounter with Leo – and Danny, and Joe.

Diamonds of water cascaded in streams from the eaves of the veranda. She stretched, trying to catch hold of her thoughts. 'No, not at all. I just need a little time to acclimatise and then you won't see my tail for dust.' Laura smiled. 'I was finally getting used to the heat when it started to rain. How did the shopping expedition go?'

Belle slumped down on a chair and looked heavenwards. 'Hardly shopping, darling. If it had been anything that exciting you could have come along for the ride. The roads are really tricky in this sort of weather but I have to pick up a trailer-load of staples – rice, pasta, that kind of thing – from a lorry off the ferry once a month. Shopping would be a real treat by comparison. I thought that while you're here we could have a couple of days in Cairns and go see what we can find?'

Laura nodded.

Belle peeled off her hat. 'Leo tells me you're going up to Ropey's tonight?'

Laura hesitated. It was the first she'd heard about it. She nodded, careful not to commit herself.

'Are you taking Joe along too?'

Laura pulled a face, wondering what exactly Leo had in mind for her.

Before she could reply a familiar voice answered. 'Maybe, it depends on what his plans are. We haven't asked him yet.'

Laura looked up to see Leo striding along the boardwalk carrying a tray. 'I thought you might like a drink,' he said setting it down on the small table between the women.

Belle smiled. 'Angel,' she said taking a glass. 'Everything go okay this morning while I was out?'

Leo smiled mischievously at Laura. 'Oh, just fine. Laura and I have been planning her itinerary. Ropey's tonight, then maybe out on the reef.' He took a long pull on the can of beer he'd brought for himself. 'I think I've finally persuaded her to loosen up and enjoy her holiday.'

Belle nodded her approval. 'Good.' She stretched. 'I think I'm going to go have a shower and catch up on a few hours' sleep.' She smiled at Laura. 'I'm so glad you're settling in. I've arranged with Leo to take a few days off next week. I thought we might do a little exploring. Give us chance to get to know each other better.'

'Sounds like a great idea,' Laura said.

Belle drained her glass in one and stood it back on the tray. 'Meanwhile, I'm afraid I'll have to leave you to Joe and Leo – but I'm sure, between them, they'll take good care of you.'

Laura glanced surreptitiously at Leo; his expression was enigmatic.

Belle got up. 'If you'll excuse me, I've really got to get on. I'll see you both at dinner.' She picked up the drover's coat she'd dropped over the back of the chair and headed back out into the rain.

As soon as she was out of earshot Leo turned to Laura. 'We've got a big party of clients booked in tonight for a barbecue. Belle is relieved you're going to be out of the way for the evening.'

Laura pulled a face.

Leo grinned. 'God, the hoops that woman's put herself through trying to ensure you don't find out about O'Malley's – if only she knew.'

Laura picked up her book. 'You don't have to make it sound so two-faced, Leo. She's only trying to protect me – and you're going to help her by taking me to this Ropey's place.'

'Not exactly. I thought maybe we could go up there for a quick drink, wait until the evening gets going and then drive back here. I promised you a guided tour and I'm a man of my word.'

'Won't Belle see us?'

Leo took another slug of beer. 'Not if we're careful. Take a tip from Belle, and get some sleep – it's going to be a long hot night. I've got to be getting back and give her a hand to check the stock.'

He glanced at Laura and then leant forward and ran a hand over her long, smooth legs. Almost idly he slipped his hands up under her dress, his fingers outlining the mound of her sex. His caress made her shiver.

'You were really good this morning.' He pulled a little roll of money out of his trouser pocket and dropped it into her lap. 'You left this behind.'

Laura stared at him; it was the money Danny Collins had given her at Home Cove.

He kissed her gently. 'You're going to enjoy this,' he said in a whisper, and then winked. 'And so am I. Sweet dreams.'

Laura waited until Leo had disappeared before moving. His casually intimate caress had made her ache for more. What was happening to her? She collected her things together and went into the cabin.

On her way to the shower she heard the phone ringing. Throwing her towel and book onto a chair she picked up the receiver.

Before she could say more than 'Hello', a familiar voice said, 'Oh, so there you are.'

Laura sat down heavily on the edge of the bed. 'Hello, Gareth, how are you?'

Although her boyfriend was twelve thousand miles away the line was as clear as if he was in the next room.

'It's after midnight here.' There was an edge of annoyance in his voice. Although she instantly recognised who it was, it felt as if Gareth was an echo from another lifetime.

'I thought you would have rung me by now. I've really been quite concerned. Forgotten about me already have you?' His question mirrored her thoughts almost exactly and Laura reddened. There was no warmth in his words.

'I rang my family,' she said lamely, 'but I just—'

'Don't tell me,' Gareth said. 'You didn't think and you haven't had the time. You really need to get yourself more organised, Laura.'

She was about to protest but Gareth continued. 'Well, it doesn't really matter. This is just a quick call. I'm not going to be long, I ought to be in bed – long day tomorrow. Squash with Philip first thing, meeting of the senior partners after lunch. You know how these things go. The reason I called is that I wanted you to know that I've arranged an interview for you as soon as you get home.'

'An interview?'

Gareth snorted. 'Yes, Laura, you remember. A decent job, something with a proper career structure, and a pension plan? I've had a word with Gerry Lloyd in H.R. and he thinks he may have found you the perfect niche. Actually, I've pulled a few strings – the interview should be just a formality. I've already told him all about you.'

Laura stared at the receiver. 'Really, and what did you tell him?'

Gareth sniffed. She could imagine him sitting by the phone in his dressing gown, cradling a small Scotch. 'That you'd just passed your exams with flying colours – mature student, good steady sort, and all that – he seemed most impressed with your current CV.'

Laura lay back on the bed. Outside, through the open door she could see a couple walking hand in hand across the grass, apparently oblivious to the cascading rain. They looked like bright birds. The girl's blouse clung to her, revealing every curve, every plane of her ripe body. Something about the way they moved told Laura that their liaison was business. She smiled. Business and pleasure; a perfect combination. The idea amused her.

'Gareth, I don't have a current CV.'

'You do now, I had my secretary type one up for you this morning. Anyway, they're looking for a managerial trainee in data processing. I thought it would be the perfect job for you.' He paused to let the words sink in.

Laura sighed. Perfect for Gareth.

Outside, unaware that she was being watched, the girl, a stunning brunette, ran her fingers back through her wet hair and arched her back. Her nipples, hard and dark as thunder clouds, showed through her thin cotton blouse, Laura stared at her – she was an erotic masterpiece.

The man turned towards her, every molecule of his body shimmering with desire. The girl grinned mischievously and, breaking away from him, ran towards one of the cabins. Laura craned forward, curious to see what might follow next.

'We'd be working in the same building,' Gareth continued in his dry monotone. 'We could travel in to work together, perhaps even have lunch together occasionally. Though we shouldn't make too much of the social connection. The bank aren't awfully keen about executive managers fraternising with . . . well, you know.'

69

Laura couldn't help but smile. She could hear his discomfort and wondered what he really wanted to say. 'Minions and underlings' sprung to mind.

With the view of the lovers obscured by the tumble of vines and bushes, Laura rolled over onto her belly and tried to concentrate on Gareth's voice. It wasn't easy. The temperature was beginning to rise, in spite of the downpour. A trickle of sweat glistened in the valley between her breasts.

She and Gareth had been dating for years. Only her reluctance had stopped them from getting married. What was it that had stopped her from making a commitment? Gareth was safe and strong and ultimately reliable. It was just that there were so many parts of her nature he wasn't aware of.

She slipped the shoulder straps of her dress off her shoulders, pushing the fabric down over her breasts and hips until she could wriggle out of it. The air from the overhead fan caressed her naked skin; she had already begun to tan. She ran a hand over her nipples and then down over her belly, relishing the smoothness of her taut skin. It was sad to think how much he was missing.

Gareth hadn't even been prepared to consider anything as normal as their living together. He was the product of a bygone age. She wondered what he would think if he could see her now. She brushed the dark corona of hair around her sex and the light touch made her shiver.

'So,' he said, 'I'd better get off to bed. Having a good time are you?'

Laura could hardly bring herself to reply.

The drive up to Ropey's Bar was rough going, the road slewing back and forth between densely packed trees. Out beyond the headlights the night was unimaginably dark. Laura watched nervously as the track climbed at an impossible angle up through a rocky gorge and wondered what she was doing and where exactly they were going. It was hard to believe there was anywhere habitable this far out in the wilderness.

Although it was no more than eight o'clock they had

passed no cars and seen no other signs of life. In the driver's seat Leo's concentration was entirely fixed on the route ahead. Finally the road levelled and she sensed him relaxing – surely they had to be nearly there?

'We really didn't have to come all this way, I wouldn't have minded giving Ropey's a miss.'

Leo grinned. 'Now she tells me,' he said with mock indignation. 'Ropey would have noticed though. Belle was on the phone to him this afternoon – he's expecting us.'

'So we had to come?'

'No reason to make Belle suspicious.' He nodded towards the back of the jeep. 'I've brought along a little something for you to change into before we go back to O'Malley's. Hope it fits.'

Laura turned round. Resting on the seat behind her was a small overnight case. 'What's in it?'

Leo grinned. 'You'll see. Here we are.'

Ahead of them on the curve of the road was a large area of grass encircled by lights set into the ground. In the centre was what looked like a cowboy bunk house, with a long veranda. The only incongruous feature – besides the heaving mass of people drinking – was an enormous sugar-pink neon sign that, in italics, read, '*Ropey's Deluxe Bar and Grill.*'

Laura stared in astonishment. It was like an oasis in the desert. Heavy rock music throbbed out through the moist night air, while at the open-air bar customers were queuing three or four deep, waiting to be served.

'Where the hell do they all come from?' she said in amazement.

'Down out of the hills some of them, but most of the customers here are back packers – Ropey's got cabins, tents and dormitories that he hires out for peanuts. He makes his money on the booze and food. And if you can't settle your bill, it doesn't worry him. See that big coloured girl serving behind bar? That's Layla. She came up here three or four seasons ago, couldn't pay, so Ropey let her work it off. She liked it so much she just stayed. Sometimes he sends the odd girl down to O'Malley's and Belle settles up for her. Come on – let's go mingle.'

71

Laura could hardly believe it. For the next two hours, in the middle of the jungle, in the darkest night Laura had ever seen she danced and drank and laughed with Leo and a crowd of the students staying at Ropey's.

Ropey himself – a weather-beaten hippie in his late fifties – once introduced and standing her a beer, went back off to get on with business – and it was booming.

Finally, just as she was beginning to feel as if she could dance all night, Leo came up behind her and dropped a hand onto her shoulder. 'We really ought to be getting back. Unless of course you've changed your mind about the guided tour of O'Malley's.'

Laura smiled. 'Back to Belle's party?'

Leo nodded. 'Yeah – should be swinging by now.'

Without another word Laura stood her glass on a nearby table and followed Leo back out into the tropical night. To her surprise, once they were outside, instead of getting back into the jeep, Leo handed her the little suitcase from the back seat and headed down a gravelled track beside the bar.

'Where are we going?'

Leo, carrying a torch to show the way, grinned. In the sallow yellow light his features looked uncanny.

'Jut a little detour. Nothing too demanding.'

Two hundred yards down the track it was impossible to believe that Ropey's existed. Forest surrounded them like a blanket and the only sounds were the song of the frogs and insects.

Walking around another sweeping bend Laura could hear the distant roll of the ocean and between the trees pick out the raw orange flicker of flames.

Leo indicated the bonfire with the torch. 'There we are, babe, your first official assignment.'

Laura stared at him. 'What?' she whispered in horror.

'Don't look so worried. They're expecting you. Get changed.'

Laura took a step back. 'They?'

Leo grinned. 'Two very close friends of mine.'

Laura stared at him. 'I don't understand.'

'You will.' Leo took the case out of her hands and opened it. Inside was a tiny black lycra mini-dress and a pair of patent sandals. She bit her lip, apprehension mingling with a certain mischievous desire.

Leo looked at her. 'Well?'

'What do you want me to do?'

'Remember this morning in the office? Just follow your instincts. You'll be fine.'

Laura unzipped the cream sun dress she had been wearing and let it drop to the road. She was about to pull the black outfit on when Leo stopped her.

'Take the rest off too.'

She reddened, already feeling exposed in her tiny white lace bra and bikini knickers.

Leo retrieved her discarded sun dress before she could change her mind.

She stared at the roll of black material in her fingers.

'Doesn't pay to keep your customers waiting, babe,' he said softly. 'You've come this far.'

Laura took a deep breath, unhooked her bra and handed it to him. Leo smiled. 'God, you're lovely,' he purred, eyes moving rapidly over her pale flesh. 'I wish I'd recruited you.'

Laura laughed dryly. 'You did, didn't you?'

Leo shook his head. 'You did that yourself.'

Laura slipped her panties down. Leo held out a hand and she passed them over. Before he dropped them into the case he pressed them to his face and took a deep breath, as if savouring the sweetest perfume.

Laura's colour deepened.

'Off you go,' he said, waving her towards the trees.

Laura took one faltering step and then turned back, her face pale, expression tight and nervous. 'Aren't you coming with me?' she said.

Leo shook his head. 'Nope, this is your first real solo flight. But don't worry, I'll be close by if you need me.'

Laura swallowed hard and headed towards the beach.

Leo walked back to the jeep, dropped off the suitcase, and picked up a beer before wandering back down to the sea.

He had rung two of the men who sailed the tourist boats out onto the reef. They were acquaintances rather than close friends, but both of them enjoyed a good time. He'd seen them in action at Belle's on more than one occasion. Neither were rough or heavy-handed. The perfect introduction for Belle's precious little niece.

Guided by the firelight he switched off the torch and moved in close to watch his protégée at work. He was not disappointed.

Laura was sitting between the two sailors, and although she looked nervous, it seemed the initial introductions were over. One of them handed her the bottle he was drinking from and she took a long pull. Her companion moved closer and slipped his arm round her shoulders. Laura's eyes flashed with panic like a nervous filly. She took another mouth full of liquor and then one of the sailors pulled her closer, kissing her hard. She didn't resist as the second slid his hand up inside her dress.

Leo could sense the tension in Laura's body and willed her to relax – she was sprung tight, her fists clenched. He guessed it wouldn't take very much for his latest pupil to turn tail and run.

She flinched as the man found her quim, hidden beneath the black fabric, while the first man, his lips firmly fixed on Laura's, slipped the straps of her dress down to explore the uptilted curves of her small, pert breasts.

The firelight highlighted his work-roughened finger tips – a stark contrast to Laura's creamy white flesh – as they twisted and nipped at the sensitive peaks, rolling them into erection.

Guiding her back onto the sand the man began to stroke her breasts and belly, mouth working furiously against hers. There was no way she could resist their advances. They appeared totally mesmerised by her body, stroking her gently like some precious treasure washed up for their pleasure by the ebbing tide.

Leo could see Laura finally beginning to respond to the sensations, buoyed up by the power of their adoration.

She moaned thickly, her hands moving up over the first

man's chest, nervously seeking the buttons of his shirt. Between her legs the second man rolled her dress higher and pushed her thighs apart.

Laura appeared to freeze for an instant, caught up with her own inhibitions but the sailor had no such reservations and plunged his tongue into her sex.

Leo knew they had been waiting all night for Laura to arrive, and although they weren't the type to force her to do anything she didn't want to they had neither the time nor the inclination for a prolonged and subtle seduction.

To Leo's surprise, Laura cried out in pleasure, thrusting herself up to meet her lover's lips. Leo smiled; he was right, she really was a natural, and with that single cry she surrendered to the two men, letting her body be absorbed into the moment.

The man crouched between her legs gasped and murmured his approval, fingers working deep into the tight, wet crevices of Laura's now compliant body.

His companion, still kissing her, moved his fingers lower and dipped into the same fragrant sea, spreading her juices out in a silken web over her sex and belly.

Leo could sense the trio's growing excitement. Laura began to writhe as the man brought her closer and closer to the brink. Her excitement was contagious.

As if by some prearranged signal, the two men turned her gently. Her body was like liquid, moving instinctively under their guidance. All resistance and fear had gone, all she wanted was pleasure – theirs and hers, every inch of her seemed to pulse with barely controlled hunger.

Between them the two sun-tanned seamen lifted her up onto all fours, exploring the ripe curves of her body as they did so, fingers, tongues and lips stroking and touching, until there could be no fraction of her skin that they hadn't kissed or caressed.

While one man slid his hand up over her thighs, fingers splaying the wet, glistening curves of her sex, the other teased and toyed with her nipples. Slowly, the man who had been kissing her got to his knees.

'C'mon, sweetheart,' he whispered thickly, undoing his

shirt and guiding her hand into his groin. 'You know what I want. Take me in your mouth, suck me dry.'

His companion laughed. 'I would have thought you wanted to fuck this one. Christ, she's tight and wetter'n hell. You could drown in here.'

The first man laughed. 'Maybe we could take turns.' He looked down at Laura. 'What are you waiting for?' For a moment he pulled her close, rubbing his chest against her breasts and then he pushed her head down into his lap. Laura, eyes alight with a mixture of passion and fear, resisted for an instant.

Leo held his breath, wondering if now was the moment that she would pull back from the brink, then she unzipped the man's trousers and guided the head of his cock between her lips.

As she did so her hips thrust up and back. The rounded curves of her backside looked like molten gold in the fire light. Behind her, the sailor dragged off his tee shirt and shorts and, without prelude, he buried his shaft to the hilt in her gaping quim.

Leo let out a long, shuddering breath as the trio began to move. While one man fondled her breasts the other worked his fingers into the sopping pit of her sex. Leo knew the instant that he found the epicentre of her pleasure. Laura made a soft, baying noise, the sound trickling out around the other man's cock. And then she thrust back in triumph, eager now to set the rhythm.

Beads of sweat lifted in ridges along her spine as she flexed her hips. The sailors needed no further encouragement. Thrust for thrust they matched her, driving on towards release, the pace imperceivably quickening as both men began to lose control.

Leo saw Laura shudder, her thrusts growing ragged and instinctive as the first contractions of orgasm rolled through her. Her little convulsive movements and soft throaty gasps were too much for her companions. An instant later their bodies began to jerk like broken marionettes as the pleasure engulfed them all.

* * *

76

Laura shivered, trying to get some sense of place, some sense of control. Her breath came in ragged, noisy sobs. Above her she could feel the heat of one sailor, his chest brushing against her spine, while her mouth was flooded with the taste of the other man's seed.

The sensation of being a bridge between them, linked to them both, was all-engulfing. At the height of orgasm she had felt as if they were all joined, undivided, a single organism. Now as the sense of awareness returned she noticed the smell of their bodies – a sensual mix of sweat and sea – and the raw, rough sand beneath her knees.

The man above slipped out of her, rolling over onto his back, still breathing hard. She rolled into the sand alongside him and stared up at the ocean of stars. Her whole body felt alive, suffused with pleasure and satisfaction. The second man got to his feet, did up his trousers and added more logs to the fire.

'Want a beer?' said the man laying beside her. 'We could maybe take a breather and then start over? The night's young yet.'

His tone was so matter of fact that Laura couldn't help laughing. 'I think Leo's got other plans for me,' she said, taking the beer he offered her from the cooler. He seemed completely undisturbed by the fact that she was naked except for the black dress scrunched into a knot around her belly. The second man squatted beside her and ran a hand over her breasts, now coated with a fine covering of white sand.

'You're good. How much do we owe you?'

Laura reddened. 'I'm not sure—' she began.

From the shadows, right on cue, Leo strode across towards the fire. 'Don't worry. I'll take care of the business side of things.'

Laura felt her colour intensify. He waved her to her feet. 'If you want to wait for me by the trees, I won't be long and then we can go back to Belle's,' he said in a matter of fact voice. His tone was almost dismissive.

Laura nodded and pulled her dress back into some sort of order. At the tree line she hesitated and then looked back. The three men were crouched by the fire, sharing a joke in

77

low voices as the money changed hands. One of the sailors glanced towards her and lifted a hand in salute.

'See you around,' he said pleasantly.

Hastily Laura looked away.

Leo jogged over to join her. 'Nicely done,' he purred, resting a hand on her hip as they made their way towards the jeep. 'They really wanted you to stay. How was it for you?'

Laura snorted. 'Do you really want me to answer that?' She guessed he had watched her performance.

Leo aped hurt. 'No need to be angry with me, babe. I told you I wouldn't leave you on your own. Besides you looked as if you were having a good time. Certainly had the right effect on me.'

The humour in his voice stoked the little flare of indignation in her belly. He caught hold of her hand and pressed it into his groin. She could feel his cock throbbing, hard and unsatisfied under the soft cotton. If he was expecting her to be contrite or embarrassed he was wrong. She was annoyed that he had set her up so effectively but at the same time was elated by the raw animal desire that had coursed through her veins like magma. Heady stuff.

Without a second's hesitation she rounded on him, taking him by complete surprise, fingers tearing at his zip.

'Is this what you want? It is, isn't it?' she hissed, catching hold of his hand and pressing it up into the sopping pit between her legs.

'Jesus,' he gasped as she pushed him back against the trunk of a palm tree.

Undoing his zip, and with his cock held firmly between her fingers she guided him home into her throbbing quim. Wet from the sailor's orgasm, it almost seemed to suck him inside and close tight around him.

Leo snorted in surprise and then slammed up into her, filling her to the very brim. She gasped as pain and pleasure mingled.

'You really are something,' he hissed between gritted teeth as she met his stroke with one of equal ferocity.

She looked up at him, her grin mirroring his grimace. 'You surprise me,' she said and thrust forward again.

Chapter 7

They drove back to O'Malley's in silence, both wrapped up in their own thoughts.

Laura stared out at the stars. She felt an odd sense of disconnection. The Laura who had spoken to Gareth earlier on the phone was a very different creature from the one who had crouched so willingly on the sand between the two unknown men. Or the Laura who had caught hold of Leo, working through her sense of anger with her body . . .

In some ways it felt as if she was walking inside a dream. What would Gareth have made of the events on the beach? Would he be horrified or excited? She had often wondered what dark fantasies lurked inside his mind; what it was in there that he kept so tightly locked away. Did he think she might be shocked?

How little he knew about her – perhaps that was why she could never bring herself to accept his proposals of marriage. Ghosts of their earlier conversation floated up in her mind. She suspected that his offer of a secure job in data processing told her all she had ever needed to know; there was nothing in Gareth's imagination to excite them both after all.

Only a matter of weeks and Laura would be home with him. Wasn't there some part of her that believed once she got the Australian trip out of her blood that she would be happy to settle down – hadn't that been their unspoken bargain?

Laura glanced across at Leo. He had not been unsettled by her desire – far from it. Cloaked in darkness, her anger had quickly dissolved as they had struggled towards release, pressed up against the rough, unforgiving bark of the palm tree. Even now the memory of his wild, frantic love-making lingered in her mind and made her body ache.

The two sailors? She reddened; there had been a glorious sense of freedom making love to two complete strangers, tapping into a well-spring of uninhibited, guiltless desire she never knew she had. At the same time, some part of her sensed it could easily become addictive.

In the darkness ahead she saw the sign for O'Malley's. There was a momentary sensation of coming home and then the realisation that, as far as Leo was concerned, their evening had only just begun.

He glanced across at her and pointed into the distance. 'We'll head down the road aways, park up and walk back along the beach. Okay?'

Laura nodded and turned to retrieve the case from the back seat. He shook his head. 'Stay just as you are – you'll be less conspicuous if anyone happens to see you.'

Between her legs, Laura could still feel the moist traces of the sailors' and Leo's passion, tangible remains of desire that made her shiver. What was it that had lifted the restraints that had held her so tight for years? The last few days were like a strange erotic madness. Was it that, so far from home, she could unleash a passion that she had always held in check? Or that, so far from Gareth, she was unaccountable for her actions? Before she could consider the answer, Leo drew the jeep to a halt behind a stand of palm trees and killed the lights.

'Keep your eyes peeled,' he said. 'We don't want Belle catching us. Keep close to me.'

Laura nodded and slipped out of the jeep into the velvety black night. Walking behind Leo, Laura could hear the sound of dance music carried towards them on the breeze. The earlier rain had left the air crystal clear, so that the string of lights along the shoreline glittered like jewels. She stopped for an instant – these had been the lights she'd seen from the look-out point on the first evening. That night seemed like a lifetime ago.

Caught in profile against the soft glow, Leo beckoned her to follow him towards the shadowy row of cabins. Silently, they approached the window of the first and peered inside. Laura's jaw dropped as she took in the scene.

The room's interior was lit by table lamps so that each of the players seemed to be caught in their own pool of light. A beautiful blonde youth, perhaps nineteen or twenty and as naked and as ethereal as Michelangelo's David, was crouched in front of an expensively dressed young woman.

Laura realised, as her eyes adjusted to the light, that the boy was one of the hotel waiters. Seated in an ornate rattan chair in the far corner of the cabin, watching the tableau, was an older man, dressed in a black silk dressing gown and cradling a glass of brandy.

Laura recognised them as one of the couples she had seen at breakfast. The young woman took a long pull on a cigarette, her face obscured by a tumbling cloud of smoke.

Close behind Laura, Leo whispered. 'That's his wife in the chair.'

Laura nodded and looked at the woman again. Between the tendrils of smoke her eyes were dark, pupils dilated with excitement. With one hand she slowly lifted her skirt up over her waist.

She was wearing spiked patent high heels, black stockings and a matching suspender belt. The straps of the belt framed her sex which was trimmed close so that every fold and contour was exposed. The boy nuzzled up against her, a cat courting its mistress.

His tongue, pink and inviting, lapped eagerly at her quim. The woman, still smoking, settled back into the chair and opened her legs, while across the room her husband watched without moving, though Laura could see the glitter of pleasure in his eyes.

The woman moaned appreciatively and rested a hand amongst the boy's flaxen curls, encouraging him closer.

'Oh, that feels so good,' she purred as she drank in every nuance of the boy's movements. The boy moaned and doubled his efforts.

Laura felt a flurry of excitement in her belly. The old man, totally immersed in the scenario, leant forward a little to get a better view of his wife's seduction.

The woman moved lower in the chair, thrusting herself

up to give the boy more freedom. She unfastened the buttons of her shirtdress, revealing the heavy curves of her breasts and the rounded plane of her belly beneath. Her husband murmured his appreciation as she ran a single fingertip around her engorged nipples. Her fingernails were painted scarlet, the colour almost matching the excited flesh.

The boy pulled away a little and sat up, chasing her caresses with his lips while his fingers still worked deep inside her sex. Eyes closed, the woman moaned. The boy's mouth left a trail of moist pleasure, marking his passion over her pale golden skin.

Behind them the old man stood up and undid his robe. Moving closer to the couple, he stood over them like a dark, malevolent crow, eyes alight with need and desire. Without faltering the boy turned and lifted the old man's cock to his lips, planting a single kiss on the grizzled foreskin. The old man shuddered.

Drawing the old man's shaft deeper into his mouth the boy's fingers cupped and stroked the wrinkled bag of his testicles as if handling a holy relic. The old man's cock hardened almost at once, a scrawny, excited finger that pointed skyward. The woman, who had been watching from behind hooded eyes, lifted a hand and snapped her fingers. Immediately the boy stopped and turned towards her.

Although it would appear that the boy was totally submissive – a slave to their game – Laura knew instinctively that this was a complicit pantomime, played out by the three of them, carefully choreographed to give the couple maximum pleasure.

Between the boy's muscular thighs she could see the imposing arc of his cock thrusting up like a meaty sword.

The boy, on his knees now, slipped his hand under the woman's thighs and pulled her closer before guiding his shaft deep inside her.

Whimpering with delight, the woman strained up to meet him. Her expression was ecstatic, almost angelic. The old man closed his eyes for a second as if to fix the image in his mind and then knelt down behind the boy.

From the pocket of his dressing gown he produced a

tube of cream from which he began to anoint his cock. Leaning closer he slid his fingers between the boy's shapely, bronzed buttocks. The boy groaned softly, lifting himself up for the old man's caresses. Slowly, with great deliberation the older man eased forward, working his cock into the tight contours of the boy's eager body. The old man's hands stroked the boy's muscular back tenderly, before reaching forward to cup his wife's straining breasts.

'My God,' Laura whispered, her tone uneven and broken. She looked away with a mixture of horror and complete astonishment. Her pulse was racing, her stomach twisting into a knot as she tried to imagine the heady palette of sensations.

In the softly lit cabin the lovers were already moving towards the moment of climax, thrusting eagerly, hungry to harvest the tremors of passion growing between them.

Laura turned and stared at Leo. He seemed unmoved by the events on display.

'Belle caters for all tastes,' he said casually in answer to her unspoken questions. 'Have you seen enough?'

Laura looked back. From inside the room she could hear the thick, guttural noises that indicated the lovers had reached their own particular brand of paradise. She nodded, feeling a strange tremor of pleasure, as if the waves of the trio's orgasm had set something vibrating deep inside her own body.

The old man's head was thrown back as he plunged again and again into the boy's compliant body. A sheen of sweat had lifted on the boy's back and shoulders, making his body seem to shimmer in the golden lamp light. The woman was sobbing, thrusting again and again against the boy, milking every last drop of pleasure from him.

The scenario made Laura tremble. She glanced back over her shoulder – Leo was already heading across the grass and she hurried to catch him up, the images of the threesome glowing, white-hot in her mind.

She wasn't sure whether he intended taking her back to the jeep, instead they took a detour through the garden. She was grateful for the darkness – it hid the glimmer of need in her eyes. The scenario had rekindled her desire so effectively that Laura was tempted to grab hold of Leo, and wondered fleetingly what he would think of her if she did.

She could see other figures moving around the main hotel. Several were guests she vaguely recognised. The only area that was brightly lit was the outdoor dining area, and in the centre of it Belle O'Malley was holding court, pouring champagne, dressed in a shimmering strapless evening gown.

'Where are we going?' whispered Laura, as they skirted the main building.

Leo grinned. 'Just trust me.' Taking her arm he guided her up a steep path towards another cabin.

Inside, two girls were asleep under a mosquito net, naked above the tangle of sheets, they lay back to belly. One had her arm around the other, her long fingers gently cradling a sleeping breast.

Leo groaned; it seemed whatever had been going on under the soft lights they had missed it. Far from being disappointed Laura was touched by the tenderness of the two sleeping lovers. The women were both at ease, relaxed, sated after sharing pleasures that she could only imagine.

There was something deeply comforting and at the same time intensely erotic about the picture. As she stared at them she realised that one of the women was Eva, the blonde girl who she had driven to Home Cove.

Leo waved her away in frustration and, taking her hand, led her further along the winding path. Even before they got to the next cabin Laura heard the noise – a cutting, cracking sound that seemed to reverberate through the night air.

'What if we get caught?' she murmured as they stepped up onto the shadows of the veranda.

Leo grinned. 'Half the people here would love to think they had an audience. Why do you think Joe comes to stay here so often?'

He lifted a finger to his lips and Laura peeped in through the open door. A metal fly screen hid them from the players within, though once she had seen what was going on inside Laura doubted whether the couple concerned would have cared even if they knew she and Leo were there.

Laura recognised the girl instantly from the morning on the beach – it seemed as if the brunette took the need to be conquered to extremes. Bound hand and foot, she was tied spread-eagle fashion to a wooden frame that dominated the otherwise empty room. Her thick-set body was slick with sweat, her heavy curves emphasised by a black leather G-string tied so tight that it nestled up between the lips of her shaved sex.

Her heavy breasts were supported in a kind of halter, made up of straps that framed, but did not cover, the ripe mounds and her dark, engorged nipples. Behind her a tall, athletically built man, stripped to the waist, masked and wearing jodhpurs, drew back a ferocious looking whip and with a single sweeping gesture brought the lash down across the woman's back.

She shrieked, surging forward against her restraints, mouth frozen into a provocative moué. The tasselled end of the whip curled around her torso, a dark finger of pain that left a red welt behind on her flushed skin.

Laura took a step back, astonished by the scene. And yet, deep inside, she felt a tiny surge of excitement. The idea of being tied up had always intrigued her, though when she had suggested it to Gareth he had dismissed the idea, with a dry laugh, as perverted. She had never asked him again.

Now, confronted by an image from one of her fantasies she felt her pulse quicken. She swallowed hard and looked back into the room, imagining the sensation of the tight leather harness nipping her flesh, the leather straps pulled tight around her wrists and ankles as the whip found its mark.

Behind her she could feel Leo drinking in the details of the scene, and was almost afraid to look at him in case he could see the growing excitement in her eyes. He dropped a hand to her waist, pulling her back against him so that he could whisper in her ear.

'She loves to be tied up. It sets her free to enjoy whatever's on offer. The rest of the time she's the CEO of a chemical company – you'd never guess looking at her now, would you?'

Laura flinched as the whip cracked ferociously.

'In real life when she tells someone to jump they ask how high. Look . . .'

Laura needed little encouragement. The jodhpured man ran his hands over the woman's helpless body, his fingers invasive and apparently unfeeling. He unfastened the side straps on the leather G-string and dragged it away. The woman moaned, writhing under his brutal touch.

Even from her hiding place Laura could see the glittering traces of pleasure seeping out onto her thighs and shivered as the man began to finger her, dipping inside her again and again, smearing the silky liquid over her belly and hips.

He appeared to be rough, but Laura realised he knew exactly what he was doing. Under his skilled hands the woman was experiencing a subtle combination of pleasure and pain that quite obviously excited her beyond measure.

His fingers moved down to the little pleasure bud that peeped provocatively from between the lips of the woman's sex, while his other hand worked on her breasts, twisting her nipples, rubbing them back and forth between his finger tips until they were scarlet.

The woman threw back her head, gasping with excitement. Sweat trickled down her face, dripping in tiny crystal facets from her chin. His hands moved to her waist, dragging her back against her restraints. Her body strained against the ties. Laura saw the triumphant grin on his face as he parted her buttocks and jerked her back toward him, sinking his teeth into the meaty curve of her shoulder. With one final thrust he drove his cock home.

The woman shrieked and Laura looked away, reddening as she imagined the sensation of his cock opening her up, driving into those moist welcoming depths.

Her own sex pulsed instinctively, desire bubbling up through her as the man began to thrust furiously. The woman cried out again, helpless to resist her seducer. Some part of Laura recognised in her tone that strange mixture of pleasure and pain. Surrender to this unstoppable sexual force was as compelling as any magic.

'Seen enough?' whispered Leo.

Laura jumped. She had almost forgotten he was there. Her body and her mind had been transported into the steamy interior of the cabin; every thought centred on the intricate dance of the two lovers. She turned towards him, eager to be back in the safe shadows of the hotel garden. To her horror, Leo caught hold of her, and tipped her face up towards him. She already knew what he would see in her eyes.

He grinned triumphantly. 'Well, well, well,' he said with amused satisfaction. 'So that's it, is it? Have we found a little something you'd like to try for yourself?'

Laura felt her colour deepen. She couldn't bring herself to reply. What could she say? That the idea of being tied up and taken by a man was something she had always fantasised about?

In her dreams she had imagined Gareth tying her to the bed, consumed by a desire to possess her totally. She had thought about how exciting it would be to have a man who lusted after her, wanting to make use of her body until every fibre, every cell was sated.

Pulling away from Leo, she hurried down the steps into the darkness. Leo followed close behind.

'Ring a bell, did it?' he said mischievously, catching hold of her arm. 'Is that the kind of thing you and your precious Gareth get up to on those long dark winter nights? I did wonder. I always thought from your letters he was one of those repressed public-school types. I should have guessed.'

Laura spun round to face him. 'Well, you're wrong,' she snapped furiously. 'Gareth's not like that at all. He'd run a mile if he seriously thought that I . . .' she stopped, reddening furiously.

Leo moved closer. 'What? If he knew that that kind of thing turned you on? Come on. After all we've been through, you can tell me, Laura.'

Laura glared at him. 'No, I can't. That's the trouble – I don't know how to. Gareth is so bloody staid. He thinks making love is something you do with the lights out, once a week. A simple, necessary physical function like eating, sleeping. I don't know how to tell him or you what it is I really want, what I need. If I tried to talk to him he'd . . . he'd . . . Oh, I don't know! Since I've been in Australia it's been like finding a part of myself I didn't know existed. A part of me that is so hungry – I'm afraid of what I feel. How the hell can I go home to Gareth like this? Having done what I've done, felt what I've felt . . .' she stopped, eyes filling with tears. 'I could use a drink,' she snorted, rubbing the tears away with the back of her hand.

Leo pulled her closer and kissed her gently. His tenderness surprised her. She moaned, feeling the desire flicker, glowing like a torch flame in her belly, and leant against his strong body. His arms soothed her.

'It's all right,' he whispered. 'Let it go, it doesn't matter. We'll go back to my cabin.'

With his arm still around her waist he led her down through the trees back towards the beach. Away from the main cabins, behind a stand of wind-bowed palms, was the staff accommodation.

Laura shivered. Slung across the front of Leo's cabin was a canvas awning, so much like the one at Danny Collins's place at Home Cove that it gave her an unnerving sense of *déjà vu*.

Laura sat at the table out on the deck, watching the surf roll up onto the gently sloping beach. Leo reappeared with a bottle of wine and two glasses. She didn't know whether she wanted to speak. Her mind was a mass of jumbled, erotic images that left her with a sense of unfulfilled desire and an exhilarating flutter of fear.

Leo handed her a drink without speaking. She nodded her thanks and drained the glass in one.

Leo refilled it. 'Better?' he said, sipping his own glass.

Laura snorted. 'What the hell am I going to do?'

Leo settled back in the canvas chair opposite her, gaze locked on her. 'Why not just enjoy it while you're here? You're so far away from home, no one else need ever know. When you get back on the plane you can just leave all this behind.

Take what's on offer.' He smiled and, leaning forward, stroked a finger down over her cheek. 'Let me show you just how good it can be.'

Laura shuddered. If only it was that simple. 'How can I go back and be the same as I was? I'm afraid of what I feel.'

The amused look didn't leave Leo's eyes. 'No need.'

Out on the rim of the horizon Laura could see the twinkling lights of a boat, sailing home. Like her it was in limbo, caught between two places. She took another sip of wine, this time letting the rich flavour flood her taste buds. Perhaps Leo was right. This was a place out of time. In under a month she would be home in England, safe with Gareth, with a job in data processing. Maybe this was her last chance to do something crazy.

She looked up at her would-be guide. 'So where do we go from here?' she said in a low voice.

Leo indicated the cabin. 'Bed – and then tomorrow I'll take you up into the rainforest.'

She stared at him. 'The tourist thing?'

Leo laughed. 'Not exactly.' He ran his hand over the curve of her breast. The cool sea breeze had chilled her nipples into hardness.

'Why don't you take this off?'

Laura hesitated.

'I don't know about you but I could do with a shower.'

Slowly she got to her feet and pulled the little black dress up over her head. She could sense Leo watching her every move. The night wind skittered over her naked skin like the furtive caress of a nervous lover. Leo smiled.

'You know, you're very beautiful,' he said softly. 'Gareth is a complete fool. If I was him I'd give you everything you wanted.'

The moonlight painted her pale skin with highlights of silver and ivory. Almost as if he was moving in slow motion Leo leant forward and planted a single kiss on the soft hair that curled around her mount of Venus.

'Go and have a shower. I'll clear up out here. You need some sleep. It's going to be another long day tomorrow.'

★ ★ ★

Closing the bathroom door, Laura discarded her clothes onto the cool white tiles and stepped under the torrent of icy water; it was bliss. She ran her hand over her body, relishing the sensation of the water as it coursed down over her. Every bone, every muscle, in her body ached.

The memory of Leo's arm around her shoulders, the feeling of his body close to hers, replayed in her mind. She smiled, soaping her breasts, teasing her taut pink nipples until they stiffened under her finger tips. Just as she had hoped, Leo stepped into the shower behind her. His hands joined hers, soaping her breasts, making her glow with need. Without a second's hesitation she turned in his arms and kissed him. He was already hard, and she knew she was already wet. He was so tender and gentle that she thought she might cry.

Leo's lean, sun-tanned body pressed against her, his muscular frame a sharp contrast to her own slim form. He leant forward and kissed her furiously, tongue seeking entry, lips working against hers, hands gliding down over her narrow waist and broad hips, pulling her close to him.

Her breasts brushed the soft covering of curls on his chest. Slowly, he sank to the floor, kissing her nipples, her ribs, her belly, his tongue outlining the contours of her navel.

Laura shivered, her fingers tracing Leo's journey. As she parted the soft contours of her sex she was stunned to discover how wet she was, her body totally ready for his attention. One finger glided inside, whilst with her other hand she circled the engorged ridge of her clitoris. His tongue echoed her journey. The first brush of his tongue against its sensitive hood sent a lightning bolt of pleasure through her body. Her sex tightened instinctively around his exploring fingers, drawing him deeper. As he began to stroke rhythmically at her pleasure bud, she became oblivious to the water, her mind suffused with the sensation of Leo's tongue and fingers as they worked their magic on her body. She thrust forward, milking the sensation as her mind and body were consumed into a white-hot cascade of pleasure.

Gasping, she slumped forward, head resting against the icy wet tiles while she caught her breath. She was grateful that he had satisfied the raw sensual hunger in her belly. In all the years she had known him, her boyfriend, Gareth, had never made her feel like this.

Getting to his feet, Leo pressed her up against the tiles and, before the contractions of her orgasms had abated, he slipped inside her. Her body welcomed him, absorbing him as if he was some necessary part of her, and within seconds they were both caught up in another journey towards release.

An hour later Laura was curled up in Leo's arms, deep in a dreamless sleep.

Chapter 8

If Belle noticed that Leo and Laura arrived together for breakfast the next morning she said nothing.

'Have a good night?' she asked, as Laura sat down at the table.

Laura nodded, careful to keep her expression fixed. 'Very interesting.'

Across the table Leo busied himself with arranging cups, careful to avoid the eyes of both women.

'Ropey's is a great place. He came up here in the sixties, staked his claim up at the Cape and just stayed,' Belle said. 'I've known him since I opened up the hotel. He's a great guy.'

Despite her game attempt at making light conversation, Laura noticed that her aunt's eyes were ringed with dark circles. It had obviously been a long night. Belle toyed with a slice of French toast and then dropped it, untouched, back onto her plate.

Leo poured them coffee. 'You know I've got a couple of days off now?'

Belle lifted an eyebrow. 'I'm hung-over, Leo, not senile,' she snapped and then winced. 'You'll have to excuse me this morning. I'm feeling a little fragile.' Laura noticed the apology was aimed at her, not Leo.

'I thought maybe I'd take Laura out to my place and show her the pole house,' Leo continued casually.

Belle glanced down at the large diary beside her. 'Fine. As there's nothing much going on next week, Laura and I'll drive down to Cairns, book into the Piermont Hotel and have a few days R & R there.' She looked up at Laura for her agreement.

Laura nodded. 'Sounds like a great idea.'

'You're right, it does,' Belle said with a smile. 'I'll book it up then. I can't remember the last time I cut loose and played hookey from this place. It'll do me good to get away for a little while.'

Laura drained her coffee cup. 'If you'll excuse me I'll just go and finish getting packed.'

Belle waved her away. 'Sure.'

When Laura had left the table, Belle smiled at Leo. 'Thanks for keeping Laura out of the way last night. It was complete madness here. I didn't get to bed until nearly four.'

Leo said nothing, so Belle continued. 'I feel guilty that the place is booked solid, but let's face it, I really can't afford to turn trade away, not at this time of the year. Do you think she's having a good time?'

Leo, poker faced, nodded. 'Oh yes, I've made sure of that. Laura's doing just fine.'

Belle stretched. 'And she doesn't suspect?'

Leo shrugged. He didn't feel it was his place to tell Belle that Laura knew exactly how Belle made her living – and besides, it was much more fun to keep her in the dark.

'I still think it would be a good idea if you had a quiet word with her.'

Belle dismissed his comment with a wave of the hand and then looked up at him from under her thick dark lashes. 'I really missed you last night, I could have done with a little something to help me sleep. You just be careful what you get up to while you're away.'

Leo grinned and was struck again by how similar Belle and Laura were. There was something about the way each held her body, the look in their eyes. Although Laura lacked Belle's confidence they could easily be mistaken for mother and daughter, and both exuded a subtle sexual energy that was difficult to resist. It was a shame Belle wouldn't come clean with Laura, though Leo felt it was really just a matter of time before they discovered each others' secrets.

'Don't worry,' he said. 'She's in good hands.'

Belle laughed. 'I wish I believed you.'

'Oh, my God, it's beautiful,' Laura said, staring up in amazement at the elegant house nestled up amongst the trees. Built on huge tree trunks driven into the ground, Leo's cabin seemed to hang in mid air, the wide verandas and windows level with the rainforest canopy. Constructed from raw timber, it blended in totally with its surroundings.

Leo grinned. 'Glad you like it. I built it myself. Wait until you see inside.' Dropping the four by four into first, he crept slowly up the steep hill and pulled in between the poles, so that the house was above them. Laura almost leapt out of the seat and swung round to admire the view. Rolling down the hillside, trees stretched as far as the eye could see and close by she could hear the sound of running water.

'What's that?' she said. 'A stream?'

Leo was getting the box of supplies out of the back of the truck. 'I'll show you later. Help me get this lot upstairs, will you? And then we'll get the shutters open and make ourselves at home.'

Though it had been hours since they left O'Malley's, Laura's exhaustion was rapidly receding. Unlocking the security gate, she and Leo climbed the open tread stairs up into the tree-top bungalow. Inside it was dark, the air fragrant with the heady smells of cut timber. The polished wooden floors were criss-crossed here and there with straps of sunlight that cut through the closed shutters. What struck her most was the sheer beauty of the huge room that opened up in front of her. Completely built from honey-blonde wood, the room was sparsely furnished with a high, vaulted ceiling. There was a simple table and chairs in one corner, a cream sofa in the other and an open kitchen area that gleamed with stainless steel and copper.

Leo set the food box down on the kitchen bench and began to undo the shutters. Laura was stunned – out beyond the balcony the rainforest rolled away from the wide veranda in a jewel green carpet. Brilliantly coloured birds fought and wrestled on the nearby branches. Clinging to the overhang of the roof crouched a bright green tree frog, with eyes so huge and hypnotic that he could easily have been created by a cartoonist.

'Laura?'

She turned round slowly. She had been so taken in by the view she had almost forgotten about Leo and the sexual tension that had been growing steadily since they left O'Malley's. It was hard to put into words – there had been a growing feeling in her stomach that something was about to happen and now, looking at Leo standing in the half light inside the stunning tree house, she knew she had been right. In one hand Leo held a studded leather collar and in the other a pair of handcuffs.

Laura swallowed hard and instinctively took a step back.

His eyes glittered as he held the collar out towards her. She shivered. Wasn't this what she had dreamed of?

'Get undressed,' he said softly.

Laura bit her lip and then, very slowly as if her fingers had a mind of their own, she began to undo her blouse. Leo sat down on the sofa to watch her. He seemed almost uninterested, cool and aloof and, though she doubted that was the case, it seemed to add to her excitement.

The blouse dropped to the floor revealing her black lace bra. Leo waved it away. She unfastened it and dropped it alongside her blouse and then slid her skirt down over her hips. Before she could remove her tiny matching black knickers, Leo beckoned her closer. She moved slowly, nervously, torn between the desire she felt and a tingle of fear at what she was agreeing to.

'This is what you wanted, isn't it?' he said, smiling thinly.

She could already feel her nipples hardening, her sex throbbing with expectation. She nodded, throat dry, afraid to speak.

Leo pulled a face. 'Oh come on, Laura. We're friends. I want you to tell me that you want me to tie you up and fuck you until you beg me to stop.'

Laura blushed.

'That is what you want, isn't it? Maybe it would be better if you asked me – why don't you say please?'

'Please . . .' she stammered thickly, aware of the way his

eyes took in her nakedness. She felt so vulnerable and yet at the same time almost overwhelmed by expectation. 'I want—'

'Yes?' Leo encouraged, his expression hawkish and dark. 'What is it you want?'

'I want you to – to . . .' she couldn't find the words.

'To fuck you,' he said again, more slowly this time. 'To tie you up and fuck you.'

'To tie me up and fuck me,' she said looking away, feeling the heat course through her body.

'Good,' said Leo, 'Now turn round and hold your hands behind your back,' he murmured. Laura did as she was told, trying to control the tremor in her body. The cuffs, as cool as ice against her warm skin, snapped into place around her wrists with an air of finality.

Leo indicated she should kneel. Wordlessly she complied and didn't resist as he slid the collar into place.

He smiled triumphantly. 'Very nice,' he said in a low voice. 'All ready for your first lesson. Get up.'

Laura did as she was told, struggling to keep her balance. Leo ran a hand over her hips and belly. His touch was proprietorial, fingers stroking the outline of her sex, lingering for an instant on the crease where her outer lips met.

'Now I want you to bend over the table and wait for me.' She looked at him. 'What do you . . .'

'Sssh,' he said, holding a finger to his lips. 'If you want to be a perfect little slave, the first thing you have to learn is complete obedience. Just do as I tell you.'

Laura glanced round. What choice did she have?

The table was polished wood, so highly buffed that she could almost see her reflection in it. As she struggled to bend over it, the cool wood sucked the heat from her body, lifting goosebumps on her pale skin. Totally exposed, she waited while seconds ticked by. She struggled hard to quell the rising sense of panic and strained to hear Leo. Was he moving? What was he doing?'

Just as she began to feel uncomfortable she heard the sound of a car engine and struggled to push herself upright.

'Stay exactly where you are,' Leo snapped as the sound of the engine died.

'But someone's coming,' Laura protested.

She heard Leo laugh. 'How very perceptive of you.'

From the corner of her eyes she saw him get to his feet and head towards her. 'This might help you relax. Just let go and let it happen – that's what you dream about, isn't it?' he said softly as, gently, he slipped a folded kerchief around her eyes and tied it tight. Plunged into darkness Laura cried out in protest. Leo ran a hand over her spine.

'Trust me,' he whispered, and then she heard him move away.

Whatever she had anticipated, however potent the fantasy her mind had concocted, the reality was very different. She was afraid and at the same time felt a surge of excitement. From behind the blindfold she strained to pick out sounds she could recognise, but all she could make out for certain was the frantic beat of her heart and the sound of her pulse thundering in her ears.

Somewhere behind her she heard muffled voices and then a hand slid over her buttocks, making her jump. The hand was cool and smooth. Slowly, it insinuated itself between her thighs, opening her legs, stroking her sex through the thin black silk of her knickers. She knew she was already wet and moaned softly as knowing fingers slid up towards her belly and brushed over her pleasure bud.

And then the caress was gone – a tantalising touch snatched away. A split second later she felt something cool and hard trail along the contours of her spine. Her senses strained to pick up another clue and then – in the instant she guessed what it might be – something exploded across her buttocks making her scream, not just in pain but in astonishment.

The blow ricocheted through her body. The pain was breath-stopping, a red-hot tide roared through her. She barely had time to catch her breath before a second blow cracked across her skin. This time the pain was like a raw, abstracted heat.

The hand that had touched her seconds before tugged

her knickers down and plunged a hand between her legs, seeking the soft, vulnerable places, finger plunging into her sex. The contrast to the heat glowing in her buttocks was breathtaking. Without thinking she lifted her hips, her body instinctively seeking out the comfort of the caress. As she did so the fingers withdrew. Again the pain cracked across her backside, this time its bitter tongue catching those places she had been so careful to conceal.

The tears that formed in her eyes were instantly soaked up by the bandanna. While her body was being overwhelmed by the sensations, her rational mind reasoned that whoever it was – Leo or his mysterious companion – had to be using a riding crop or a whip. The angry stripes across her backside seemed to radiate heat – and then there was another blow and another.

The intense pain fragmented the voice of reason, all she could do now was surrender herself to it. Every nerve-ending in her body seemed to glow white-hot. Overwhelmed by feelings, she was afraid she might faint. Just as the blackness threatened to overwhelm her, cool hands pulled her upright and turned her round.

One pair of hands slipped under her armpits, taking her weight, while another tugged mischievously at her panties, pulling them down around her ankles.

Fingers and lips stroked at her throat, her nipples, kissing and sucking their swollen peaks with a tenderness that was almost unnerving. As her unseen lover pressed a kiss to her lips Laura stiffened; she could smell perfume.

An instant later she felt the delicate brush of flesh against her own and knew without a doubt that it was a breast – her unseen tormentor was a woman.

She gasped as the woman's tongue traced the valley between her breasts, lingering for an instant to kiss the pit of her navel before sinking lower, lapping at her sex, drinking in the juices that Laura knew pooled there. Her revulsion and fear was tempered by the compelling need of her body.

The woman's tongue moved like quicksilver, tapping out a rhythm, circling, nibbling, sucking.

Laura leant back against the hands that were supporting

her, legs opening wider to receive the fingers that joined the tongue. The other woman's caresses were propelling her into a realm of sensation she had never dreamt existed. Time and again the woman's skilful attentions brought Laura to the very brink of ecstasy and then, just as Laura was about to plunge into the abyss, snatched her back.

It was divine torture. Laura struggled to breathe, struggled with the sensations, struggled to maintain her equilibrium against all the odds. The blindfold meant her mind was focused inwards, each caress exploding like a fusillade of sparkling lights inside her imagination. Just as she thought she might be going mad the person holding her lowered her gently towards the floor. At first Laura thought it was her mind playing tricks until she felt the cool smooth wood under her shoulders.

An instant later she felt the most fleeting brush of flesh against her face and then gasped – all she could smell was the heady perfume of the other woman's sex. Her unseen lover's tongue teased her sex open, and Laura knew, without a shadow of a doubt that the woman was crouched above her. Despite her fears she found herself reaching up. The taste that filled her mouth was both deeply shocking and at the same time strangely familiar, the scent not unlike her own but subtly different.

The woman groaned; Laura felt the soft noises of pleasure reverberate through her body and knew then she was lost.

The moments that followed were surreal; she thrust upwards, plunging her tongue deep inside the woman above her. Behind the darkness of the blindfold she imagined it was like making love to a twin soul. A kindred spirit. Stroke for stroke, caress for caress, the two women seemed to be linked by some instinctive thread. Each movement was echoed in the other. The woman ground her quim onto Laura's tongue and mouth, compelling and inescapable, Laura felt her buck and then began to moan; she too was caught up in the current, drawn down into the maelstrom.

Seconds later Laura heard a dark throaty moan and was stunned to realise that the voice was her own. Thrashing to and fro, oblivious to everything but the sensations spiralling out from the warm damp pit between her legs, Laura rode on and on, until finally, exhausted, she slumped back on the cool wooden floor.

It took several minutes before her senses began to return, almost as if she was waking from a vivid dream. Her arms, still locked behind her back screamed out in protest, her buttocks still glowed from the beating, and between her legs, alongside the liquid heat, was a glowing sense of satisfaction that filled her belly like a good meal. Beside her she could still feel her unseen companion and hear her laboured breathing. Cautiously Laura attempted to roll over and was rewarded by someone unlocking the handcuffs. Laura wriggled free, reluctant to remove her blindfold but at the same time deeply curious about the identity of her lover.

After a second or two she pulled the bandanna off. The sunlight made her eyes water. Naked, curled on the floor beside her, with a pillow under her tumble of blonde hair lay Eva, the girl Laura and Joe had driven to Home Cove.

She looked up at Laura with a lazy, satisfied grin.

Leo was sitting on the sofa, watching them both. His expression was triumphant. As Laura focused on him he smiled and began to clap. 'Very, very nice,' he said with a smile.

Laura reddened. On the table beside her was a small black leather riding crop, the handcuffs alongside it. Eva uncurled and slowly got to her feet. She was stunning. Heavy breasts, tiny waist, and generous hips – she looked as if someone had carved her body into an erotic masterpiece. At the junction of her long legs, her quim, still glistening with droplets of moisture from Laura's kisses, was framed with a quiff of white blonde hair that barely covered the plump outer lips.

She stretched like a pedigree Persian. 'I'm starving, Leo. Why don't you cook up something wonderful while Laura and I go for a swim?'

Leo nodded and then waved them away. 'Fine.'

Eva smiled and then extended a hand to Laura. 'Come on,' she said. 'You must see Leo's waterfall.'

The invitation was completely unselfconscious; in spite

of herself, Laura felt the last remaining shreds of embarrassment receding. Eva picked up a pair of sandals from the floor. 'I'll find some towels – just put something on your feet. No one will see us, there's no one else up here.'

It felt strange to be naked outside – even stranger to be in the company of a woman she barely knew, who moments earlier had given Laura one of the most intense orgasms of her life. If Eva guessed what Laura was thinking she gave no sign of it. She seemed completely at home with her nakedness.

Out beyond the confines of the pole house's small garden, a narrow, winding path ran between a stand of trees. Eva giggled and broke into a run.

'Race you,' she called back over her shoulder and hurried into the forest gloom. Laura felt compelled to follow, twisting back and forth between the trees, catching glimpses of Eva's lithe golden brown body, she already knew she had no chance of catching the beautiful blonde. A final turn and Laura found herself on a grassy slope running down towards a deep pool. Above it, cascading over a dramatic outcrop of silvery grey rocks was a waterfall, and away to her left the overflow from the pool tumbled down into a boulder-strewn stream.

A streak of gold caught her eye and Laura looked round just in time to catch Eva plunging into the water, shrieking in delight. Laura stared in to the bubbling water, waiting for the blonde to surface. A few seconds later Eva broke the surface, her hair slicked down like an otter's pelt. She grinned and spat out a mouthful of water.

'Come on in, it's lovely – freezing, but lovely.'

Laura hesitated for an instant, then dropped her towel onto the grass and jumped off the rocky edge. The water exploded over her aching body was like a thousand icy crystalline fingers, embracing her, sucking every last molecule of breath from her chest.

Gasping, fighting for air Laura surfaced. Eva grinned, rolled over on her back and floated idly towards her. As their bodies touched, Eva stood up and, leaning forward, kissed Laura gently on the mouth.

'Leo's right,' she said in a soft, almost tender, voice, her hand lifting to stroke Laura's cold breasts. 'You are very good. You made my whole body hum. Maybe we could do it again and take a little more time?'

Laura shivered as Eva pulled her closer and unbuckled the leather collar. The blonde's body was so warm compared to the icy mountain pool. Laura had never touched another woman until the events in the pole house – it filled her mind with all kinds of complex contradictions and fears – but in spite of that Laura knew it wouldn't take very much for her to take Eva up on her offer.

Beside her the blonde threw the collar onto a nearby rock and then jack-knifed under the water. It was so clear in the shallows that as she swam away her body looked as if it was made from mother of pearl. As exquisite as any mermaid, Eva headed towards the bubbling cauldron at the foot of the falls. Laura took a deep breath and followed her, the icy water closing over her like a silken sheet.

Chapter 9

Later, laying on a sun-warmed rock, naked as a baby, Laura rolled her towel up under her head and closed her eyes. The noise of the waterfall filled her head, shutting out all other sounds and thoughts. She could feel herself being lulled into sleep. Alongside her, Eva stretched, dropped an arm over Laura's waist and curled up close to her so that their bodies touched. The other woman's casual familiarity was strangely comforting.

Eva wriggled closer, getting comfortable and pressed a chaste kiss between Laura's shoulder blades. The fleeting brush of her nipples against Laura's damp back made her shiver.

She wasn't sure whether it was minutes or hours later that she heard Leo's voice over the lyrical music of the running water.

'Great picture,' he said, his voice trickling in through her dreams. 'You two look like the babes in the wood.'

As Laura stirred into wakefulness Eva laughed and rolled onto her back. 'I hope you've come down here to tell us dinner's ready or the next thing you're going to be looking at is the bottom of the pool.'

Leo snorted and squatted down on the rock beside them. Laura could see the interest in his eyes as he drank in the details of their nakedness. Eva was totally unselfconscious. Reaching out towards him she tipped his face toward hers and kissed him gently. Eva made Laura think of mermaids. Her lithe body was naked and lightly tanned. As she pressed herself tight against Leo, Laura knew the exquisite blonde would be a temptation that would very hard to resist.

'So,' Eva purred, as she pulled away, 'is dinner ready or are you going for a swim?'

He grinned. 'It's waiting for you on the table, getting cold. It seemed a real shame to wake you up.'

Eva grimaced and got to her feet.

Leo turned his attention to Laura. 'Did you enjoy your swim?'

She nodded, feeling her colour deepen as Leo's eyes moved on to her body. Despite the obvious approval she wasn't as comfortable with her nakedness – her first instinct was to cover herself with the towel. Casually, he stroked a finger over her breast; her nipples stiffened instantly. She guessed that for him her exposure was completely natural – he and Eva were at ease in a way she truly envied.

He held out his hand and helped her to her feet. Her body felt stiff and sore – both from her earlier encounter with the riding crop and from sleeping on the unwieldy rock.

'Come on, babe, supper's spoiling,' he said, indicating the path.

Eva draped her towel around her shoulders and, without another word, she and Leo headed back to the house with Laura following close behind.

Around them the daylight was already fading fast. Overhead a thunder head of fruit bats headed out across the night sky to feed in the forest. The air was heavy with the scent of wood mould, and the heady perfume of creepers and torch ginger that filled Leo's jungle garden.

As they climbed the stairs back at the pole house Laura could make out the rich perfume of fried peppers, tomatoes, onions and garlic curling out towards them on the evening air. Her mouth began to water; she hadn't realised how hungry she was.

Before she could speak, Eva stole the thought. 'God, that smells wonderful. I hope you've made plenty. I'm starving.'

'Of course,' said Leo, taking a bottle of wine off the counter. 'I'd hate to have gone to all this effort and nobody be interested. Sit down while I open this.'

Upstairs, by the open windows in the sitting room the table was set for three, with beeswax candles burning in a sconce set amongst glittering crystal and crisp cream linen.

Laura smiled and took the seat Leo indicated. The feel of the table top pressed against her naked breasts was seared on her memory like a brand. Now, set for dinner, the table would have looked more at home in an exclusive London restaurant than a lonely jungle hideaway.

Eva went into the bathroom and reappeared carrying two thin black cotton robes.

'Here,' she said with a grin, dropping one into Laura's lap. 'Trust me, there's nothing worse than Leo's pasta sauce on naked skin.'

The daylight seemed to be seeping away – there was no evening in the tropics – just a few moments when the sky darkened from blue to grey and then it was night. From behind the forest canopy the moon rose like a single all-seeing eye set in a dark ocean of bright stars.

Surrounded by the smell and the sounds of the trees, despite the events of the day, Laura felt strangely at ease. Sitting between Leo and Eva, she realised she was really enjoying herself. Leo set a huge bowl of pasta in the centre of the table, alongside salad and crisp hot rolls and invited them to eat.

Eva leant forward and dipped into the pasta sauce. Laura shivered as Eva licked her fingers, her long tongue winding round to catch every last drop. The image was intensely sensual. The blonde closed her eyes and groaned her approval.

'Oh yes, God, that is wonderful,' she purred, helping herself to an enormous plateful. 'Food and sex, my two favourite things in the whole world. I've always thought a man who can cook as well as screw like a rattlesnake has got to be a real find – food is the sexiest thing.'

Leo laughed as he filled their glasses. 'Really? I'll take your word for that.' He glanced at Laura. 'You'd better help yourself. Eva's appetite for both is insatiable.'

The laughter and the conversation rolled back and forth between the three diners, the wine taking effect on all of them.

As Leo cleared away the remains of the pasta, Laura

stretched. Her body still bore the marks of the riding crop and as she moved she could feel the tight little arcs of pain on her buttocks. The sensation added a tiny *frisson* of expectation – despite the warm relaxed atmosphere the weals reminded her that this was no ordinary dinner party.

After a few minutes Leo reappeared carrying a huge dish of exotic fruits: grapes, mango and papaya, jack fruit and rambutans lay alongside thick, juicy slices of fresh pineapple.

'Here we are, ladies, the second course. Would you like some cream?'

Eva giggled. 'Of course – and some more of that wine.'

Laura felt as if they had been shipwrecked, washed up on some lonely paradise island; they could be the only people left on earth.

As Leo set the cream on the table the atmosphere altered subtly. All evening there had been a relaxed air of expectancy between them but now that promise intensified. Laura felt a flutter of anticipation in her belly.

As if at some given signal, Eva got to her feet and began to untie her robe, pushing it back off her shoulders. In the candlelight she looked breathtaking; broad-shouldered with those astonishing high, heavy breasts and long, slender torso she looked as if she had been carved by a maestro.

She ran her fingers through her hair, twisting the long blonde tendrils up into a make-shift knot. Her body seemed to have an exquisite luminescence in the subtle light, every curve, every inch of her lightly sun-tanned skin glowing with vitality. It was impossible to ignore her. For a few seconds she posed for them both, pouting provocatively and then, very slowly, she climbed onto the table, stretching out like a pampered cat between the flickering candles.

Leo looked at Laura and grinned.

'Dessert?' he said, and dropped a single grape into Eva's navel.

Laura swallowed hard, nervousness bubbling up alongside a plume of desire.

Leo picked up the cream jug and poured a stream of white liquid onto Eva's prone body, a glistening white river that extended from the pit of her throat down between her breasts to her navel. The cream was so thick that it clung to her skin in thick waves.

Eva giggled again and the tiny movement made the cream ripple like silk. She smiled lazily and lifted her arms in a languid invitation.

'Come on,' she said in an undertone to Laura, her eyes dark with excitement. 'It's all right – why don't you touch me? You were so good this afternoon. Come and lick the cream off.'

Laura stared down at her, wondering if she and Leo had planned this scenario, and imagined for an instant what it must be like to have sat through supper knowing this was to follow.

The blonde drew a painted fingernail across the rapidly hardening peaks of her nipples, dipping into the cream and drawing it around the pale pink circles of her areolae. Laura watched, totally ensnared by the image, while Eva's other hand slid down gracefully over her belly and insinuated its way between the lips of her sex. The tableau, caught in the soft glow of the candlelight, was so deeply erotic that Laura found it impossible to look away.

She could almost feel the sensations Eva was experiencing rippling through her own body and she rose to her feet, propelled by some need that she had no name for.

Leo stood up, too, gently guiding her between Eva's open legs.

'Here,' he whispered taking hold of her hand and resting it gently on one of the blonde woman's breasts. 'Touch her, just feel how good it is.'

Eva's skin was like liquid velvet, warm and inviting, her heartbeat pulsing up through Laura's fingertips. From where she stood Laura could smell the subtle perfume of Eva's body, a mixture of heat and the soft oceanic scent of her sex.

To her surprise and horror her mouth began to water. Shaken, she jerked her hand away.

'Sssh, don't fight it, baby, go with it. Feel your way.' Leo whispered his encouragement and kissed her neck, his lips making her tingle with delight as his fingers tugged at the tie fastening her robe. As the belt gave way his hands moved

109

up over her hips and waist, cupping and fondling her breasts. Laura moaned and rubbed herself against him, ensnared by his desire.

'Here, let me show you,' he murmured, taking hold of her hands again and leading them back towards Eva's prone body. 'Remember how good it felt this afternoon. Feel your way . . . follow your instincts. Let go . . .'

Laura could already feel the press of his cock against her spine. Nervously, she began to stroke the other woman's pert nipples. On the table, the blonde closed her eyes, as if she was certain the pleasure would continue and somehow that subtle gesture of surrender set Laura free.

Bending over Eva, she planted a chaste kiss on each of the puckered, cherry-red peaks – and then another kiss. The flavour and feel of the cream added a strange counterpoint to the taste of Eva's warm, salty skin. This time, opening her mouth a little, Laura let her tongue work a tight circle around Eva's areolae, lapping at the cream, drawing the little bud into her mouth and sucking the warm liquid off.

Eva moaned, writhing provocatively, encouraging Laura on. The invitation to continue was explicit even without words. As she closed her lips tighter around one exquisite peak and drew it further into her mouth, Laura could feel the other woman's body trembling with anticipation.

She flicked her tongue back and forth, imagining what the sensation would be like on her own body. Eva moaned again. The little sounds of appreciation made Laura's flesh tingle. While fragments of reason and fear held her in check, her body ached to let go, to be engulfed by the power of her desire. Understanding Eva's needs – so much like her own – made it all the more difficult to hold back. She knew exactly what fires each caress, each kiss was igniting in the other woman.

As she looked down again at the blonde's astonishing body, Leo's hand fluttered lightly over Laura's belly. His fingertips seemed to stir little flurries of passion, each one more compelling than the last.

She already knew sensation would win – why fight, why hold back?

She drew back for an instant to catch her breath, relishing the sensation of Leo's fingers on her flesh, already anticipating the instant when he would slide a finger into the warm folds of her quim. Beneath her, Eva's hand snaked up and caught hold of her neck. Pulling Laura close the blonde woman kissed her full on the lips, opening her mouth, easing a tongue in to tease her own.

Laura gasped; the woman's kisses were as sweet as the tropical fruits, mixed with a subtle taste of wine. Laura's breasts brushed across Eva's, their journey lubricated by the warm cream.

Eva's kisses were insistent, making Laura hunger for more, and in the same instant that Laura surrendered to the pull of the other woman's embrace Leo pressed a finger down the engorged ridge of her clitoris.

Laura moaned with pleasure, flexing her hips, pushing her buttocks into his groin, feeling the last of her reluctance dissolving like ice before the thaw.

The blonde began to stroke along Laura's spine, fingers working over her vertebrae as if she was playing notes of an hypnotic piano concerto. Between her legs, Leo's fingers were busy picking out a compelling tune of their own. Wriggling free of Eva's kisses she renewed her attention to the blonde's voluptuous breasts, nipping them gently between her teeth, licking and nibbling at the throbbing peaks, lapping away their coating of cream.

Eva made a dark throaty noise of delight and thrust up towards her. Laura felt the brush of the other woman's sex caress her belly, the blonde curls calling her like a whispered invitation. Almost without thinking, Laura began to spiral her kisses lower, lips sliding back and forth over the sticky slick of cream, lapping at Eva's navel and drawing the single grape in between her lips.

On cue, Eva lifted herself higher, demanding more, wordlessly begging Laura to guide those kisses down to that moist fragrant seat of pleasure. The perfume of Eva's sex suffused Laura's senses, making her head reel. From behind her she heard Leo murmuring his approval, but she didn't need it now. It was if her body was being directed by something else, some wild free spirit, hell-bent on pleasure and satisfaction. She could feel the insistent press of his cock, free, seeking entry between the sore, bruised orbs of her backside, and his hunger helped to drive her on.

Eva's sex was like an open, exotic flower, scarlet with desire. As Laura ran a tongue tentatively over the delicately perfumed petals, Leo rewarded her by guiding his cock deep inside her.

She gasped, feeling her body tighten around him, eager to draw him deeper, but he would not be hurried. He moved slowly, deliberately, so she could savour the first breathtaking sensation of penetration. It was almost as if a bow wave of pleasure preceded his cock, rolling out from her body on an unseen current.

When Leo began to move she began to lap at Eva in earnest, tongue seeking out the secret places that gave so much satisfaction. Leo, sensing her growing excitement, started to move more quickly, powering in and out of her throbbing sex, all the time his fingers working on her clitoris, multiplying the sensations that were rapidly growing inside her.

She pushed her fingers into Eva's body and was stunned by the way the woman's smooth, silken juices eased the pathway. As she reached the full depth her fingers would allow, she felt the muscles in Eva's quim sucking at her like a hungry mouth, closing again and again as she began to explore the exquisite contours deep inside the beautiful blonde.

Eva made a strange guttural sound as Laura ran her tongue around her pleasure bud. As the heat intensified Eva began to flex her hips, spurring her on. Laura knew that she was nearing the point of no return. Her skin was flushed, her eyes tight closed, mouth open to let out a series of tiny, whimpered cries. The sounds touched the instinctive core deep in Laura's being; these were ancient animal sounds of pure unadulterated pleasure.

Laura shivered, wanting nothing more at that moment than to bring the blonde to the very edge of oblivion. Leo's caresses had already brought her close to the abyss.

And then suddenly Eva caught tight hold of Laura's head, fingers locking in her hair. Laura's tongue pressed down hard, all subtlety lost as Eva's body demanded release. An instant later Eva began to convulse, her body jerking in wild, ragged thrusts as she was consumed by the raging fires of pleasure.

Laura gasped in astonishment. It felt as if Eva's climax was ricocheting through her belly, igniting her own as effectively as any fuse – there was no way she could hold back now or extinguish the roaring flame. An instant later orgasm roared through her, driving away everything except the mesmerising taste of Eva's sex and the heat of her body.

As Laura thrust forward, tongue and hips working in tandem, deep inside her Leo's orgasm pulsed through the already throbbing confines of her quim. Inside her mind, crystal fragments of pleasure exploded like a mortar shell and spiralled away into velvety darkness.

On and on it went, until Laura felt she might die from sheer pleasure. Gasping she finally collapsed down onto Eva, her face resting on the blonde's taut belly. Under her cheek she could hear Eva's pulse beating out a frantic rhythm and closed her eyes, relishing the intensity of the satisfaction that glowed in the pit of her stomach.

Laura woke in the middle of the night, consciousness pulling her from a tangle of wild, erotically charged dreams. Through the mosquito nets and the fly screens she could pick out unfamiliar stars and for an instant wondered where she was. Outside the sounds of the forest were so loud that it almost seemed as if it was breathing. And then the memories came flooding back. She was in Leo's bed. After they had finished their erotic dessert and had coffee, Leo had suggested they might like to retire to the comfort of his huge bed. She had fallen asleep cradled between them.

Despite the overhead fan, she was hot now, sweat trickling down in the valley between her breasts and the pit of her belly, her skin slick and smooth. Her waking movements disturbed her companions, and images of the previous day, as hot and all engulfing as the night air, filled her mind.

On her lips she imagined she could still taste the perfume of Eva's sex, and the subtle smoothness of the cream. Beside her, Leo lay on his side, curled like a big cat, naked, his musculature emphasised by the discreet gloss of sweat on his chest and belly. His long dark hair was loose now, spread out on the pillow like a tangled mane. As she watched, he rolled over onto his back and stretched; he was leonine – even in sleep his body exhuded a dangerous sexual promise that was compelling.

It was tempting to touch him, run a hand down over that glorious body, slip a hand beneath the sheets and stroke the magnificent cock that slept between his thighs.

She imagined it stirring into life – it would wake before he did – and before he was fully conscious, she would roll over on top of him, guiding him into the molten void between the lips of her quim. The idea made her shiver and sparked a realisation that there had never been a time in her life when she had given her sexual hunger free rein.

Until now that well-spring had been buried deep, controlled by a sense of propriety. Gareth hadn't been her only lover, but until now she had always chosen men like him; safe, repressed men, who offered her no threat – and no real satisfaction. Perhaps there was some part of her which understood the power of her desire and had held it safely in check until now.

Leo stirred again. The desire to touch him was growing like a hungry ache.

On the other side of the bed, Eva moaned, and Laura glanced across at her. Sleep seemed to have softened her body, and taut, heavy curves of her breasts and belly diffused by the heat, dissolved into a golden glow.

Caught on the high-water mark of sleep Eva stretched out and ran a hand over Laura's back. The touch wasn't sexual but a sleepy gesture of comfort and tenderness. The caress earthed Laura out, stilling the strange sexual energy that was pulsing through her.

She curled up against Leo, relishing the smell of his body. Although his scent still stirred the animal need in her loins, Eva's sleepiness was infectious. It seemed to seep into Laura's mind like a warm grey fog, dragging her back into unconsciousness.

Chapter 10

Laura found herself reluctant to think about leaving Leo's pole house; it was a place out of time, so far away from reality that she felt she could easily have stayed forever and explored the dark new energies that drove her on.

Eva had left before Laura woke. Discovering she was gone, Laura felt cheated, wishing the blonde – who had shown her so much – could have at least waited around long enough to say goodbye. As Laura sat with Leo, eating breakfast, she wondered if they would be able to renew their acquaintance at O'Malley's.

Leo handed her a coffee, breaking her chain of thought. She was dressed in the robe Eva had loaned her and realised as she took the proffered cup that she hadn't even bothered to tie it up. Leo, dressed in an unbuttoned white shirt and navy sweat pants, smiled as she began to pull the belt tight.

'Why bother?' he asked lifting an eyebrow.

She blushed and shook her head. 'No particular reason.'

'Then leave it undone. We're the only two people here and I don't mind – it's good that finally you're relaxed enough to just be. Why don't you stand up and let me look at you?'

Laura did as she was asked, letting the robe flow open around her.

Leo nodded, gaze moving down from her eyes to her breasts and the corona of dark hair that trimmed her sex.

'Now take it off and turn round,' he said in an undertone.

The robe slithered to the floor at her feet and she turned as he had asked. She heard Leo move and then shivered as he kissed one of the weals on her backside. Overnight the red marks had changed into arced bruises, a tangible record of every stinging blow. Behind her, Leo sank to his knees kissing each bruise in turn.

His kisses brought back the memory of the need she had felt in the middle of the night, when only Eva's sleepiness had drawn her back from the edge.

She turned round a little more so that his tongue and lips moved to her hip and then moved again so that now he was kneeling between her legs, his face level with her pussy.

He looked at her and grinned.

'Oh yes, very good. You know, you've got the markings of a great whore,' he said wryly and planted a kiss on the mount of her sex, tongue easing its way between the lips. She gasped as the very tip brushed her clitoris, sending a minute electric pulse through her.

'But what are you going to do for me in return?' he said pulling back a little, eyes alight with mischief. She could see he was already excited, his cock straining against the thin cotton of his trousers.

She smiled. 'I don't know. What do you want?'

He sat back on his haunches and pulled the waistband of his trousers lower; his cock sprang forward like a scimitar. 'I think I'd like a little of what you're begging for,' he said.

She nodded and dropped to her hands and knees, creeping towards him, eyes lowered, aware that it was an act of submission – an act as contrived as the beautiful blonde boy's in the cabin at O'Malley's. Leo hooked a cushion off one of the chairs and, slipping it under his head, lay back on the bare boards, while Laura nuzzled his belly, kissing the broad bands of curls that encircled his stomach. He groaned and then caught hold of her chin and tipped her face up towards him.

'Why don't you bring that sexy little arse of yours up here and let me kiss you too? Kill two birds with one stone?'

She hesitated, imagining herself crouched above him on her hands and knees, her body totally exposed and open. She shivered. Under cover of darkness she wouldn't have been so reluctant but in daylight the idea disturbed her. He was watching her face, his eyes dark with desire.

'Well?' he said. 'That's what this particular client fancies.

116

This game's like any other service industry – the customer's always right.'

He reached out towards her. 'What are you waiting for?'

Laura stared at him, realising the sexual confidence she thought she had been developing was a very fragile thing.

Leo smiled at her again. 'Come on,' he whispered. 'Why so shy? I want to slide my tongue inside that delicious little cunt of yours, taste you, slide my fingers into you, make your whole body hum. I want to feel your mouth on my cock, I want you to suck me dry.'

Slowly Laura crept up over his body, the sensation of the hairs on his chest brushing her breasts making her tremble. His hands slid up over her, and then gently but firmly turned her round so that she was crouched above him. He stretched up, pressing a moist kiss to her inner thigh.

'Relax,' he purred, his breath warm against her skin. 'You know we're both going to enjoy this, don't you?'

Laura had surprised Leo – he had never imagined just how willingly she would play along with his and Eva's game, however keen she was to explore the wild sexual frontiers. It delighted him that he had underestimated her.

As she bent down to take his cock deep into her mouth he could feel her trembling. Her lips were as soft as oiled velvet, gently drawing him deeper, her tongue working nervously back and forth across the sensitive glans.

Above him her sex was open, the delicate inner lips already blood red, flushed with excitement. In spite of her nervousness she was wet and eager, her quim a ripe flower that demanded his attention.

He slipped a finger inside her, and was instantly rewarded by a moan that vibrated through his balls. Her sex tightened around his touch. He grinned; hard to imagine that the girl crouched above him was Belle O'Malley's tight-lipped little English niece. In her letters Laura had always sounded like a repressed, naive school girl, always afraid, always holding back from the extreme of life's outer edge.

It had been Joe Blanco who had confirmed his suspicions that Laura wasn't all she appeared – though Leo had thought as much from the minute he picked her up from the airport. It had been Joe who had told him about the mysterious dark-haired girl watching the couple making love on the beach. But nothing could had prepared him for the speed and enthusiasm of Laura's conversion.

He ran his tongue over the ripe inner petals of her sex, the taste of her arousal flooding his mouth. As her fingers closed more tightly around his shaft he shuddered. Laura was good already, but there was so much more he intended to show and teach her before the month was over. He grinned; she would go back to England a very different woman. Her boyfriend, Gareth was in for a pleasant surprise – Leo almost envied him.

He gasped as her fingers moved down to stroke the delicate, puckered skin around his balls. She was beginning to set a rhythm with her hands and mouth, and as she did so Leo found it impossible to hang onto the thoughts that had been forming in his head, instead he surrendered to uncluttered instincts that drove them both out into the realms of pleasure.

Laura hung her clothes for the long drive home to O'Malley's over the towel rail and then stepped into the shower. The water washed away the remains of Leo's moist kisses but not the memory. It was so strange, the pleasure she had discovered was like a compulsion, almost an addiction. Like a fever, it warmed her body and her mind and she wondered, fleetingly, whether she would ever fully recover from her Australian odyssey. Even though her body still glowed with the intense satisfaction Leo had given her, some part of her psyche was already hungry for more. The thought both excited and unnerved her.

It was almost midday when they finally left the pole house. Leo locked the doors and closed the shutters whilst Laura waited for him in the jeep. He seemed to be taking a long time. When he finally appeared from the shadowy stairwell under the house he was grinning.

'Change of plan,' he said, pulling on his bush hat and clambering into the driver's seat.

'I'm not with you.'

Leo turned the key in the ignition. 'I've just rung a friend of mine on my mobile. Fredo. You met him and Jack the other night on the beach at Ropeys? He's got a trip booked to go out to the reef this afternoon. I thought you might fancy tagging along for the ride.'

Laura hesitated, thinking about her encounter with the two sailors, wondering what the trip might entail. 'Isn't Belle expecting us back at the hotel?'

With his mind fixed on reversing out into the sunlight Leo made a dismissive gesture. 'Not a problem, it was Belle who chartered the boat, and besides they're sailing back to O'Malley's afterwards.'

Laura bit her lip, trying to find a way to frame the next question.

'Are they . . .' her voice faded as her eyes met Leo's; she could see the amusement there.

'Are they what?' he asked, with a grin.

'Are they just guests on the boat or are they . . .' She struggled to find the right word to describe Belle's sexual clientele and failed. 'Or, you know,' she said, realising the words sounded slightly pathetic.

He laughed as he steered the jeep down the steep track, back towards the main road. 'You'd better get used to the idea that all Belle's guests are "you know" in one way or another.'

Laura stared at him. '*All* of them? Are you serious?' she gasped in astonishment.

He nodded, while Laura let the idea and its implications catch hold. All those faces she had seen over breakfast, all those ordinary looking people, on holiday, casually dressed, smiling and talking in low voices across the tables, came back to her in vivid detail.

She shook her head. 'My God. Did Belle honestly believe I wouldn't guess what was going on?'

Leo nodded. 'That was the plan. O'Malley's has got a reputation for complete discretion. She thought it would work out okay, particularly if someone took you out and about, did all the tourist things. I did try and talk her out of

119

it, but, well, it's too late now, eh?'

Laura stared at him. 'And you were supposed to take me out and about? Keep me away from the hotel?' She paused. 'Wasn't that a bit like putting a wolf in charge of the sheep pen?'

Leo aped hurt. 'Ouch, ouch, ouch,' he snorted with a wry laugh. 'You can be so cruel. I was on scout's honour – and besides, if you remember, it was you who took yourself off to Home Cove. And after Danny Collins rang me . . .' he shrugged. 'I dunno, I reckoned that maybe you didn't really want the kind of tour Belle had got in mind for you.' He pointed ahead of them. 'Look – that's where we're going.'

As Leo slowed the jeep to a crawl Laura looked through the trees in surprise. She hadn't realised they were so close to the sea and tried to fix the view from Leo's balcony onto the vast landscape. Below them a sheltered cove wrapped its tree-covered arms tight around a shallow saucer of azure blue ocean. The water was edged with a perfect crescent of white coral sand and, moored a little way off shore, was a sailing boat, so small from their view point that Laura found it hard to get a sense of scale.

As she stared down through the forest, tiny figures began to unfurl a milk-white sail.

'We had better be going,' said Leo, putting his foot down. 'They're getting ready to catch the tide.'

Laura glanced at him in surprise. 'You're coming too?'

He grinned. 'I was planning to keep an eye on my latest apprentice – why? Do you mind?'

Laura shook her head. 'What about the jeep?'

'One of the shore crew'll drive her back for me.'

Without another word he accelerated and Laura closed her eyes. The hillside road dropped away like a stone, clinging to the rock face between the trees like a twisted grey ribbon.

A few minutes later they pulled up alongside a weather-beaten hut under the trees that framed the beach. As they got out a figure, dressed in white polo shirt and matching shorts, waved to them from the water's edge. Laura reddened as she realised the man was one of the sailors she had last encountered on the beach behind Ropey's bar. In the water floated a small, empty painter, waves lapping up against its dark blue bow.

'Hi,' he called as Laura and Leo headed towards him. 'I thought you weren't going to make it.' The man grinned. 'Everyone is already on board and cracking open the bubbly.'

Laura noticed that although he was speaking to Leo his eyes were firmly fixed on her, his gaze working down over her body, taking in the details of her curves and the way her thin, sleeveless dress clung to her.

He extended a hand. 'Better get aboard, babe. We're all set to cast off.'

She slipped off her sandals and paddled out towards the little boat. Clambering aboard she was aware of the way the sailor's hand lingered in the small of her back.

'Two seconds, Fredo,' said Leo and hurried back to the four by four. He was back an instant later carrying a holdall. 'I've left the keys in the ignition.'

Fredo nodded. 'No worries, mate – I've already arranged for someone to come out and pick her up for you.'

'Sun block and towels,' Leo said, in answer to Laura's unspoken question as he dropped the bag into the bottom of the little boat. 'Out here you'll burn red raw in half an hour.'

He and Fredo pushed the tender off the sand and then clambered aboard. A few feet from the beach the sailor whipped the outboard into life and they headed out across the cove towards the sailing ship. There was a fixed platform and ladder at the stern to help the passengers climb aboard. As they drew alongside, Fredo threw a rope to another man who was waiting for them. Laura glanced up at the uniformed matelot and blushed as he smiled down at her. She guessed he had to be called Jack – it seemed that the second sailor from Ropey's was part of the ship's company as well.

'Welcome aboard the Reef Rider,' he said in a low voice as he took her arm and she stepped unsteadily onto the platform. Without waiting for Leo, Laura hurried up the half a dozen rungs onto the main deck. She could feel her colour rising. It had never really occurred to her that she would see either of the two sailors again.

Once aboard Laura looked round. The main deck was covered with a faded cream sail that created a tented pool of deep shade, under it several of the ship's passengers were being served cocktails by two other crewman. Laura instantly recognised a few faces amongst the crowd and wondered if she perhaps had been foolish to accept Leo's invitation.

'Hiya, you look as if you could do with one of these,' said a familiar voice.

Laura swung round and was confronted by Joe Blanco holding a glass out towards her. He grinned. 'I didn't know you were coming on the cruise.'

Behind Joe, Leo was still in conversation with Fredo, the sailor who had brought them across from the shore. Laura took the drink without a word and drained the glass in one.

'I wondered where you'd got to,' said Joe, retrieving another glass from a passing steward. 'I've been looking for you all over the hotel. Are you okay?'

Before Laura could reply Leo joined them. 'I thought I'd show Laura my place up at the Cape. Shame you couldn't have come along too, Joe. I'm sure you would have found it most entertaining.' At his shoulder Fredo grinned salaciously.

Joe shrugged. 'I'd expect nothing less from you, my friend. Next time just give me a shout.'

Joe glanced back at Laura, as if he could sense her growing discomfort. 'Maybe you'd like to get something to eat?'

Laura nodded gratefully; it felt as if everything she had experienced in the last few days was suddenly under the spotlight.

The Italian took her arm and guided her under the canvas awning towards a long table bolted to the deck. Laura noticed that the edges were raised to stop dishes sliding around in the swell.

As she took a plate offered by a steward Laura could see the crew were making ready to set sail. An engine that had been idling, creating a backdrop to the conversation on deck, began to work in earnest as the captain slowly manoeuvred the boat out of the bay into open water.

'So, you had a good time with Leo?' Joe asked conversationally. 'His house, it is really something, isn't it?' Laura could sense there were other, more intimate questions he would like to ask.

She took a spoonful of salad from the buffet, careful to avoid his gaze.

'Yes,' she said in a low voice. 'It is an amazing place.'

He indicated a bench along the handrail and gratefully Laura sat down. 'Did you go to the pool?' Joe continued. 'You want to tell me all about it, maybe?'

She laughed. His open curiosity had a strangely innocent ring to it.

'Not today, Joe,' she said gently, taking a sip of champagne. He looked hurt and she patted his arm. 'Maybe another time.'

Around them the other passengers, at first glance, appeared at ease, eating, drinking and chatting away as the boat slowly made its way through the waves towards the open sea. But Laura could already sense the slightest edge of expectation amongst the little groups. There was a tiny *frisson*, an unformed, abstract something that hung in the air around them like a gathering storm.

She wondered what it was that gave them away. Was it that they seemed to be standing too close to each other? Or was it the air of casual intimacy, so unusual amongst strangers?

By the handrail on the far side of the deck, Laura recognised one of the dark-haired girls from her trip to Home Cove. She was deep in conversation with a plump, well-heeled man in his late forties. He was dressed in casual but obviously expensive clothes. At first glance they just seemed to be chatting and their liaison appeared innocent enough, but there was something else, just below the urbane veneer of polite chit-chat and easy laughter that gave them away.

Laura found it impossible to look way from the couple. She could almost feel the unspoken sexual promise bubbling up between them. As she watched, the man very slowly stretched out his hand towards his dark-haired companion. Laura took in every detail, as if the simple movement was being captured on film. The man's hand was lightly tanned, the hairs on his arm touched golden by the sun. Just below the wrist was a heavy gold bracelet.

His thick fingers slipped between the buttons of the girl's sun top, unpicking the fastenings with slow deliberation, and then he eased his hand inside, pushing the material back as he did so, to reveal one perfect, golden-tinted breast.

Laura swallowed hard. All her consciousness was focused on the girl and her companion. The rest of the passengers and crew, even Joe and Leo, seemed to have faded into insignificance.

The girl's ripe, flawless skin was pale in contrast to the man's hand, her breast a delicate upturned peak tipped with a scarlet bud. The man smiled wolfishly and rolled her nipple between her thumb and forefinger as he might an expensive cigar.

The girl's face was impassive, almost as if she was awaiting instructions from her client. His other hand lifted to join the first and pushed her sun top back off her shoulders. Her slim body could have been sculpted from creamy marble. As his hand reached her shoulders she leant back against the hand rail, posing for his approval. The two of them seemed oblivious to the rest of the people on deck.

The man ran his hand over his prize and the girl thrust her breasts towards him. Laura thought she heard the old man moan; he leant forward and sucked one of the peaks into his mouth. The girl closed her eyes and Laura finally looked away, feeling the sensation of that tender kiss echo through her own breasts and belly.

She had been unaware that Leo had joined Joe on the bench and as she looked down she felt and then saw a hand slide up over her thigh.

'Welcome to the pleasure dome,' Leo said, following her gaze. 'Belle calls these her special pleasure cruises,' he continued, pressing his lips to the curve of her neck. 'And trust me, that is exactly what they are. Now, would you like to go and mingle?'

Laura stared at him. 'I . . .' The words dried in her throat as she realised what he was suggesting.

Slowly she got to her feet. Around them the sails were being raised by the crew as the boat entered the main shipping lanes. Leo's eyes were fixed on hers, as dark and compelling as a tropical night. 'Maybe you'd like me to introduce you to a few people?' he said, taking her glass and plate.

She shook her head, afraid to speak, and looked around the various groups of passengers. By the buffet a grey-haired man in his late fifties smiled at her and extended a hand. Standing beside him was a tall, good looking young man, dressed casually in shorts and tee-shirt, his relaxed manner a sharp contrast to the older man's sharp military bearing.

'Don't think we've been introduced,' he said briskly. 'Perhaps you would care to join us for a drink, my dear. The name's Guy, Guy Faber.' He spoke with a clipped English accent. 'And this is my dear friend and companion, Harry Renshaw.' He indicated the young man, who murmured a greeting.

Laura took one final glance back at Leo. He encouraged her on with a barely perceivable nod of the head. She turned back to the older man and his youthful companion and painted on a brittle smile.

'I'd be delighted,' she said with a confidence she didn't feel.

'Is this your first time in Australia?' Faber continued.

'Yes, yes, it is.'

'Marvellous place, isn't it? Harry and I spend at least two or three months a year here. I've got business interests in Sydney.' The man handed her a glass of champagne. 'Perhaps we could take our drinks below, out of this damned heat. I've booked a cabin. We could relax a little more, don't you think?'

The boy nodded before she could say anything. 'It's much cooler down there too with the air conditioning.' His accent was pure public school. 'And I can tell you exactly what it is that Guy wants.'

Laura hesitated for an instant. Guy, the older man, smiled pleasantly. 'What is your name, my dear?'

From the bench by the hand rail, Leo said, 'You don't

have to worry about her name, Guy, just that she's new and very, very willing to please.'

The old man reddened with pleasure and then tapped the side of his nose in a conspiratorial gesture.

'Whatever you say, Leo, old chap. Mum's the word then.' He indicated the hatch that led down into the bowels of the boat. 'In that case I won't ask again. Why don't you go downstairs with Harry and get ready?'

Laura shot Leo one final nervous glance. Leo waved her away. 'All you have to do is exactly what Guy and Harry tell you, and remember, the customer is always right.'

Laura glanced nervously at Joe, but his attention had moved on to the couple by the hand rail that she had been studying earlier. The girl was naked now except for a leather belt cinched right around her narrow waist and a pair of tiny silver high-heeled mules.

Chapter 11

The nervousness and expectation Laura had held in check since she had climbed on board the vessel seemed to percolate up in her belly as she stepped down into the shadowy confines of the ship.

Ahead of her, Harry turned and smiled. 'Guy prefers me to get his women ready for him – you know, touch, suck, get them wet, turn them on. All that foreplay stuff. He likes to watch us perform and then he'll want to screw you.' He grinned as Laura looked anxiously back up over her shoulder. Guy was still standing by the buffet, seemingly engaged in conversation with someone else.

'Actually we both will but he always likes to go first.'

Harry was standing by an open cabin door. Laura noticed the names of the two men were printed on a card in a holder above a spy hole.

Harry continued, 'And he won't speak to you – he spent a lot of time in the Far East. He likes his women obedient, compliant and above all, silent. So . . .' he lifted his hand in a boyish gesture of apology that was deeply disconcerting. 'Please don't be offended if he more or less ignores you. When you get to know him, Guy's really a nice guy!' He laughed at his own weak joke and waved her ahead of him.

Laura stepped inside. The cabin was small, the decor utilitarian with an loosely nautical theme. The centre of the room was dominated by a single bed, covered in a crisp white sheet. There seemed to be very little else to look at other than a row of cheap anchor ornaments tacked to the wooden clad walls.

'Haven't you got the little whore's clothes off yet?' snapped Guy from the gangway. 'You know I don't like to be kept waiting.' His brusque manner – totally at odds with the unctuous tones he had used above deck – made Laura jump.

'Strip her off and let me see what you've got for me this time.'

Harry nodded and then turned to Laura. 'Just take your clothes off nice and slowly. Here . . .' He indicated a spot in front of a mirror that backed a cupboard door.

Facing Guy, Laura began to undo her dress. The old man looked away in disgust.

'No, no,' said Harry gently. 'I want you to look in the mirror, not at us. This might help.' He took a small tape recorder from the bedside cabinet and switched it on. Trickling through the speaker came an indifferent pop melody.

Laura stared at him but Harry waved her into action. She turned to face the mirror and tried to ignore the nervous tension in her stomach.

What had Leo said? *The customer is always right.* She swallowed hard and tried to concentrate on the image in the pitted mirror. Lifting her hands to undo her zip she could just see Guy's bright eyes reflected in the glass. Very slowly she divested herself of the little sundress. Underneath she was wearing a tiny, cream lace bra and pantie set. Made from the thinnest cotton, they clung to her in the heat.

Guy poured himself a drink from a tray on the side table and settled back in the chair.

Laura looked away – she could have been alone in the room for all the effect she appeared to be having on the two men. She fixed her attention firmly on the mirror. The volume of the music seemed to increase and she let herself be caught up by the rhythm, moving her hips from side to side, admiring her reflection.

Her skin had already began to tan – to a golden veneer over her smooth flesh. As the beat finally took hold, she eased the shoulder straps of her bra down over her shoulders and then rubbed her hands across the ribs, caressing the skin as she had imagined Harry might.

She thought about the old man and the dark-haired girl

up on deck and pushed the lace cups down so that she could toy with the little pale pink buds that nestled beneath. They hardened in seconds. She spiralled teasing fingers down over the taut, flat muscles of her belly, stroking the mound of her sex and then, cupping it, felt its heat and the promise of wetness beneath her fingertips.

It was surprisingly easy to get lost in the image she created in the mirror. She ran her fingers through her hair, lifting it up onto her head, posing as much for her own pleasure as the effect that the picture might have on the two men. She unfastened her bra, let it drop to the floor and then teased her fingers through her hair again, this time twisting it into a top knot. Stray tendrils dropped back to frame her face.

Caught in the unforgiving eye of the mirror, Laura had become a study in the erotic; the idea entranced her. Her pupils had dilated, eyes dark now with sexual promise, her nipples jutting forward like cherry stones. The image captivated her – it was almost like looking at a stranger.

Leo had helped her to discover this sensual creature that had lurked unseen for years, and whatever else might happen she was glad he had helped her let this particular genie out of the bottle.

As her fingers retraced their journey over her belly and breasts she imagined it was Eva stroking her. She could almost visualise Leo looking on in approval. Anticipation and desire began to rise inside her like the incoming tide. She struck another pose, running her tongue around her lips, eyes narrowed, thrusting a hip forward, stretching provocatively.

Part of her had forgotten that Harry and Guy were watching her too and she was surprised when Harry stepped behind her and ran his hand up over her waist to cup her pert breasts. She could feel the heat of his body behind her and was fascinated to see his caresses in the mirror as well as feel them. For the first time she was aware that – for all his apparent indifference – Guy's chair was carefully positioned so that he could see every movement.

Harry gently turned her round so that they were now facing their one man audience. His hands seemed to be all over her, teasing and stroking at her nipples while his other hand glided over her waist and caught hold of the side of the moist reaches of her quim. His intimate, knowing caresses made her shiver. Almost casually he splayed the outer lips wide, so that no part her was obscured from the eyes of his elderly friend.

When she looked across at Guy he still seemed completely unmoved. He nodded, taking another sip from his glass. 'I suppose she'll do, though you know I prefer bigger women. What does she feel like. Is she tight?'

Without a word, Harry's fingers plunged into her, making Laura gasp. Between them they were rapidly reducing her to a sexual commodity. Although in some ways it was an exhilarating experience, she began to move against Harry's invasive fingers, determined to assert herself over the two of them. To her surprise, Guy snapped. 'Stand still, damn you. I want to look at what's on offer.'

Harry guided her closer to Guy's chair and with his foot pushed her feet apart so that the old man could see every part of her – and touch her too.

Guy leant forwards and stroked a hand down over her buttocks in a gesture she imagined he might use to calm a nervous animal, and then slid a single finger deep inside her. His fingers were smooth and icy cold. He could easily have been judging horseflesh for all the passion he showed. Slowly he withdrew and ran his tongue along the single digit. After a moment or two, as if he were the connoisseur of a vintage wine, he nodded.

'She'll do, but you'll have to get rid of some of that.' He indicated the thick veil of pubic hair that framed her sex.

Laura felt rather than saw Harry nod. 'Get on the bed,' he said in an undertone, his lips level with her ears. 'This won't take very long and I promise not to hurt you.'

Up on deck, as the crew trimmed the sails and guided the Reef Rider out into the currents, Leo stretched and then looked across at Joe. 'You want to come and watch the show?'

Around them other couples and threesomes had formed. Some of the passengers had already vanished below deck, while others preferred to remain above to savour the view, flirting, touching, deep in conversation or just watching the sea go by.

The Reef Rider had caught the edge of a stiff breeze that eagerly pushed it out towards the distant reef. Behind the vessel the coast line was slowly shifting out of focus until it was little more than a chiffon streak of grey and green against an increasingly blue ocean.

Joe glanced around the passengers who had chosen to stay above deck and drained his glass. 'Why not?' he said. 'Not much going on up here to hold my interest.'

The two men got to their feet and clambered down the open tread of staircase into the body of the ship. Both knew where they were headed; tiny cabins adjoined each of the main rooms, allowing unseen observers to watch the activities in any two cabins at once if the fancy took them.

Joe opened the door that abutted Guy's cabin. There, behind a two way mirror was a long narrow central bench. In the fetid gloom they settled themselves down to watch the show unfolding out in the main room.

Laura was naked, hands above her head, clutching the bed frame, stretched out on the white sheet while Harry crouched between her legs. As Leo's eyes adjusted to the gloom he realised the boy was using a pair of nail scissors to trim her pubic hair. Leo could sense that Laura was nervous, eyes tightly closed as the scissors moved back and forth across the impressive mound of her quim. Harry sat back on his heels to admire his handiwork, gently blowing away the discarded curls.

Sitting behind them, Guy watched, apparently unmoved, by the girl's preparations. Harry got to his feet and poured a little oil into the palms of his hands, and began to rub it into Laura's skin. Laura visibly relaxed as the young man began to work on her tense muscles. Gracefully, he swept up over her breasts and down over her belly, leaving a glittering trail in his wake. It was soon apparent that Laura and Harry were both enjoying the experience.

She stretched like a sleek cat under his caresses, her body moving appreciatively under the attentions of his fingertips.

131

Her nipples had hardened into dark peaks. She moaned softly, allowing her body to roll back and forth with the strokes, lifting her hips up to meet him as he leant forward.

Guy sniffed. 'What the hell are you waiting for?' he growled, slamming his glass down. 'I'm not paying her to have a body massage.' He sounded like a petulant child.

Even through the mirror Leo could sense Laura's growing ambivalence; though Harry's hands were lighting fires of desire in her, Guy's cold, business-like approach was unnerving. Harry paused, looking down at his prize, thumbs resting casually in the little valleys either side of Laura's sex.

Guy waved him on. 'I'm waiting,' the old man snapped.

Harry nodded and then traced a finger through the now shorn curls of her quim, the oil making the remaining hair glitter like jet. He added a little more lubricant and then bent forward to lick her open sex. Leo saw Laura shiver – almost flinching – as the boy's tongue found the secret spot, now barely covered by hair.

'Open yourself up for me – hold yourself open,' Harry murmured. As if they had a will of their own Laura's fingers moved down to her quim, holding the heavy outer lips apart for the boy's devilish tongue.

The taste of her body was fresh in Leo's memory. He shivered as Harry lapped at her, tongue spiralling around the engorged ride of her clitoris, concentrating on its sensitive hood. He knew only too well how she smelt and tasted and envied Harry his task.

Gently, Harry slipped his hands under Laura's buttocks and lifted her up towards him, pushing a cushion under her hips so that no part of her was concealed or beyond his reach.

Leo guessed what would follow. He could already see the boy's hand gently working the oil back over the sensitive bridge of flesh that lay between her sex and the tight little closure between the cheeks of her backside.

He wondered if Laura would protest as the boy's finger traced its contours, but his tongue – as pink and subtle as a kitten's – was keeping her occupied, still working the scarlet

132

bud that peeped so provocatively between the open lips of her sex.

Harry moved away fractionally and Laura moaned, lifting herself up so that she shouldn't miss one single stroke, one single pass of the boy's clever, clever tongue. And, as Leo had suspected, as soon as Laura lifted clear of the pillow, the boy, oh-so-gently, slipped a single finger into the tight, dark depths of her backside.

For an instant he saw Laura stiffen, her body resisting Harry's advances, eyes flashing open in surprise and shock. In the very instant when she might protest, Harry renewed his attentions to her clitoris, this time moving lower so that as she moved to chase his tongue she lowered herself further onto his waiting finger, guiding it deep inside her most secret places. His strategy was faultless.

Laura gasped but the boy was relentless. Another finger slid into her quim, impaling her again and again, both fingers working in tandem now to bring Laura to the very edge of orgasm. She bucked, fighting the need that was bubbling like a cauldron in her belly.

Leo could see her need and her revulsion, the muscles in her neck and jaw were tight, fear and desire caught up in a running battle through her hot, writhing body. And then, as the boy's tongue executed another scintillating pass over her quim, he saw her relax and knew she had surrendered to the pull of desire.

She began to move instinctively, oblivious now to everything but the wild ride towards release – but just at the split second when her orgasm seemed inevitable Harry pulled back.

Laura gasped in disbelief, her body searching him out, but she was to be denied. Behind the couple, Guy had got to his feet and was unzipping his cavalry twills.

As the boy moved away, Guy, with his cock jutting out in front of him like a flag-pole, crouched between Laura's open thighs and, almost as if she was a rag doll, pulled her up towards him. Her body tensed, still instinctively seeking Harry's expert caresses, and at that moment Guy took her weight and pressed his cock home.

She convulsed as he breached her, her body straining up to draw him in. She was so close to the edge that Leo guessed that she was almost oblivious to the change of partner. Desperately, she began to thrust up onto the rampant cock of the older man, fighting for her prize.

Her fingers, still holding those slick, engorged lips open and so close to the seat of her pleasure, sought out her clitoris and began to caress it frantically in an attempt to keep the passion boiling.

Leo saw the first wave hit her, careering through her like a tropical cyclone, sweeping away all reason as she was engulfed in the ecstasy of orgasm.

Above her, Guy strained forward, his face reddening, features contorted with pleasure. Leo imagined the sensation of Laura's tight, wet pussy closing rhythmically around him, sucking that desiccated cock deep inside her.

But there was more. As the old man breathlessly pulled out of her, seed spilling out onto her thighs and belly, Harry, naked now, stepped closer and caught hold of Laura around the waist. Her body was so enmeshed in the backwash of orgasm that she seemed almost liquid, unable to resist them as she gave herself over to the younger man to do with as he pleased.

Harry, seemingly without any effort, turned her over onto her belly, up on all fours, her face pressed down onto the bed. With one hand he renewed his attention to the tight little gathering between her buttocks, smearing it with the mingled juices of their mutual desire and the remains of the glistening oil, while his other hand strayed back between her legs, stirring the fading fire back into a bright flame.

Leo could hear Laura starting to moan, the intense sensations lighting a mixture of protest and pleasure.

'No, no, please . . . oh, my God,' she gasped, wriggling away from Harry's invasive touch, but her body was saying something very different. Harry moved closer, and as he pressed his finger home, Laura's body opened up for him like a ripe fruit.

Guy seemed to be equally eager to see Harry's needs answered and moved closer to the bed so that he could work more oil over the boy's throbbing shaft. Leo saw Harry gritting his teeth – he too was close to the edge and the old man's touch brought him that fraction closer.

It was obvious that Harry's touch had found the magic spot for Laura was straining back against him, her whole body glowing with desire. At the zenith of one of those glorious thrusts, Harry slipped his finger out of her anus and nuzzled his cock against the same tight little spot.

Laura's body resisted for a few seconds, apprehension and taboo contracting the muscles that he sought to breach. He worked his fingers along her spine and then, just when Leo feared Laura might call a halt, renewed his attentions to her clitoris and she was lost.

Leo shivered as he heard a thick, animal moan, part protest, part passion, trickle from her open mouth. Harry ran his hand over her hot flesh, a tender touch to still her obvious fear and then, very slowly, he eased his slick shaft home.

Laura moved too, though she was more tentative, but her tiny movement was more than enough to topple Harry over the edge. His face reddened, his jaws locked and he thrust forward, gasping for breath.

Leo shivered, imagining the intensity of the sensations. Laura's body would be so tight, unbroken, that secret dark passage as all engulfing as a tightly clenched fist. Sweat dripped off Harry's chin as he fought to hold on, to milk the pleasure that would be building in his belly – but it seemed he had underestimated the beast that drove Laura.

Suddenly, she bucked and fearlessly lifted her hips to draw him deeper. Leo could see the boy was rapidly losing the struggle – he closed his eyes, threw his head back and surrendered, tossed back and forth on the wave of pleasure until both of the lovers finally fell forward onto the bed, sweat, baby oil and juices smeared over their prone bodies a tangible record of their mutual desire.

Leo, who realised he had been straining forward, mind totally caught up in every nuance of the lovers' performance, slumped back in his chair, breathing hard.

Beside him, Joe Blanco sighed. 'My God. She is a real

find, eh, Leo? I'm surprised Belle didn't say anything about her.'

Leo glanced across at Joe. 'That's because Belle doesn't know anything about Laura's little adventures, and I'd really appreciate it if you kept it that way.'

Joe frowned. 'You're not serious? I thought that was a joke?'

Leo shook his head. 'Uh huh, Belle hasn't got a clue.'

'I always thought she could weigh someone up at a glance.'

Leo shrugged. He had always thought so too, perhaps it was just that in the case of her niece, Belle didn't want to believe what her instincts told her.

He waited until Joe had gone and then looked back into the room. Guy and Harry had left quickly, leaving Laura alone on the bed.

Her eyes were dark with sated passion, but despite the events that had unfolded in the tiny cabin she retained an almost uncanny air of innocence. Her face and body appeared completely untouched by the ravages of the men's desire.

Slowly she got up and ran a sink full of water. She obviously had no idea that she was being watched. Leo found something incredibly erotic about her unselfconscious movements as she washed the last traces of the men from her slim body. In a strange way the simple act of washing was far more erotic and appealing than the animal passion he had witnessed minutes earlier.

Finally, Laura approached the mirror, still naked, tidying her hair and applying a touch of lipstick. She looked at her reflection and smiled before picking up her summer dress and slipping it on.

Even though he knew Laura couldn't see him, Leo smiled back. It was as if she had shared the best part with him and him alone. Bending down, revealing an acre of long lightly tanned leg she picked up her underwear and dropped it into her handbag. With one final glance around the room she opened the cabin door and strode back into the corridor.

Chapter 12

Laura stood at the stern of the boat and looked out across the vast open ocean. The coastline had vanished. Below her the sea was slowly changing colour, getting shallower and even bluer as the Reef Rider approached the waters of the inner reef.

The crew were busy furling the sails, working in virtual silence like a well-oiled machine. The canvas sheets flapped furiously for a few seconds as the sailors unleashed the wind that had carried them so far out, and then gave up the fight as the men pulled them in and secured them to the boon.

Laura had chosen the relative seclusion of the rear deck, away from Harry and Guy and the rest of the passengers. Although she could hear their voices and the bass beat of music, muddled and distorted by the stiff breeze, the sounds didn't encroach on her thoughts.

With the wind in her hair and the sunlight reflecting off unnaturally blue ocean, it was so easy to let her mind drift away. Her head was full of fragmentary images of her life in England, Australia and the strange initiation she had so willingly undertaken.

Her body ached, every movement reminding her of Harry and Guy's attentions. Even now she could smell the musky scent of the oil Harry had rubbed into her skin. She shivered thinking about his fingers and cock working into her secret depths. There was a lingering pain and a sense of violation even though it would be a lie to say she hadn't enjoyed what he had shown her. How strange that her body could respond so eagerly to something so alien . . .

'Penny for them?' said a voice behind her.

Laura jumped.

Leo smiled as she turned. 'I brought you this,' he said and handed her a tube of sun block.

She laughed aloud; it seemed such a deadly practical offering after everything else she had experienced under his tutelage.

He sat down on the bench beside her. 'Are you okay?' Laura wondered.

'I couldn't find you,' he began.

She peeled a stray tendril of hair off her face. 'Maybe you were looking in the wrong places.'

'How did it go with Guy and Harry?'

Laura sighed. 'I don't know. The more I think about it the more uncertain I am. I'm not sure if I'm really cut out for this, Leo. They just wanted a compliant body. Someone to take part in a performance they'd already planned. I enjoyed it – physically, at least – but I could have been anyone, what I wanted and needed wasn't really part of their agenda.'

Leo nodded. 'The whore's lot. Have you considered turning the tables for a little while?'

Laura stared at him. 'I'm not with you.'

Leo pointed back towards the prow. 'Three or four of the guys on board work for Belle, nice guys, male escorts – that's the polite euphemism – take your pick. They're all up for hire. They'll give you anything you ask for and more besides. Why don't you try calling the shots next time?'

Laura grinned. 'Are you serious?'

Leo laughed and handed her a glass of champagne. 'Sure, why not? You're on holiday. Mind you, your name isn't on the official guest list so you'll have to settle up with them personally, but don't worry; they'll let you have a price list and they all take travellers' cheques.'

Laura snorted and choked on her champagne. Leo grinned and banged her on the back. 'Do you fancy a swim before you make up your mind?'

'A swim?'

Leo nodded. 'A few more minutes and the crew will anchor up near one of the coral cays. They provide all the equipment so that the passengers can snorkel, swim . . .' He pointed to the small tender that was slung from davits across the stern of the boat. 'And they've got a glass bottom boat. If you fancy something a little less strenuous then we can take a trip out over the reef and look at the fish in comfort.'

The warm, friendly tone of Leo's voice was strangely comforting. She nodded. 'I'd like a swim and maybe the boat ride too.'

'Great. I'll go and fetch us some towels.'

Watching Leo make his way back along the deck, Laura was surprised to realise how much she liked Belle's good looking second in command. Whatever the strange things he introduced her to she also knew the feeling was mutual. As if reading her thoughts he looked back and grinned; lifting a hand in salute. She could see genuine affection in his eyes and was touched.

The sea, despite the warmth of the sun – was icy cold and strangely effervescent, like soda water. Laura gasped as the first chill hit her and then bobbed up to the surface, supported in the cork vest the crew insisted they all wore. A few yards away Leo ran his hands back over his head, hair slicked down like a glittering pelt, and grinned. 'Good, huh?'

The water hung in diamond droplets to the dark hairs on his chest and belly.

Laura laughed. 'Cold.' The sea water seemed to have found every bruise and sore place as effectively as any physician.

Behind them, on a glittering white coral cay, the small rowing boat they had dived from was being pulled ashore by one of the crew. A stand of palm trees offered a little shade for the crewmen who stood on watch over the party of swimmers. Moored a few hundred yards away from the little tropical island, the Reef Rider seemed to be no more than a dark outline against the unrelenting sun.

Laura tugged at her swimsuit; her body was keen to remind her of Guy and Harry's attentions. Leo beckoned her towards the outcrops of coral that spread out towards them like dark fingers.

As he struck off towards the nearest, he called back over his shoulder. 'Try not to touch the coral – besides being delicate it's bloody sharp. Just look.' And with that he glided out into the glittering blue ocean. Laura fitted her snorkel, pulled on her mask and let the water embrace her.

Below them the water was crystal clear, the sand as white as salt and as Laura reached the first corals – like giant pincushions of ribbed, soft maroon velvet – tiny electric-blue and gold fish darted out to meet her.

Laura was so astonished she almost forgot that she was in the water. Beyond the first pillows of coral the ocean floor shelved away steeply and at the bottom of the undersea ridge a giant clam closed as her shadow passed over, coyly hiding the deep purple inner folds over its dark and tender heart. It was so magical that Laura was oblivious to Leo being there with her, until she felt his hand on her thigh. He pointed down to the sea bed. Below her, skirting in and out of the multicoloured coral ridges, was a huge shoal of tiny silver fish, glittering like coins falling as they twisted in and out of the fantastic landscape in an intricately choreographed, silent ballet.

Laura had never seen anything so beautiful or so awe inspiring in her life. Leo pointed things out to her as they passed over the undersea world – a bed of shocking-pink sea anemones swaying in time to an unseen current, a moray eel, with his bad-tempered and churlish mouth, peering out from a crevice, clown fish, parrot fish and pipe fish, shoals of tiny fish as bright as birds – a thousand variations on a theme, the spectacular colours and textures of the reef and its inhabitants laid out like a painter's palette for their pleasure on the ocean bed.

Even though she was tired Laura was reluctant to head back to the cay. Her limbs felt leaden when she finally stood up and waded through the water to the beached tender. Leo, a few feet ahead of her, pulled off his flippers, picked up a towel from the sand and threw it to her.

By some instinctive agreement neither spoke, as if words might somehow detract from the intensity of the visual images from the reef.

It was the ship's crewman who broke the spell. 'Are ya' ready to go back yet?'

Leo nodded and, throwing their equipment into the boat, helped the sailor push the painter back out into open water.

Laura paddled out after them and climbed aboard, still not wanting to break the precious silence.

The sun was sinking by the time they got within sight of the mainland. The Reef Rider headed for a sheltered cove. Laura, who had spent most of the return voyage dozing on a sun-lounger, could see the glow of a bonfire and the bright flares of flaming torches stuck into the sand. Leo, lying on the next sunbed, rolled over onto his side and brushed a stray curl off her face.

'Barbecue time – and then home. Did you give any more thought to my suggestion?'

She stretched and yawned. 'What suggestion?'

The atmosphere on the boat was more subdued now, everyone tired after the long day. From the stairwell Laura could just hear the strains of music from the bar below decks. Leo grinned, and pointed to three good-looking guys idling against the hand rail, sharing a beer.

'Belle's beefcake,' he said, eyes twinkling mischievously. 'Looks like they've got time on their hands.'

She looked heavenwards, but he continued, 'Come on. Everyone else is all partied-out. Too much booze, too much of everything else that's on offer. Only we professionals are stone cold sober, or,' he grinned and glanced at the three young men, 'still full of stamina. Would you like me to arrange a little light entertainment for you?'

Laura sighed. 'I thought you said we were going to land and eat? I'm starving.'

He nodded. 'That's right, but the beach is very secluded. Which one do you like the look of?'

Laura reddened. 'It's like choosing a puppy,' she said, but nevertheless her eyes moved slowly over the bodies of the three men; one was tall, with Nordic features and cropped blond hair, the second was thick-set – Laura thought she remembered him from the first morning on the beach bringing down the curvaceous company executive. The memory caught hold and replayed in scintillating detail while her eyes moved on to the third guy.

Laura knew she hadn't seen him before. He was of mixed race, though she was unsure whether he was of Caribbean or aboriginal origin. His skin was the colour of *café latte*. Thick set and muscular, with long, curling black hair, he looked like a pirate. He was dressed in faded blue jeans and a white tee-shirt that emphasised the broadness of his shoulders and the soft golden glow of his skin. She could see an earring glittering in amongst his tight curls.

As if he sensed Laura was studying him, he turned to look back along the deck; a phalanx of dark curls rose above his shirt neck. He had a kind of intense, languid grace. For an instant she imagined what it might be like to look up and see him above her, dark eyes locked on hers, slim hips grinding into her sex.

Leo, who had been watching her, grinned broadly.

'Gabriel? Nice choice.'

Laura blushed.

Leo waved her embarrassment away. 'Don't be so bloody coy. Why don't you just go downstairs and have a drink, while I take care of business? My treat.'

Without a word Laura slipped off the sun-lounger and headed towards the bar. She found herself a secluded corner, careful to avoid Guy and Harry, ordered a bottle of wine and two glasses and then turned her attention to the view from the porthole. A few minutes later she felt someone slide onto the bench next to her. When she turned Gabriel was no more than a hair's breadth away from her, although somehow, even though he was so close, he didn't seem to invade the space around her.

He smiled, revealing perfectly pearly teeth set off by a generous mouth.

'Enjoy your swim?' he said refilling her glass and then pouring himself a drink.

She nodded. 'It was amazing. I've never seen anything like it.'

He nodded. His voice was low and cultured. 'I know

exactly what you mean. The first time I swam on the reef I was so overwhelmed I nearly drowned.' He laughed with genuine good humour. 'Forgot all about breathing through my mouth – the two guys I was with had to haul me back into the boat.'

Gabriel, like Leo, was remarkably easy to talk to. As they shared the wine and laughed and chatted about her trip, some part of her was aware just how good he was at making her feel comfortable. He really was a professional.

Above them they could hear the crew making ready to drop the anchor. The chain rumbled over the side. Gabriel drained his glass and offered her his hand. 'Would you like to go ashore and eat?'

His palm was dry and warm and engulfed hers. She smiled. 'Sounds like a wonderful idea.'

Up on the deck the night was as black as velvet, stars overhead tumbling like a waterfall towards the hills that surrounded the cove. As they reached the top of the stairs Gabriel slipped his arm through hers and guided her towards the platform where the passengers were disembarking for the beach barbecue. The gesture was so natural, intimate and gentle, that she couldn't resist a smile.

'Oh, you're good,' she said, letting the humour linger in her voice.

His eyes twinkled. 'Why thank you, ma'am,' he said and touched his forelock in a gesture of mock subservience. 'It's our aim to please.'

As the painter pulled away from the Reef Rider, Gabriel moved closer, hand searching for hers, an arm sliding around her shoulders.

The evening was still warm despite a tropical breeze ruffling the sea into tiny white coronets. On the beach under an open shelter, roofed with palm fronds, was a buffet, a bar and a small stage where a group had already begun to play. At the barbecue pit a uniformed chef was ready, waiting to serve the passengers.

The food was glorious – chargrilled prawns and mouthwatering steaks served with potato wedges and salad. Gabriel was attentive without being obsequious and gradually Laura relaxed, remembering what Leo had said about this being her chance to call the shots. Around them, as supper was finished, couples began dancing on the sand.

It was a strange feeling – some part of her was expecting Gabriel to make the first move. She wondered if she ought to tell him that. As if he had read her mind he stood his glass down and moved a little closer. His dark features were thrown into relief by the flames of the bonfire – he really did look like a pirate, she thought.

His eyes glittered. Leaning forward he slipped off her sandals. The gesture took her completely by surprise. She moaned softly as he began to massage her feet, fingers working down over the toes and soles, rubbing in soft compelling circles that were at once both remarkably pleasant and strangely erotic.

Laura looked up at him. 'God, that feels incredible! I've never done this kind of thing before – do I have to tell you what I want you to do?'

Gabriel smiled lazily. 'If you want. Or you could let me seduce you, pamper you . . .'

She bit her lip as his fingers found a spot that ached and eased the pain away. 'I'm not sure what it is I want—'

He lifted a foot to his mouth and ran his tongue between the toes. It lit an intense flame of pleasure in her belly. She shivered.

'Then why don't you just let go and let me spoil you.'

His tongue wormed its way back again, making the hairs on the back of her neck rise.

'Because I'm supposed to be calling the shots,' she murmured.

Gabriel nodded. 'I know, but if you don't know what's on offer how can you choose?' He licked along the arch of her foot and then drew her big toe into his mouth. She closed her eyes, unable to believe that something so simple could be so erotically charged.

'So do you like this?' he purred.

As if she needed to answer! 'Yes,' she whispered, arching her back as his tongue worked on and on along the sensitive plains and peaks of her foot. His hands worked up onto her

144

calves, massaging the muscles. His fingers seemed to find magical tender spots that she had no idea existed. Her whole body responded instinctively to his knowing hands.

Almost without her realising it, Gabriel was working slowly up over her legs and thighs, kneading and massaging her flesh. It felt heavenly. And then gently he set her foot back in the sand, moving closer so that he seemed to be towering above her. One hand lingered between her thigh, his touch so deceptively light that it was impossible to believe he had left it there by accident.

'Dance with me?' he murmured, his lips working along her throat and shoulders, a single finger tracing along the taut muscle of her thigh.

She nodded and got to her feet, feeling as if Gabriel had ensnared her with some kind of magical potion. Every inch of her flesh was tingling with anticipation. He kissed her gently, his lips as soft as spun silk, and then taking her hand, guided her towards the other dancers.

The music had a heady, earthy beat, echoing her mood perfectly. Gabriel was so close that it felt as if they were sharing the same breath. He smelt of sea and sand and a soft male musk that made her mouth water. His body brushed hers, driving her crazy with desire. His gaze was locked onto hers excluding everybody and everything else. As they began to move all she was aware of was the heat of their bodies and the soft rise and fall of Gabriel's broad chest against her breasts.

His hands worked their way up over her hips and back, his touch was unhurried and oh, so beautiful. She wondered if it was possible to come while dancing. He ran his tongue over the lobe of her ear, teasing back and forth until she thought she would faint from sheer longing.

As the music faded he kissed her again, more emphatically this time, holding her tight against him. Her mouth opened to receive his tongue. He ran it gently around the frame of her lips making every nerve-ending flash white-hot.

Laura surrendered to his embrace and, before she had time to protest or encourage him, he slipped his hands under her thighs and picked her up. She seemed to float up into his arms, her body moulding seamlessly against his. In his arms it was as if she weighed no more than a feather.

They headed away from the bonfire towards a secluded stand of palms – it seemed that someone had already planned her seduction. Beneath the trees someone had spread a blanket on the sand and left a pile of pillows and the spot was marked by a single storm lantern. Laura smiled. Leo had apparently thought of everything.

Gabriel lowered her onto the blanket as if she were made of the most delicate porcelain. He tucked a pillow under her head and then, with knowing fingers he began to undress her, eyes locked with hers, his attention fixed entirely on her to the exclusion of everything else.

His touch lit a trail of beacon fires in her mind. His lips worked over her breasts, teasing at the swollen peaks while his fingers stroked the rise of her sex. When she was naked, he stood up. She watched him intently, hungry for the satisfaction her whole body demanded.

Without a shred of self-consciousness Gabriel undressed. His body was perfection, everything she could have possibly imagined. His skin was like taupe silk, draped over slabs of sculpted muscles. His chest was covered with a vee of dark hair, with a line of curls drawing the eye down like an enticing invitation over a taut stomach to the prize below. Something glittered – another magpie call to look down.

His cock was already hard, a great curved beast that begged for her attention, nestling amongst a nest of dark hair, and through his foreskin was a narrow gold ring that matched the one in his ear. Laura shivered, imagining the sensation of the smooth metal gliding deep into her.

She swallowed hard. Gabriel was beautiful, and what was more he was all hers, bought and paid for. He knelt between her legs and rubbed his body against hers. The gold ring tickled against her belly and thighs, a delicate taste of what was to follow.

Gabriel's heat and raw masculinity stirred up a maelstrom of need in her gut. She reached up and pulled him down towards her, relishing the weight of his body on hers.

Laura felt his hand between her legs, guiding his shaft

home. She was already wet – every second they had spent together had been part of an intricate, unspoken game of foreplay. She was so ready that she didn't want to be denied another instant and then, just as the head of his cock nuzzled at her sex, begging for entry, she froze, holding back from the edge, some part of her crouched on the edge of the abyss, caught up in the raging torrent of passion, afraid of the sheer intensity of what she felt.

Gabriel stopped too, his dark eyes reflecting the lantern light and an unspoken question. Laura licked her lips, aware of their breath and the glowing hunger in her sex, and then she closed her eyes and surrendered to sensation, passion drowning out the tiny voice of dissent.

She lifted herself up towards him, the tiny movements an explicit invitation. Slowly, he brushed the delicate inner lips of her quim, working his shaft deep inside her. His cock felt huge, opening her up in its path. The gold ring was cool, a stunning contrast to the heat of his throbbing phallus. The sensation was almost more than she could bear.

What she was feeling was raw passion, unmuddied by intellect and reason, an animal hunger that drove away all thought but pleasure. Full to the brim, her sex humming, Gabriel began to move slowly, stroking his pelvis and belly against the throbbing bud that lay between the lips of her quim. She gasped as he found it, amazed that she could be so close to release so soon.

As he found his rhythm, every movement designed to tease her clitoris, she grinned and then laughed aloud, thrusting up to meet him, making the most of every stroke. Eyes wide open she looked up at Gabriel: he was grinning too.

'Feel good?' he said at the pinnacle of a long artful thrust.

'Oh, my God, yes,' she moaned, arching back to meet him, milking the pleasure curve. 'Leo was right, you're a real professional, this is amazing.' The last word crumbled into a sob as the first intense wave of orgasm crashed over her.

Deep inside she could feel the ring in Gabriel's foreskin echoing the scintillating rhythm, beating out a pulse in the hidden depths of her body. It was too much. She linked her fingers around Gabriel's neck and wrapped her legs around his waist, holding on tight, his hot flesh a touchstone, a beacon fire to guide her back from the shores of madness.

Chapter 13

It seemed like hours before Laura and Gabriel finally returned to the welcome glow of the beach bonfire. Laura's body felt as if it was full of stardust. Exhausted, she sat down by the fireside and didn't resist as Gabriel folded a blanket around her shoulders and then went off in search of coffee.

Leo and Joe Blanco were standing just outside the circle of the firelight. Leo grinned and lifted his glass in a silent toast. Laura was so tired she could hardly be bothered to acknowledge him. Gabriel returned a few seconds later, handed her a mug and then sat down in the sand next to her.

'Are you okay?' he asked, poking at the embers with a twig.

'And then some,' she said. Her body was still bathed in the afterglow of his expert touch. 'That was astonishing.' Wrapping her hands around the mug she leant back against him. The wind had dropped away but it was cooler now; it felt good to have his body to curl up against.

Gabriel slipped an arm round her shoulders and pulled her close.

'You were pretty good yourself. Leo tells me you're Belle's niece. Are you thinking of joining the family firm?'

Laura took a mouthful of the hot coffee, savouring the rich, dark taste. Despite her tiredness it still seemed as if every sense was intensely alive and receptive.

'Not if my aunt's got anything to do with it. I'm only here on holiday. A month in the sun. I haven't seen you around the hotel before.'

Gabriel grinned, making himself comfortable. 'I don't work for Belle if that's what you mean. You could say I'm

149

freelance. I live in a cabin at Pears Point. When I'm not servicing rich bitches . . .' he paused and reddened furiously, 'Sorry, present company excepted. I'm an artist. I sell my work to the tourist trade mostly, acrylics, landscapes, seascapes . . . I've got a little gallery up on the high road, I just fill in occasionally for Belle. It helps to make ends meet when business is slow.'

Laura nodded, feeling wonderfully at ease cuddled up alongside the pirate artist. Odd to be discussing making a living by selling your body. She grinned – but what a body! 'And you don't have a problem with that?'

He shook his head. 'It certainly beats bussing tables. I've met some great people – and a lot of satisfied customers stop by the gallery to pick up a memento.' He paused, a smile broadening into a good-humoured grin. 'And, beside that, I really enjoy my work.'

'I can tell,' Laura said with a laugh.

Gabriel nodded towards the boat. 'They'll soon be getting ready to board.'

'Are you coming back to O'Malley's?'

He shook his head. 'No, I've got my motorbike stashed up in the trees over there – my place isn't far from here.' He pointed along the beach. 'O'Malley's is only about half an hour's sailing time, just round the next point, but it's a lot longer by road. Why? Would you like me to stay with you a little longer?' His eyes twinkled mischievously.

Laura laughed. 'The thought had crossed my mind. But I think I'm just too tired to do you justice.'

Gabriel kissed her gently. 'How long did you say you're here for?'

'Just a month, and then it's back to reality.' She paused, trying to imagine what it would be like to go home to England. Her old life with Gareth seemed abstract and so far away – both in time and geographically – from the things she had experienced since she arrived in Australia, it was hard to believe the memories were hers.

Gabriel smiled. 'Maybe we could get together some other time?' It was a tempting idea. He had made her feel wonderful, irresistible, which was exactly the antidote she had needed after making love to Harry and Guy.

He pulled a card out of his back pocket. 'Here's my phone number – just give me a call if you ever get a little lonely. I'd really like to see you again.'

Across the beach on the water's edge the painter was beginning to ferry passengers back out to the Reef Rider. Reluctantly, Laura stood the mug down in the sand. 'I think it's time I was going.'

Gabriel nodded and then brushed his lips against hers. The gesture made her flesh tingle. 'Give me a ring,' he purred. 'I mean it.'

As Laura made her way across the sand she tucked his card into her bag and smiled, wondering if he said that to all the 'rich bitches' he serviced.

She didn't resist as the sailor helped her into the row boat and didn't look back to shore until she was safely aboard the boat. By the time she was on deck the beach was practically deserted. Gabriel had gone, leaving only the catering staff clearing away the remains of the barbecue.

Laura and Leo were the last two passengers to be put ashore at O'Malley's. Belle had come down to the beach to greet her returning guests and, as neither Leo nor Laura had any desire to be caught by her aunt, they waited until the crowd had dispersed before getting ready to disembark.

When the little boat returned for the last time to pick them up, the sailor working the outboard caught hold of Laura's arm.

'You don't have to go, you know,' he said in a low voice. 'Fredo and Jack told me all about you the other night up at Ropey's – maybe you'd like to stop for a while and have a drink with the crew? Have a little fun? We could sail round the next point and have little party of our own?' Laura froze. Although the request sounded polite enough, she could see the flicker of lust burning in the man's eyes.

Leo waved him away. 'Another time, mate – we wanna get home, it's getting late.'

The man snorted. 'You've got yourself a good-looking bit of tail here. If it's money you're worried about,' he patted the back pocket of his jeans. 'I can pay whatever you're asking for her. No worries. Name your price.' He turned his attention back to Laura. 'I've been watching you all day. I'd like a piece of what you've got on offer. What's the matter? Likes of me not good enough for you?'

Laura struggled to fix a smile, but her hands were shaking.

This man was very different from all the other men she had met and made love to since she'd arrived in Australia. Rough and crude he wanted only one thing from her; there was no pretence of civility.

Cat-like he sprung forwards, sliding his hand up between her legs. Laura was stunned, frozen to the spot as he reached up under her dress.

'Come on, you know what I want,' he murmured. He was so quick that he was pressed close up against her before either Leo or Laura had a chance to move. His fingers were like talons seeking out the pit of her sex, his face contorted into an obscene leer. She could feel the press of his cock against her belly and shivered with revulsion as he forced his lips against hers. His breath was foul.

To her relief Leo grabbed him and dragged him away.

'Stop it. Maybe another time, mate,' he said more firmly, his brusque tone emphasising the Australian edge to his voice. 'Leave her alone. It's been a long, hard day. We don't want any trouble. Just get us ashore.'

The man wriggled free of Leo's grasp, his expression murderous.

'Long day? What the fuck d'you mean? You've been sitting around on your arse all day knocking the booze back. And anyway what's one more shafting to a whore?' The sailor grinned and wiped his mouth with the back of his hand. 'She'll be lying down.'

The commotion on the landing stage had alerted other members of the crew. Amongst the men that appeared above them on the deck Laura could see the two sailors, Fredo and Jack, who had made love to her on beach and her heart fluttered. Although they hadn't been rough with her, she doubted that they would be sympathetic, after all they saw her as just another whore too.

152

The man beside Leo lifted his hands in a gesture of surrender.

'What's the matter – never seen a sailor pick up a tart before? I was only asking what the price was.'

Fredo swung over the side and shinned down the ladder. 'You've been drinking again, haven't yer Mac? Just leave her alone – she's way out of your league. I'll take them across – why don't you go below and sleep it off?'

Mac's shoulders slumped forward. Deflated by the man's comments, all bluster gone, he began to climb the rungs. Half way up he stopped and looked down at Laura. 'Next time, darling,' he said with a sly grin. He cupped his groin. 'I've got just the cure for you – I'd wake you up.'

Laura shuddered.

Their rescuer indicated the boat. 'Sorry, about that, we've warned him about keeping off the sauce before. He doesn't mean any harm.' His remark was casual, almost throwaway, but the man had completely unnerved Laura.

It had been a mistake to think that being with Leo, being part of Belle's stable – even if unofficially – kept her safe. So far she had been exploring in the confines of a magical erotic garden, secure in the knowledge that Leo would keep an eye on her.

Up until now she had had a choice whether to play or pass, but the sailor had undermined those assumptions in the matter of a few seconds and made her realise how her impression of security was in fact built on sand. The sailor didn't think of her as Belle's niece or even as a woman – just another whore for hire.

Trembling, Laura let Leo guide her into the painter and sat down in the prow.

'It's all right,' Leo said in a low voice. 'Don't let it worry you. He'd been drinking.'

Laura nodded dumbly but his words offered little comfort. As the boat reached the sand she clambered ashore, glad to be back on dry land. Leo hurried after her.

'Laura, hang on – we need to talk,' he began as she ran towards her cabin.

Laura swung round. 'No, Leo. I don't want to talk to

you. You might convince me that everything is all right, but it isn't. That guy out there – they're all like that, aren't they? Okay, so he was rougher and drunker than most, but that's what they will see if I carry on with this – just another whore up for hire. Not a woman, not a person, just a body to be used. That was all Harry and Guy wanted too. This is just a game to you, isn't it, Leo?'

She realised she was shaking like a leaf.

He caught hold of her shoulders and pulled her close. 'You're right,' he said, eyes alight. 'They see you as another whore, but you know you're a lot more than that. Belle could really use you here at O'Malley's. You really ought to stay.'

Laura wriggled free of his embrace. 'Oh, right – and who's going to tell her? As far as she's concerned I'm a naive little hick up from the sticks who's got to be chaperoned around. God, she doesn't even trust me enough to tell me the truth about O'Malley's. I think you've got it all wrong. I should never have started this. I thought I was . . . I was . . .' tears bubbled up in her eyes. 'Shit,' she snorted angrily. 'That man out there really frightened me. I saw the look in his eyes – pure lust, animal desire. He couldn't have cared less who I was or what I wanted, he just wanted to have me. If you had agreed a price he would have screwed me there and then up against the boat.'

Leo nodded. 'You're right, but he didn't. I'll ring Fredo tomorrow and sort it out. We don't want our clients or our girls exposed to that kind of thing.'

'Your girls? Your clients?' she said incredulously. 'You make it sound as if it was a complaint about a cold supper. If you hadn't been there that guy could have raped me,' snapped Laura, furiously.

Leo sighed. 'Okay – I do understand. I'm really sorry. Belle would be furious if she knew.'

Laura looked away in disgust. She couldn't convey how confused or upset she was. Leo had helped to light this fire inside her and only now was she realising what a potent and dangerous thing it was.

'Why don't I walk you back to your cabin?'

Laura nodded and made no objection to him sliding his

arm through hers. She glanced around the hotel grounds. Several of the cabins were occupied – their windows looked like cats eyes glowing in the darkness. Her mind replayed the vivid images from the guided tour Leo had given her. It was hard not to wonder what was going on behind each of those apparently normal facades.

Under the umbrella of O'Malley's hotel, everyone's little fantasy could be indulged, every taste catered for, safely tucked way in the privacy of one cabin or another.

Laura took a deep breath – maybe she was overreacting. She rubbed her hand over her face. The man had made her feel vulnerable.

She didn't invite Leo inside, instead, struggling to still the contradictions that filled her tired brain, she showered and climbed into bed.

Her dreams were turbulent – images of Leo, Gabriel, Harry and Guy, mixed with strange abstracts of England, followed her eagerly into the darkness. Tossing and turning she sought peace and was relieved to find herself back by Leo's mountain stream. In her dream Eva uncurled alongside her on the sun-warmed rock and cupped her breasts, planting a single kiss on her bare shoulder. Laura stretched, finally relaxing under the woman's gentle, non-threatening touch.

The tender caress brought Laura back to the edge of consciousness and she was astonished to find that the sensation followed her out of the dream. She blinked, trying to focus in the darkness, suddenly wide awake.

Laura could smell Eva's perfume and feel the soft brush of fingertips against her ribs. Rolling over she snapped on the bedside lamp and was astonished to find the blonde really was stretched out alongside her.

'Hello,' Eva whispered in her low, even voice. 'I just thought I'd come over and see how you got on with Leo.' She laughed softly. 'But you looked so beautiful in the moonlight – too good to resist. You don't mind if I stay a little while, do you?'

Laura shook her head, blinking in the lamplight. In her dream Eva's caresses had been like balm. Now, too tired to

155

resist, too tired to worry about her inhibitions Laura snuggled down in Eva's arms, relishing the comfort of the woman's closeness.

The blonde smiled and stroked a stray tendril of hair back off Laura's face.

'Long day?'

Laura snorted. 'And then some.' It struck her that that was the same expression she had used to compliment Gabriel. 'Have you seen Leo tonight?'

Eva nodded. 'Yeah. He dropped by for a coffee. He told me about your run-in with Mac. But don't worry, I understand, and I've got everything you need to make it better.' She spoke in a whisper and then, lowering her head, drew one of Laura's nipples into her mouth.

Laura moaned. The feeling was pure heaven, the woman's knowing lips a delicate contrast to the attention of the men who had made love to her that day. Eva must already know what it would feel like and could gauge the effect.

Pulling away, Laura's nipple, outlined by the damp ministrations of Eva's tongue, had hardened into a tight, pink peak. Gently, Eva guided Laura's hand between her thighs, murmuring words of encouragement. Laura's fingers brushed the corona of blonde hair that framed the blonde's sex. It was so much like her own body and she marvelled at how soft and warm Eva's skin felt.

As Eva persuaded her hand lower, Laura could understand exactly why men were so eager to explore this sacred spot, for the blonde's pussy unfolded under her fingertips like the petals of an exotic orchid, a magic box, moist and fragrant, drawing her fingers inside as if they were being carried on the same unseen current that had flowed around the sea anemones on the reef.

Eva moaned as Laura's finger eased into the tight confines of her sex. Her response was to do the same to Laura. As her finger glided home, Eva kissed Laura full on the mouth, with lips as soft as velvet, breasts gently pressed against hers. Eva's skin, her whole body seemed to be incandescent, glowing with an intense, but unthreatening, sexual promise that was impossible to resist.

156

As Laura turned her attention to the little bud that rose between the outer lips of Eva's sex, Eva did the same to her. Laura stifled a nervous giggle – it was a game, an intricate electrifying game of follow the leader. She wriggled down the bed so that she could kiss the blonde's heavy breasts, her inhibitions pushed aside by the rising call of her desire.

When her lips moved away from the hard peaks Eva, giggling too, wriggled lower and followed suit. Laura gasped and then relinquished her fears, casting her body adrift on the heady ocean current of sensation.

Every touch seemed to echo through them both until it was impossible to tell who was leading and who was following. What was certain was that as they stroked, kissed, and caressed each other, the excitement was slowly building up until it hung in the air around them like an electric storm.

Laura remembered just how good Eva had been at bringing her to the very brink of release and then denying her the final prize, over and over again until Laura had thought she would go insane, and she now followed Eva's earlier example, making the blonde writhe with a mixture of frustration and pure, unadulterated pleasure. Under her fingertips she could feel Eva quivering – a low resonant hum that electrified her.

She wondered how long they would be able to sustain the intense dance – and then Eva slowly rolled away and smiled slyly. Laura heard a strange little noise, not unlike a mosquito.

'What are you doing?' she murmured. It was hard to find a voice after her mind had spent so long quelling logic under a tidal wave of pleasure. Eva smiled triumphantly. 'Close your eyes,' she purred. 'Trust me.'

'Are you serious?'

The blonde nodded. 'Indulge me – indulge us. Relax – you'll love this.'

Laura lay back amongst the tumble of pillows and did as she was told.

She felt something brush her nipples and then gasped as

an intense vibration spun down through her skin to her very core. Her eyes snapped open.

Eva was crouched over her cradling a shiny black vibrator. Although Laura had never seen one before she knew exactly what it was. As smooth as polished ebony it was cock-shaped with a disproportionately large head. Eva lifted it to her lips and ran her tongue over the dimpled end, her kisses leaving a slick trail in their wake. And then, as Laura watched, Eva guided the dildo between her thighs, burying its throbbing head into the soft recess of her sex. Laura gasped. It was such an overwhelmingly erotic image that her pulse quickened.

The blonde slowly drew her hand away. Laura looked down – it was impossible not to. The smooth black cock was a stunning contrast to the blonde's creamy skin. It was then that Laura realised the vibrator was double ended. Curving towards her was a matching bulbous snout, glittering in the lamplight.

Eva, eyes hooded with desire, licked her lips and beckoned Laura closer.

'Here,' she purred, her expression ecstatic. 'Why don't you come and play too?'

Laura shivered. The blonde extended a hand, her face already registering the intense effects of the cock shimmering away inside her. Nervously, Laura moved closer, clambering up onto her knees, crawling nearer, and slowly the blonde guided the curved end of the dildo into her. Laura gasped as her body drew it in. At first it seemed cool and unwieldy, and yet the vibration was so intense that Laura thought she would pass out.

The intense burr seemed to start a chain reaction. Even before the dildo was fully home she started to come, a sensation that swept up through her in series of tight, reeling pulses.

Eva gasped and caught hold of Laura's breasts, her fingers nipping viciously at her nipples. Laura cried out in astonishment – the pain and pleasure roared through her like magma, and without thinking she kissed Eva full on the mouth, biting down hard on her bottom lip, pulling her closer, almost afraid to let her go. Eva mewled in protest and thrust her hips forward, driving the dildo deep inside them both.

Laura snorted and instinctively flexed her hips. On and on and on the waves of pleasures went, until Laura could barely draw breath. Finally she knew she just couldn't take any more and gasping for breath, wriggled away. The dildo slithered out of her, slick, dark and unforgiving. Laura stared at it, she could hardly believe that something so ugly could possibly give so much pleasure.

Eva, still gasping, slid the vibrator out from between her legs and rolled over onto her back.

She was grinning widely. 'Well?' she said triumphantly.

Laura shook her head. 'I really don't know what to say.'

Eva laughed aloud. 'My little friend often has that effect on people.' She switched the vibrator off and dropped it down beside the bed. 'I think we really ought to get some sleep,' she said leaning over and kissing Laura gently. 'I've got to work tomorrow.'

Laura rolled over and switched off the bedside light. The image that lingered in her mind was the glow of satisfaction on Eva's face. In the darkness the blonde pulled her close, curling around her so they lay back to belly.

'Good night,' Eva purred sleepily. 'Sweet dreams.'

Laura closed her eyes. The sensation of Eva's breasts rising and falling against her back were the last sensations that trickled through her mind as sleep called her back into oblivion.

Chapter 14

Laura wondered if Eva's visit had been another dream when she woke again just after seven. The little cabin was empty – no sign remaining of her unexpected nocturnal visitor. Perhaps the intense sexual images had just been her imagination – another reminder of the things she had discovered about herself on this voyage of self discovery.

She slipped out of bed, pulled on a robe and headed for the bathroom.

On the hand basin, between the taps, was a black silk drawstring bag.

Laura grinned; the distinctive shape left her in no doubt what the bag contained. It seemed that she hadn't imagined Eva's visit after all. There was a note tied to the string, and in a strong round hand the stunning blonde had written: 'Take care of my little friend for me. Sweet dreams. E.'

Laura picked it up and turned it over in her fingers. A rogue thought surfaced in her mind – perhaps she could take the vibrator home for Gareth as a souvenir of her trip. The idea was so ridiculous it made her laugh out loud. She dropped Eva's gift into her makeup bag and turned on the shower.

An hour later, dressed in shorts and a shirt, she was about to put on her make-up when there was a knock at the cabin door.

'Morning,' called Belle from the veranda. 'Can I come in?'

Laura glanced at her reflection, wondering whether there was any outward signs of the changes that had taken place in her since she had last seen Belle. Would her aunt guess? She pulled her hair back into a pony-tail. The light tan she was now sporting had brought out a flurry of freckles across her nose and cheeks. Added to her casual clothes and the uncomplicated hair-style it made Laura look like a schoolgirl. She smiled and then called, 'Sure, come in, it's unlocked.'

Belle smiled. 'Morning, sweetheart – I'm sorry I didn't hear you come back last night. Leo said it was very late. Did you have a good time up in the rainforest?'

Laura nodded as her aunt made herself comfortable on the side of the bed.

'I just thought I'd come and remind you about the Cairns trip. Maybe if you're up to it we could drive down later this afternoon?'

Laura nodded. It might be a relief to have a break from the electric atmosphere of O'Malley's. She caught a glimpse of Eva's gift protruding from her make-up case and surreptitiously dropped her towel over it.

'Sounds like a great idea. We hardly seem to have had any time to talk since I arrived.'

'That's exactly what I thought, and I could really do with a couple of days away from it all. All girls together: it should be fun. Right, well in that case I'll confirm the booking. Have you had breakfast yet?'

Laura shook her head.

'No worries. I'll get chef to send you a tray over.' Belle looked jubilant. 'Time off – that'll be a treat. I'm really looking forward to having you all to myself. Oh, before I forget, how was your trip out to the reef?'

Laura stiffened. She had no idea that Belle knew she and Leo had gone out on the Reef Rider, and was immediately thrown into total confusion. If Belle knew Laura was on the trip what else did she know? Laura was about to speak when Belle continued, 'Leo said you managed to go out on the Wave Crest – I envy you. It's a lovely old ship.'

'Yes,' Laura said cautiously.

Belle was already on her feet. 'We sometimes hire her sister ship, the Reef Rider, for the guests. Leo said you went snorkelling – isn't the reef something?'

The tension eased in Laura's stomach. She would have no problem at all talking about the beauty of the reef, snorkelling, or the voyage out there, but she was spared even that, as Leo stuck his head around the cabin door. He was obviously surprised to see Belle there.

'Oh hi,' he said, quickly regaining his composure. 'I thought you were in the office. I just nipped over to see if . . .' Laura could see Leo fishing around to find a plausible excuse and couldn't help wondering what he had really come to see her about.

Meanwhile Leo pressed on, 'I just wondered if Laura had remembered the Cairns trip.'

Belle grinned. 'You don't fool me, what you mean is you were skiving off! You really don't give me much confidence, Leo – the place will probably go to wrack and ruin while I'm away. Are you sure you can handle it?'

Leo pulled a face, and for the first time Laura noticed the intimate, flirtatious way Belle spoke to him. The realisation stopped her in her tracks. Leo hadn't just seduced her but no doubt Belle as well. Laura stared at him, thoughts exploding like mortar shells; Leo was Belle's lover. She could feel her colour rising.

Leo smiled at her. 'Are you coming over for breakfast?'

Belle waved him away. 'No, she isn't. I've already said I'll send a tray over. Why don't you come back with me and give Laura a chance to get herself organised.' She turned to Laura. 'See you later, babe. Oh and pack your glad rags – I'm planning to paint the town red.'

When they had gone Laura stared into the mirror. She had been so caught up in Leo's exquisite little plans that she hadn't given much thought to why he had stayed with Belle – or what their relationship might be. She turned the thought over in her mind.

'Leo?' said Belle, pushing a stray tendril of hair back over her ear. 'I met him while I was in Sydney about ten years ago. Why?'

Laura and Belle were idling along the Cook highway in the hotel's four by four with the windows wide open. The sky above was cloudless and away to their left the Coral Sea lapped lazily along the shore line. It was a perfect day.

Belle had her elbow resting on the window ledge, one hand on the steering wheel. Laura thought her aunt looked very beautiful with the wind in her hair – certainly the most relaxed than she had been since Laura arrived at O'Malley's.

Laura nodded. 'I just wondered, are you . . .' she hesitated, 'a couple?'

Belle threw back her head and laughed aloud. 'Good God, no. I don't think Leo really has any idea what a couple is. You'd have to ask him yourself. But no, Leo and I really are very good friends but nothing more.' She paused and then shot Laura a glance. 'Why? You're not interested in him, are you?'

Laura reddened.

Belle shook her head. 'Please don't be. The guy has the morals of an alley cat. He's great company, he'll make you laugh, show you a really great time – he certainly knows how to make a woman feel special – but he'll break your heart. Take my advice, even if you're just looking for a holiday romance, don't get involved with him.'

Their drive over to Cairns had been leisurely. As Belle and Laura made their way down over the hills Laura could see the city laid out around the harbour, the sprawl of white buildings like sea shells cast up a tropical beach. City blocks, modern hotels and shopping centres were punctuated by traditional colonial buildings and picturesque wooden Queenslander houses set up on stilts. The sharp corners and angles of the modern city were softened by an abundance of rich greenery, trees, creepers and vines insinuating themselves into every nook and cranny – as if the city was barely holding its own against the ever present rainforest.

They drove in along the esplanade under rows of palm trees that lined the mud flats and the harbour. Belle stretched as they slowed for the traffic lights. Away to the right the roadside was lined with brightly coloured shop fronts and crowds of tourist looking for bargains and souvenirs.

'God, I could use a shower,' Belle said and then pointed between the buildings that framed the pier. 'We're staying along there – it's a really nice place run by an old friend of mine. We should have a great time.'

Laura nodded. After the solitude and isolation of the Cape it felt strange to be back amongst so many people. The colours and the bustle of the cosmopolitan resort seemed almost overwhelming.

Laura had been tense when they left O'Malley's, anxious not to give away any of the secrets she had discovered nor to share her thoughts about Belle and Leo, but had gradually relaxed as the miles rolled by.

Talking about family and friends to Belle it seemed as if O'Malley's and even Leo were part of another existence – though, other than her question about Leo and Belle, Laura had been careful to keep the conversation to safe topics.

Gradually the tension in her shoulders and belly had eased – they were just two women, connected by blood and more than friends, escaping for a couple of days.

Down past the pier and the marina towards the docks, the new Piermont Hotel overlooked the harbour – and after the warm colonial beauty of O'Malley's it came as quite a shock to be back in the twentieth century. The huge, modern vaulted lobby was wonderfully cool and as silent as a church.

Laura stared in astonishment at the hotel interior. The cream marble foyer exhuded an unmistakable aura of discreet luxury, from the acres of plush royal blue carpet that rolled away towards the marble reception desk to the elegantly understated chrome and leather fittings.

Two exquisite Asian girls confirmed their reservation and handed Belle a key while their luggage was swiftly dispatched by a uniformed bellboy.

As they went up in the lift, Belle said, 'Well, what do you think of it so far?'

Laura grinned. 'I don't think I've ever stayed anywhere so grand.'

Belle grinned. 'Good. Just wait till you see our room.'

The lift doors opened and to Laura's surprise instead of being in an anonymous corridor they found themselves in an exquisitely decorated hallway. Ahead of them double doors opened up into a sitting room, with huge picture windows that gave an uninterrupted view out over Trinity inlet.

While Belle tipped the bellboy Laura explored their suite – she really hadn't ever seen anywhere as luxurious. The carpets were the colour of buttermilk, cream leather sofas framed a single glass coffee table, exotic flowers, tumbling from square cut crystal blocks added the only touch of colour.

Belle took a bottle of champagne from the cooler on a side table. 'Well? Now what do you think?'

Laura spun round. 'It's amazing!'

The cork eased from the bottle with satisfying sound, Belle handed her a glass and then lifted hers in a toast. 'I can't say that I always stay in such style but I thought we both deserved the best while we were here. Nice to have an excuse to treat ourselves. Here's to a great holiday.'

Laura's eyes filled with tears. 'Thank you so much,' she murmured.

Belle laughed. 'Don't thank me, I should be thanking you – if you hadn't come over I wouldn't have had a day off for months, and I certainly wouldn't have booked the penthouse.'

She glanced down at her watch. 'I suggest we drink this and then have a little siesta, have dinner about eight and then we can hit the town. We can call in at the new casino, there's a couple of good night clubs or maybe we can just go cruising. Up in town they've got some amazing bars with live music and dancing.'

Although it had sounded like a good idea to have a siesta Laura found impossible to sleep. Her room – a spacious, split-level space with an en suite bathroom, situated off the sitting room – overlooked the harbour. She sat by the window watching the ships go by and finally decided to go and explore the city. Leaving a note for Belle she took the lift back down to the foyer.

As Laura headed towards the main entrance a party of oriental businessmen crocodiled passed her towards a waiting coach – and amongst them was a familiar figure. Laura stopped mid stride as their eyes met.

Danny Collins – the tour guide from her first night at

Home Cove – grinned. 'Well, well, well, fancy meeting you here,' he said.

Laura swallowed hard. She felt as if she had walked into a sprung trap. Danny's eyes moved over her appreciatively. She was still dressed in shorts and shirt, hair pulled back into a pony-tail and just the lightest touch of make-up.

'I'm here with Belle,' she said quickly. 'She's upstairs having a siesta.'

Danny waved his charges through the doors, where a waiting uniformed girl ticked their names off a clipboard.

'Really? Leo told me all about your little subterfuge. It's good to see you again.' He grinned. 'You're looking very wholesome today.' He glanced back out of the sliding plate glass doors. The party of businessmen were busily clambering aboard the tour bus. 'Maybe you'd like a coffee?'

Laura was rooted to the spot. 'What about the tourists?'

Danny shook his head. 'Not mine anymore, they're off on a trip up to Undarra – night-time bush walk and then on to the Lava tubes tomorrow. They'll be gone a day or two.' He moved closer and slipped his arm through hers. 'I've been thinking about you a lot since I spoke to Leo. Interesting that Belle has no idea what her little charge is up to.'

Laura stared at him. His words held a barely veiled threat.

'I've got to be getting back upstairs,' she said, realising how weak it sounded. He had already seen her heading towards the doors.

Danny lifted an eyebrow. 'I don't think so, do you? I think we can come up with a better way to spent the rest of the day. How much do you reckon it's worth to keep your secret? My place is about ten minutes drive from here. We could be there and back before Belle missed you.'

Laura closed her eyes. If she went with Danny she knew she would be lost – even though he was threatening her there was some uncanny desire to do as he asked. She shivered; at Home Cove she had been attracted to him and despite the events that followed that tiny flicker hadn't quite been extinguished. The realisation took her by surprise.

She turned to look into his eyes. 'You don't have to blackmail me, Danny.'

He laughed. 'Really? What's this, then? You're a fully paid-up member of the oldest profession now, eh? Fine – however you want to play it suits me.' He slid a hand up over her thighs, his fingers raking her flesh. 'Just make sure you remember the rules of the game. The customer is always right – but I'm sure that Leo must have told you that already. And he should know. That's how I first met him, you know. We used to pick up women in bars in Sydney. He struck real lucky when he met Belle. She knew exactly what he was and didn't care a rat's arse – in fact, one night in his company and she offered him a job up at the hotel. He really fell on his feet, that boy.'

Laura reddened. Danny caught hold of her elbow and headed back towards the lifts. The two receptionists didn't even look up.

'What are you doing?' she protested, careful to keep her voice low. 'I thought we were going back to your place?'

Danny pressed the lift call button. 'First rule of business is never take a whore home.'

The lift doors opened silently to reveal a couple of Asian businessmen. As they stepped out, one looked Laura up and down, taking note of the fact that Danny's hand was locked firmly around her arm and then smiled at Danny.

'You okay?'

Danny nodded as they passed. 'Sure thing, Nabim, just test-driving one of Belle O'Malley's latest acquisitions.'

The man laughed. 'Nice work if you can get it.'

The lifted doors closed behind them. Laura blushed furiously.

'How dare you?' she snapped.

Danny turned towards her. 'Oh come on, I thought you just told me you were a convert?' Roughly he caught hold of one of her breasts and pulled her closer, his lips working furious against hers. Against all the odds she felt her body responding. He jerked away, grinning broadly.

'You learn real fast, and I like the schoolgirl outfit – you should do really well for yourself when you've got the courage to own up to Belle. How the hell she missed you I'll never know.'

He slid his hand between her legs and cupped her sex, his lips back on hers. His touch was brutal and demanding. She felt her stomach muscles tighten and then gasped as the lift doors slid open again. This time, instead of the plush luxury of the public rooms the doors opened to reveal a concrete block wall, lined with metal pipes.

Danny extended a hand in invitation. 'Welcome to the basement of the best hotel in town,' he said with a sly smile, and guided her out into the shadowy corridor.

There were doors to the left and right but it seemed that Danny knew exactly where he was going. Overhead the way was lit by dim bulkhead lights and from close by Laura could hear the dull hum of machinery running.

'Here we are,' said Danny opening a door in a linen store. The room was lined with open slatted shelving piled high with sheets, towels and table linen. As they stepped inside he locked the door.

'Just so we won't be disturbed,' he said, pocketing the key.

Laura's pulse had quickened – there was no escape and she doubted that anyone would hear her above the engine noise even if she called out.

Danny grinned. 'So, do you want to show me what Leo's taught you so far?'

Laura shivered. 'What do you want?'

Danny groaned. 'Oh, you disappoint me. First of all take off your clothes – I'd like to see what it is I'm getting for my money.' He leant against the door as Laura slowly unbuttoned her shorts and slid them down over her hips. Where Danny had raked his nails across her leg the skin had already risen into parallel red weals. Her shirt was next, slowly she unfastened it and dropped it to the floor, leaving her standing in a soft white cotton bra and white pants – hardly the sexiest garments she had ever worn, but practical in the heat – after all, she hadn't anticipated running into Danny.

He grinned. 'The schoolgirl motif again?'

Laura reddened.

'I like it – take them off.'

Laura unfastened her bra and let it slip to the floor with her shorts and tee-shirt. She could see the desire rising in Danny's eyes and her nipples puckered into stiffness. She turned a little and tugged her panties down.

He beckoned her closer and ran his hands over her belly, fingers lingering on the trimmed contours of her quim. He murmured his approval and then pulled one of the napkins off the pile.

'Get hold of that shelf,' he said, indicating one above her head. She did as she was told, heart pounding in her chest as he tied her wrists tightly to the pine slat.

With her hands secure there was very little she could do to resist him. The idea was both exciting and frightening. She could feel the adrenaline kick in as he stroked a hand down over her arms, ribs and waist.

She could sense his excitement and wondered what he had in mind for her. He pulled off his polo shirt revealing a slim, muscular, bronzed torso and then dropped onto his knees. Taking her weight he guided her legs over his shoulders so that she was sitting on him. His skin was hot and moist against hers. Exposed, unable to resist, she moaned as he slipped his hands under her buttocks and jerked her closer, his tongue easing in to her.

He looked up, eyes alight. 'You're already wet. Being tied up turns you on, huh? Me too.'

He didn't wait for her answer, instead he plunged his tongue and fingers deep inside her. She thrust forward, gasping as he found her clitoris. His touch seemed to unleash a wave of raw desire so instinctive that she felt as if she was no longer in control but carried away in its current.

He moaned in delight as she thrust forward again and again, milking every stroke, every fleeting touch. His fingers burrowed inside her, filling her to the brim. Just at the point when she felt the first rolling pulse of her climax, he stood up. She gasped, her legs sliding down around his waist. With one hand he supported her weight while he unleashed his cock and drove into her. The movement was seamless, the effect electrifying.

She began to come as he breached her and writhed in

sheer delight as he thundered into her again and again. The muscles in her arms screamed out in protest as he slammed her back against the shelves. He was brutal, desperate to follow her into the pit.

She could feel the muscles deep inside her seize his shaft, as if they might consume him. Danny roared as his orgasm hit, sweat dripping down onto her naked breasts and face. At the very pinnacle of their pleasure he locked his fingers in her hair and forced her lips against his. His kiss was fiery and furious, his tongue emulating his cock as it plunged deep into her mouth. She gasped, struggling to breathe – and then it was done and he slipped out of her, totally sated, his hunger fed.

He leant forward against one of the shelves breathing hard and then looked across at her with a grin. 'Better, much better,' he said breathlessly. 'I'd like to know what Leo did to you.'

But it wasn't Danny that held Laura's attention but a face pressed to the re-enforced glass porthole in the door. Dark eyes took in every detail of the two lovers. Danny followed her gaze, his amused, exhausted expression not changing for an instant.

'Archie?' he said cheerfully, unlocking the door.

Outside, leaning against a broom was an ancient aborigine dressed in a crumpled boiler suit.

'How's it going, mate?' said Danny.

The old man spat onto the floor. 'Not s'bad,' he said, eyes working hungrily over Laura's naked body.

Laura was painfully aware of her vulnerability as the old man stepped into the room. Danny smiled at her.

'Archie, I'd like you to meet an acquaintance of mine. Archie was the guy who told me about this place – ideal for a little recreation.' He looked at the old man, waving a hand toward Laura. 'Maybe you'd like to try a little of what she's got to offer?'

The old man screwed up his nose and shook his head.

Danny shrugged. 'Please yourself – next time maybe.'

As he turned to leave Laura could see the mixture of disgust and desire in the old man's eyes and understood it perfectly – it was the same paradox she felt, the difference being that somewhere, muddled in the act of submission was an edge of pleasure and excitement that she had found impossible to resist. Danny closed the door when the old man left and untied her wrists.

'Get dressed. I'll take you back upstairs. Can't let Auntie Belle suspect, can we?' He pulled a roll of notes out of his pocket and threw them onto the sheets beside her.

Laura glanced at them and then rubbed her aching wrists before bending to retrieve her underwear. When she had her back to him, Danny ran his hand over her buttocks and slipped a finger deep inside her.

'Seems such a shame to waste it – the old boy really doesn't know what he was missing.'

Danny's touch was unnerving – too familiar, too invasive – as if he had laid claim to her. She moved away quickly and pulled on her shorts, her expression steely to mask her nervousness.

'Second rule of business, don't take what you haven't paid for,' she snapped in an icy tone.

Danny laughed. 'Sweet Jesus, you learn fast. You really are a chip off the old block. Come on. Best not to keep Belle waiting.'

Chapter 15

To Laura's relief Belle was still asleep when she got back upstairs to the suite. Laura crumpled up the note she had left on the coffee table and dropped it in the bin. Her whole body was suffused with the lingering scent of Danny's body and the sense of having escaped from the sexual promise at O'Malley's had evaporated. Heading for the shower she stripped off her shorts and shirt and stepped into the torrent.

The water coursed over her aching shoulders and back. Resting her forehead against the cool marble tiles Laura let her thoughts have free rein. She had to do something, she couldn't just blithely continue with the lies – especially not with Danny Collins so close at hand. Something or someone was bound to give her away.

The bubbling, prickling fingers of water were as relaxing as any massage. She closed her eyes, letting the tension ebb away as the water worked its magic on her. She would have to tell Belle, there was really no other logical answer – the question was, when?

Belle was woken by the sound of the shower running. She stretched and then rolled off the bed. Picking up a silver-backed brush from the dressing-table she pulled it through her abundance of dark hair, ruefully noting the flurry of grey hairs at the crown. Belle had carefully primed the hotel manager that she was on vacation, neither she nor Laura were at the hotel on business.

Belle hoped it would be enough – although she had always been extremely cautious and very discreet, too many people knew about her business for her to be totally certain of what would happen while she was in the city. Cairns, although a city, was still small enough for people to know everyone else's business.

She stared at her reflection. Perhaps Leo was right, maybe she couldn't blithely continue with the subterfuge. She would have to tell Laura about O'Malley's, there was really no other logical answer – the question was, when?

Through the bedroom door she could hear Laura moving around and it struck her again that under other circumstances Laura would be exactly the sort of girl she would recruit for her stable.

Belle stared into the mirror. Laura reminded her so much of the girl she had once been; but an awful lot had happened to her since then. It was these thoughts and memories that Belle carried down to supper with her.

As they ordered dinner, Belle couldn't help but notice the way her niece attracted discreet glances of interest and approval from the men in the dining room. Dressed in a little black cocktail dress and sheer, black silk stockings, the outfit emphasised the girl's slim frame and the light tan she'd picked up since her arrival. Belle was pleased to see Laura was wearing the necklace and earrings she had given her. The pearls seemed to be luminescent against the younger woman's skin. Caught in the candlelight, Laura looked radiant.

Belle shook her head to clear it. It wouldn't have been the first time she had brought a special girl down to meet a client flying into Cairns or Port Douglas. Port Douglas in particular was the playground of the rich and famous, and Belle's girls, elegant, beautiful and well-groomed, fitted their brief perfectly. Glancing round the luxurious dining room she could see a handful of faces she recognised – clients who over the years had taken full advantage of her discreet service.

Laura was the kind of girl that would appeal to them. Belle refilled her glass, just hoping no one approached her with a proposition. Perhaps coming to Cairns hadn't been such a good idea after all.

'Are you feeling okay? You're very quiet.' Laura's voice

made Belle jump. She realised with horror that she hadn't heard a word her niece had said. In front of her her first course lay untouched.

'I'm so sorry,' she said quickly. 'I was miles away. I was thinking, I must remember to ring Leo tonight.'

Laura laughed. 'Don't you trust him?'

Belle smiled and took a sip of wine. 'About as far as I can throw him,' she said with a grin and waved the waiter over to clear the plates. 'But I'm sure everything will be okay.'

Perhaps it was being away from the responsibility of running O'Malley's that made her mind run riot. The day to day round of bookings, passion and other people's indulgences normally filled her thoughts twenty-four hours a day, seven days a week.

Laura was still watching her closely. Belle smiled again, pushing the random thoughts back into the far reaches of her mind. 'Don't look so concerned. Really, I'm just fine. I'm just unwinding. Now where would you like to go once we've eaten?'

'I've never been to a casino.'

Belle lifted an eyebrow. 'High time you did, then.'

Laura slid her chips onto evens and waited for the croupier to spin the roulette wheel. Around her the gaming room seemed to be full of oriental businessmen. There were very few European faces in the casino complex, and the atmosphere around the various tables, as the cards were turned and the dice thrown, was tense with barely contained excitement.

Beside her, Belle watched the wheel turn, the ball rattling like a pea in a can. Laura glanced up and, to her surprise, saw Danny standing at the bar cradling a beer. He lifted his glass in a silent toast. Laura reddened and turned her attention back to the table.

'*Vingt-cinq, Mesdames et monsieurs,* Twenty-five,' said the croupier moving chips around the table with a long wooden rake.

'Hard luck,' said Belle, watching their money vanish into the bank. 'Do you fancy a drink?'

'Place your bets, *Mesdames et monsieurs*,' the croupier crooned.

They had been at the casino for almost an hour. The atmosphere, though opulent, was still very businesslike. Despite the chandeliers, staff gracefully kitted out in full evening dress and the plush carpets, Laura felt the clientele would have been just as happy making their bets in a garage – the turn of card, the hand of lady luck was what ensnared them rather than the elegance or beauty of their surroundings.

'No, thanks, I'm fine,' said Laura as her aunt turned away from the table. She had no wish to run into Danny Collins again. Belle glanced down at her watch.

'Will you excuse me? I'm just going to go and find a phone. I'd better check up on Leo before it gets too late. You'll be all right here on your own?'

Laura nodded. 'I'll be fine, I'm a big girl now.'

Belle grinned and dropped a handful of chips into Laura's palm. 'Put them on thirteen for me, will you? It's my lucky number. I won't be many minutes.'

Laura nodded and dropped them onto the table with a few dollars of her own. The croupier, eyes like a hawk, watched for the bets to be placed, called a halt and then spun the wheel one more time.

'Well, we meet again,' whispered Danny. 'It must be fate.'

Laura froze as his hand insinuated itself around her waist. She struggled to keep her mind on the rattling white ball as it sped around the inside of the roulette wheel. She could smell the beer on Danny's breath and feel the heat of his body pressed hard against hers.

'I thought Belle might bring you here,' he continued. 'This is where the real high dollars always hang out, it's a force of habit. Is she off turning a trick now?'

The ball dropped in thirty-one. Laura turned as the croupier scraped the chips across the baize. 'Please, Danny,' she said in a low voice. 'Don't do this. I'd really appreciate it if you just left me alone. You've already had what you wanted and Belle will be back in a minute. She's just gone to phone the hotel.'

Danny took another pull on his beer. 'I thought you might be interested in meeting some friends of mine.' He nodded towards the bar where two heavily built European men were watching them.

Laura shivered. 'Why don't you just go and have another drink. I don't need this.'

Danny laughed. 'Oh, but they do – I've been telling them what a good lay you are.' His finger lifted to outline her breasts. 'Nice body, great tits, tight little . . .' He grinned, his hand sliding up over her thighs. 'Well, we know all about that, don't we? Mmm, and you're wearing stockings tonight – very nice. Why don't you just come over for a few minutes and say hello to my friends?'

Laura stared at him in horror. 'For God's sake, Danny, I can't. I've already said I'm here with Belle.'

He leant closer. 'Ten minutes – that is all it would take.' His hand closed around hers. 'She'd just think you'd gone for a drink or off to the ladies' room. No one need ever know.'

Behind the crush of spectators was so close that Danny could slip his hand between her legs without anyone noticing, his face no more than an inch or two from hers.

Laura felt a flurry of panic – this had to stop. She had to say something to Belle or she would be caught in Danny's trap for as long as she was in Australia. At the bar the two Europeans lifted their champagne glasses in salute. She could already see the curiosity and desire in their eyes.

Danny's fingers grazed the black silk of the teddy she was wearing under her cocktail dress, toying with the fastenings. 'Well?'

She shivered, stunned that he could be so familiar, so pushy. She looked up at him. 'And then you'll leave me alone?'

Even as she said it she knew it was ridiculous – while Danny had a hold over her he was going to use it to his best advantage. The only thing that gave her any comfort was the fact that she and Belle were only in town for a few days – and her time in Australia was short.

Danny's eyes twinkled mischievously. 'Sure thing,' he said without a shred of sincerity.

Laura sighed and followed him through the crowded room. She had no doubt that Danny knew exactly where to take her. They crossed the foyer towards a bank of lifts. From the corner of her eye Laura could see the two men were following close behind.

Danny pressed the lift call button and waved the two men over. The first of them extended a hand. He was obviously uncomfortable in the tropical heat for despite the air-conditioning a gloss of sweat had lifted on his round face.

'This is the young lady I've been telling you all about.' Danny nodded towards Laura and winked conspiratorially. 'I like to think of her as Lady Luck. She's kindly agreed to give you gentlemen a little of her time.'

'Hi, I'm Ross,' the first man said in a sing-song American accent, straight from the deep south. He pumped her hand enthusiastically as if they were being introduced at a corporate cocktail party and then lifted it to his lips. 'I'm very pleased to make your acquaintance, ma'am.'

Laura forced a smile. At the very least Danny hadn't given them her real name. The second man hung back, obviously more uncomfortable than the ebullient Ross. After being introduced he held up his hands in surrender.

'No offence, ma'am, but I'm a happily married man,' he said in the rolling, blackstrap molasses accent. 'I really ain't interested in keeping you company tonight.'

Danny clapped him on the shoulder. 'No shame in that, Jed, no shame at all. Lady Luck here will take young Ross away for a trip to paradise and we'll go console ourselves at the bar with another drink.'

Danny looked at Laura as the lift doors opened. 'Take it up to the third floor. Press for the doors to open, and then before they do turn the key – the doors will stay locked. When you've done just unlock the door and push the blue button.' He grinned and patted his jacket pocket. 'Oh, and don't worry about money – Ross has already settled up with me.'

178

Laura stared at him, thoughts racing. 'In the lift?'

Danny shrugged as he dropped his arm round his slightly drunken American companion. 'Needs must, babe – and besides Ross tells me that it's always been one of his favourite fantasies.'

As the door slid closed on silent runners Laura looked over at her portly companion. He licked his lips, his eyes working up and down over her body as if she was a four course dinner.

Laura swallowed hard. His desire was so tangible that it seemed to fill the lift like a rising fog. As the lift reached the third floor she turned the key as Danny had instructed, heard the bolts slide across in the doors and turned her attention back to the plump American.

In her stomach was strange sense of elation and expectation, totally at odds with the rational fears that bubbled up alongside it. This was Ross's fantasy but she had all the power. He thought she was a real whore – to be bought and paid for. Within those four metallic walls, she could be anything or anybody she wanted.

Slowly, Laura lifted her skirt, letting Ross glimpse the black silk teddy beneath. She was wearing stockings with lace trimmed tops that left a band of ripe, creamy flesh between them and the edging of the black silk.

Ross groaned and pulled a huge handkerchief from his pocket to mop his brow. Laura smiled; the strange sense of power, mingled with elation and excitement was rising with every second. Unzipping her dress she let it slither to the floor in a glistening black puddle and, as she did, extended a hand and ran a finger down over his broad chest.

The black lace teddy emphasised her slender curves, clinging to every rise and plane like a second erotically charged skin; Ross was completely ensnared.

'Is this the kind of thing you had in mind?' she purred, in a voice she barely recognised as her own.

Ross nodded, sweat lifting in jewels cross his broad forehead.

'Certainly is, little lady. Just slip them straps down and let me get a good look at ya,' he said. His eyes seemed to have reduced to coal black spheres, dark spotlights that slid over her body like crude oil.

Laura did as she was asked; her nipples had already hardened into stormy sunset peaks. Ross grunted and jerked her closer, his hands squeezing her flesh like ripe fruit. Laura glanced down. His cock was bulging forward in his cream pants like a caged animal fighting to be released. He grinned as he followed her gaze downward. 'You want a little of that?'

Laura nodded, afraid to speak. Ross settled himself back against the stainless steel walls and beckoned her closer.

'Come here,' he grunted thickly. 'Over here. On your knees.'

Slowly Laura sank to the floor and crept towards him. He grinned. 'That's it, and now I want you to touch yourself.'

Laura nodded and began stroking her fingers back and forth across the rise of her sex and cupping her pert breasts. Ross groaned his approval. Teasing, stroking, she unfastened his zip and freed his phallus.

Like Ross himself, the shaft of his cock was short and thick-set – but even so as her lips closed around its engorged purple crown she imagined the sensation of it sliding deep into her sex. The idea made her glow with desire. Instinctively the muscles deep inside her contracted, seeking something to fill its moist, fragrant depths. While one hand cupped his balls, her fingers worked his foreskin up and down. His shaft was silky, already glossed with a patina of excitement. He seemed to grow even harder as her lips worked in tandem with her hands.

Ross grunted appreciatively. 'Touch yourself some more – play with that lovely little puss of yours,' he snorted. 'Danny tells me it's tight an' sweeter than hell itself.'

Laura let a hand slither down towards the uptilted curves of her breasts, fingers outlining the dark shadows of her areolae, and then smoothed it, palm down, over her ribs and belly until it slid between her legs. Under her other hand she could feel Ross's excitement building steadily towards crescendo, the tension puckering his testicles.

It seemed no time at all before she felt the first throbbing pulse under her fingers, and braced herself for what was to follow. Between her legs her juices were beginning to soak the thin fabric, signalling the slow building of her own arousal.

Above her, Ross suddenly grunted again, his fingers hastily displacing hers. He dragged his shaft from her mouth, holding it in both hands and pumped a glittering arc of pearly seed over her breasts. Laura gasped as the semen splashed down onto her, clinging like thick creamy pearls to her chest.

Ross, sweating hard, fell to his knees and began to lap at her skin with a long curling tongue, drawing the peaks of her breasts deep into his mouth, fingers frantically seeking out her sex. His breath was like a blowtorch against her flesh, his tongue unstoppable. He guided her down onto the floor, lapping every remaining trace of his pleasure off her skin, while his hands dragged at the fastenings of her teddy.

The smell of his seed seemed to cling to her, emphasising the unsatisfied need that now glowed between her thighs. As he freed her quim she tried to guide his fingers, encouraging him to stroke the plump little bud that throbbed hungrily between the lips of her sex, but Ross was having none of it, instead he drove his fingers deep inside her, playing in the rich ocean that engulfed him, plunging into her again and again until she was frantic with desire.

Laura arched her hips up towards him, seeking the caresses that would set her free. Roughly, he pushed her back down onto the unforgiving floor, content to stroke the fragrant foam out onto her thighs and the delicate skin of her belly.

Finally, gasping, he pulled away, his plump red face fixed into a rictal grin. Clambering to his feet he began to buckle his pants.

'Oh yes,' he said thickly to no one in particular. 'That surely was the baby – oh yes, sirreee, that was it.'

Laura felt cheated. Her sex, still glowing white-hot, ached for satisfaction, empty and unfulfilled. Ross glanced down at her, grin still fixed.

'What?' he said with an expansive gesture. 'Danny-boy's

got your money downstairs if that's what you're worried about.' He stared at her; she was still half naked, kneeling on the floor. He nodded knowingly. 'I get it – you feelin' kinda left out, huh?' He hitched his trousers, still tidying himself. Laura wondered fleetingly if she ought to have faked it or perhaps lie now.

Slowly she got to her feet and shook her head. 'It's okay. I'm fine. I'll unlock the doors.'

But she was reckoning without the power of Ross's fantasy.

'Oh, no, no,' he said, shaking his head emphatically. 'No, it's not okay. We ain't done yet.' He pushed her back against the wall of the lift. 'There's more to this, little lady. This is how it's supposed to be. You begging for it, me saying no. That's the way it goes.' His eyes had darkened again. 'What I want is for you to bring yourself off, I wanna watch you – come on. Show me how you do it.' He caught hold of her hand and pressed it to her body.

Laura, although self-conscious was so hungry for release that she needed little encouragement. Her finger glided down over the engorged ridge of her clitoris, lighting a bright beacon in her belly. She already knew it wouldn't take more than a few deft strokes before the lights exploded in her mind.

Ross, standing a hair's breadth away from her, watched her fingers working their magic. His huge hands caught hold of her breasts squeezing them tight and then he kissed her hard, almost as if his lips were sucking the breath out her chest. She fought to stay in control, circling the little bud again and again.

At the turning point, on the very edge of the abyss, he thrust her back against the icy walls of the lift, pushed her legs apart and drove his finger back inside her. Laura shrieked, crying out with sheer pleasure, body crowing in triumph as her sex closed down tight around him, sucking him into her on a wave of orgasmic euphoria.

When she had done, trembling with aftershocks, he stepped back, wiping his fingers on his handkerchief, expression smug and self satisfied.

'Danny told me you were quite a find and the boy was right, shame Jed didn't fancy taking a turn now you're good an' wet. That man just don't know what's good for him.'

He bent down and scooped up Laura's dress. 'Better get yourself all gussied up and get back downstairs. Danny tells me you're with some woman.' He grinned salaciously. 'Maybe you prefer a little pussy to what old Ross's got hanging between his legs.' As he spoke his hand cupped the bulk of his cock. 'Next time I'm in town maybe we could book up a little threesome with your lady friend. I always did like to see gals getting it together, tongues a-working.' He closed his eyes as if savouring the image.

Belle wandered back into the casino, eyes working across the faces of the guests, trying to spot Laura amongst the sea of gamblers.

She noticed Danny Collins lolling idly against the bar, deep in conversation with a portly businessman. As their eyes met she felt obligated to lift a hand in greeting. Although she disliked him he had brought her a lot of trade over the years – personal preferences did not necessarily make for good business.

Laura was nowhere in sight. Belle scanned the bar again, wondering if her niece had gone looking for her. The casino had filled up since she had gone to phone Leo and it was hard to get out of the main gaming hall, pushing her way back against the tide of incomers.

Out in the lobby Belle saw the doors to the lift, which were situated at the top of a flight of stairs open slowly, and Laura stepped out, followed by a slightly dishevelled businessman. Belle stared at the two of them and then dismissed the notion that bubbled up unbidden in her mind.

Laura and the man exchanged a few words that Belle couldn't hear and then the man headed back to the bar. Laura meanwhile, head down, turned and hurried towards the ladies' powder room, clutching her handbag to her chest. She looked slightly uneasy and unsettled.

Belle went after her, pushing her way through the crowd. As Belle opened the door to the powder room Laura was sponging the front of her dress with a paper towel.

'Are you all right? I'm sorry I was so long,' Belle said anxiously.

Laura looked up in surprise and then smiled. 'Oh, don't worry. I'm fine, it's just that some idiot spilt his drink on me.'

Belle nodded, not altogether convinced by Laura's explanation. Still hunched over the sink, her niece grinned. 'I've been all over the place looking for somewhere to clean up. I've just had a ride upstairs in the lift. I didn't realise that there was a toilet down here. How was Leo?'

There was an odd, slightly euphoric look in Laura's eyes – under other circumstances Belle would have sworn blind that Laura had had some kind of sexual encounter. She dismissed the notion as ridiculous, squashing it as it formed, and painted on a smile. 'He's just fine. While that cat's away, you know how it is. Did thirteen come up?'

Laura shook her head, still dabbing at the wet patch on her dress. 'Sorry – it was thirty-one. Shall we go back? I think I could use that drink now.'

Belle nodded, not quite able to shift the sensation that somewhere down the line she had missed something important. 'Do you want me to take a look at the stain?'

Laura picked up her bag. 'No, really. It's just fine now.'

Laura took one final look at her reflection. Her eyes were dark, glittering in the aftermath of her encounter with Ross in the lift, her body still glowing with the warm heat of orgasm. She wondered if her act had been good enough to fool Belle. She had spotted her aunt at the foot of the steps as the lift doors opened and taken a step back, watching Belle's eyes moving back and forth to find her amongst the gamblers.

Heading towards the toilet had given her enough time to compose her thoughts. Laura opened her bag and added a touch of lipstick. Until she arrived in Australia she had never considered herself a good liar nor had she ever needed to be one. It struck her that an awful lot had changed in a very short time.

Chapter 16

'Would you mind if we took a look around town?' Laura asked when they got back out into the foyer.

They looked out over the crush of people that now filled the plate glass atrium. The casino seemed to be even busier, with crowds of Orientals and Asians eagerly pushing forward to change dollars for chips at the rows of cashiers' cages.

Belle nodded. 'Good idea. I'd forgotten, the cruise ships must have docked today. Another hour or so and we won't be able to get to the bar and every night-club in town will be packed solid. They come over on package trips from the Pacific rim. The travel company arrange them especially for businessmen, offering golf and gambling and five-star service.'

As they eased their way towards the exit Laura suspected that under other circumstances Belle might have added girls to the list of pleasures that were on offer.

Beyond the heavy plate glass door of the casino the city centre was brightly lit, though the air seemed heavy and humid after the luxury of air-conditioning. Laura caught the heady scent of frangipani on the night breeze. The verges of the casino gardens were lined with palms trees, their distinctive shapes picked out by well hidden spotlights; Belle pointed across the road.

'Come on, I know just the place to start. There's a great little Cajun bar just around the corner.'

'We're going to walk?' Laura asked in surprise.

Belle grinned. 'Why not? It's a beautiful evening and it's not that far. It's a great way to get a feel for the city,' she said, and stepped across the storm drain into the road.

She was right. Cairns pulsed with life under cover of the

tropical night. Beneath the awnings that sheltered the pavements, outside the shops, pubs and clubs, diners and punters, tourists and locals, drank, ate and talked, while eddies of music seeped out over the broad sidewalks from bar fronts.

Laura and Belle meandered from bar to bar, drinking little but talking a lot, absorbing the heady ambience of the tropical city. They ended up in a jazz club and sat inside, under the balcony cradling cups of coffee while they listened to the band playing.

'Enjoying yourself?'

Laura nodded. Her mind had been carried off by the smoky blue voice of the female vocalist on stage. 'Umm hum,' she said sleepily. 'I don't know where you get the stamina.'

Belle smiled. 'Force of habit. Years of playing host to guests at O'Malley's at all hours of the night and day. That's why I always grab an hour or two in the afternoon if I can. We can go back to the hotel if you like.'

Laura admitted defeat; perhaps, for lots of reasons, she should have taken Belle's advice and had a siesta after all. It was the early hours of the morning when Laura and Belle finally arrived back at their hotel, and almost midday before Laura was woken by the sound of room service arriving.

Laura rolled over and stared at the pile of clothes she had discarded in a trail from the door to bed, and memories of the previous evening, good and bad came trickling back.

Pulling on a robe she went in search of the noise. In the sitting room Belle was sitting at a table by one of the picture windows, helping herself to freshly brewed coffee and croissants.

She smiled at Laura. 'Hiya, did you sleep well? I was going to give you a call, but the smell of the coffee got to me first.'

Laura rubbed the sleep from her eyes; the aroma wafting across the room made her mouth water.

The boy who had brought the trolley in poured Laura a cup, and as she thanked him, he pulled an envelope from under a crisp white napkin and handed it to her. Laura looked up at him surprise. To her horror the boy winked and lifted the jug.

'Cream, ma'am?' he said casually.

Laura reddened and surreptitiously slipped the envelope into the pocket of her robe.

'Milk, please,' she said.

He smiled, eyes lingering on the neckline of her robe. She glared at him and snatched the cup out of his hand.

'Croissant, madam?' he said.

Belle, who had been looking out of the window turned her attention back to Laura and the uniformed boy. 'Why don't you just leave the trolley there, Sebastian?' she said waving him away. 'We can help ourselves to what we want.'

The boy nodded, looking crestfallen.

'You've done a great job. Here—' From her handbag Belle took a twenty dollar note and handed it to him.

Brightening the boy headed for the lift doors. Just before he left he touched his forelock.

'Anything you ladies want, don't hesitate to ring. Anything at all.'

Belle thanked him, and as the doors closed, laughed. 'Maybe I ought to offer him a job up at O'Malley's. He's been fussing round me like a bee round a honey pot since he got up here.'

Laura smiled, still cradling the cup of coffee. The envelope tucked in her dressing gown pocket seemed to glow like a beacon. 'I think I'll just go and have a shower.'

Belle pushed a chair out with her foot. 'Why don't you sit down and enjoy the croissants while they're warm? I won't mind in the least that you're in your robe. I thought maybe this afternoon after we'd had some lunch we could take a cruise up the Trinity inlet, maybe go to the crocodile farm? Take a look at the mangrove swamps.' She smiled, breaking the remains of her croissant in two and popping a piece into her mouth. 'You know, I'm really quite enjoying being a tourist for a change – when we come back I thought we could hit the shops. Bring the coffee jug over here, would you?'

Laura had to wait until breakfast was over before she

could head back to her room and open the envelope. Inside was a neatly bound bundle of notes, and a short, pithy message from Danny:

'Nice work, here's your money, less a ten percent finder's fee. Perhaps I've discovered a new career?' D.'

Laura stared down at the carefully formed letters. She knew it hadn't taken very much for Danny to find out which room she and Belle were staying in, or to pay room service to bring the message up to her, but even so it gave her an unpleasant sensation low in her belly. While she was at the hotel she was at Danny's beck and call.

Laura ripped the paper and envelope into tiny, tiny shreds and dropped them in the waste paper basket before showering. Even the stinging bore of warm water couldn't quite wash away the sensation of being caught in a trap.

'Belle O'Malley! How nice to see you again.' As Belle crossed the hotel lobby later that afternoon she was surprised to see Danny Collins heading her way, hand extended in greeting. 'I was going to pop over and see you in the Casino last night but you seemed to be there one minute and gone the next. How are you?'

Belle forced a smile. 'I'm fine, Danny – and you?'

He nodded. 'I wondered whether you were here on business.' He glanced over his shoulder as if to check who was listening. 'I've got a couple of Yanks who are looking for a good time. And I saw you with that girl last night. One of your latest?' He closed his eyes and made a noise of approval. 'I'd really like to know where you get them from, Belle? I wouldn't mind a little of that one myself – very, very nice. Is she up for hire or did you bring her up here on a private commission?'

Belle's face froze. Across the foyer Laura had just emerged from the hotel office clutching their tickets for the afternoon's cruise. She was wearing a pale blue sun-dress and canvas mules, her dark hair twisted up into a loose knot. She looked fresh, an archetypal English rose, and extraordinarily innocent.

Belle rounded on Danny, eyes ablaze. 'I want you to be

very clear about this, Danny,' she said emphatically. 'I'm on holiday, that girl is my niece – she doesn't know anything about O'Malley's and I want it to stay that way. Is that crystal clear?'

Danny held up his hands in surrender. 'Certainly, not a problem. Belle.' He paused for a split second, his attention fixed on the approaching figure. 'I can see the family resemblance. Perhaps you might like to make it worth my while.'

Belle stared at him. 'I beg you pardon?' she said in her most imperious tone. Her first inclination was to slap his stupid, smug face.

He grinned. 'Can you blame me, Belle? I've always had a crush on you. You know that, don't you? I've always had a thing about older women. Brings out the little boy in me. Perhaps you and I could get together sometime?' He paused for a second and then added. 'Sometime soon?'

Belle couldn't quite believe what he had said but by now Laura was approaching fast. Danny immediately turned his attention to her niece. His face was impassive but his eyes flashed with devilment.

'Aren't you going to introduce us?' he said in a low, unctuous voice. Belle shot him a warning glance and then smiled at Laura.

Laura looked anxiously at Danny who winked at her surreptitiously. She knew then that she loathed him. She could see the disdain and the tension in Belle's eyes as she introduced them.

'So what are you doing in town, Danny?' Belle continued coolly once the formalities had been exchanged. 'I thought you'd be up in the hills conning a coach load of tourists out of their hard-earned yen.'

The blond tour guide laughed, gaze now firmly fixed on Laura's face. She suspected he was hoping to make her blush – or worse – so she forced herself to maintain a smile.

'Waiting for that special golden opportunity, Belle, you know how it is. You've always got to keep an eye out for the main chance. So, are you enjoying your stay in Australia, Laura?'

Laura stared at him, praying he would quickly tire of the game and leave them both in peace.

'Wonderful, thank you,' she said in a cool, even tone.

Danny nodded. 'Good. You know, as Belle brought the subject up, I work with a local tour company as a guide. Maybe while you're here you might like to come out with me on a trek – staff rates of course. We could get better acquainted.'

Belle broke into the conversation. 'Thanks for the offer, Danny, we'll bear it in mind, but I'm afraid we've got to go now.'

Danny tipped his bush hat in salute. 'Certainly – maybe we could all get together for dinner later?'

Belle made a noncommittal noise and turned towards the pier.

Laura's heart was picking out a frantic beat. She glared at him; Danny grinned and mouthed. 'See you later.'

Laura hurried after her aunt, realising just how easy it would have been for Danny to have let something slip.

Belle straightened her jacket. 'Sorry about that, I really don't like that man.'

Laura glanced across at her aunt and instantly understood – while the subterfuge lasted they both had as much to lose as the other. Belle had been just as worried that Danny Collins would give her away as Laura had.

Laura nodded. 'What about if we go back to O'Malley's tonight instead of tomorrow morning? He knows where we're staying and he doesn't strike me as the type whose likely to give up.'

Belle looked at her in surprise. 'Are you sure? I mean, we don't have to let an idiot like Danny spoil our break.'

'He hasn't – but I really don't mind.' Laura grinned. 'After the peace and quiet up at the Cape I'm a bit phased by all these people.'

Belle looked relieved. 'Me too – what about if we give the cruise a miss and hit the shops instead?'

Laura nodded.

190

Laden down with boxes and bags, they were back out on the Cook Highway by late afternoon and caught the late ferry across the Daintree River, both in their own way pleased to be away from Cairns and Danny Collins.

'Didn't trust me to run the place on my own, then?' said Leo, as Belle poured herself a stiff brandy from the tray in the office at O'Malley's. She had just dropped Laura off at her cabin, but all the way home she had been thinking about Danny Collins and his malevolent, scheming little mind.

Belle snorted as she shovelled in a handful of ice and added a splash of soda. 'I wish,' she said, taking a long pull on the glass.

Leo looked up at her. 'What's the matter? Something happen in Cairns?'

Belle shook her head. 'No, not really, I don't know, I'm just not used to being vulnerable, that's all. I thought those days were long gone.'

Leo looked puzzled. Belle waved his confusion aside and peered over his shoulder at the bookings in the diary. 'It's all right, take no notice of me, how's it gone while I've been in town?'

'Just fine – half a dozen old faces appeared yesterday off the cruises. I've put them in the cabins by the pool.'

Belle smiled. 'I saw the fleet was in last night at the casino. Which of the girls did you send down there?'

Leo turned the swivel chair round to face her and slid his hands up over her thighs.

'You look all in, Belle. Why don't we leave worrying about who's with who and what they want until tomorrow? Let me take you to bed and give you a massage. You know I've got the perfect cure.'

His fingers glided up into the small of her back. Belle moaned and stretched like a cat under his deft touch. He grinned, one hand lifting to undo the buttons of her blouse.

'Ummm. I've really missed you,' he said in a thick voice.

Belle laughed, glancing down to his rapidly hardening cock. 'I can tell. God, it's so nice to be back home.'

191

Leo stretched forwards, face nuzzling at the valley between her breasts, tongue tracing an intricate path across her hot salty skin, while his fingers continued to press rhythmically up the aching muscles in her back.

'Shall we go upstairs?'

Belle shook her head. 'To be honest, Leo, I don't think I can wait that long.'

Laura wasn't certain what she intended to say Belle. All the way home in the jeep she had been working on a speech, trying to find a voice, and a way to begin the things she wanted to say, but had decided it was impossible.

Now safely back at O'Malley's it seemed even more important to say something – she couldn't bear the idea of someone as manipulative as Danny having a hold over either of them. If she owned up the man's spell would be broken.

Taking her courage in both hands she closed the cabin door. There was nothing left now but the truth. Laura headed through the darkness towards the office. She could hear Belle's voice and stepped towards the door. Inside there a lamp burning on the desk which created a halo of golden light through the fly screen. Laura was about knock when she realised that Belle was in no position to be disturbed.

She cupped her hands to her face and looked in through the screen. The scene inside, picked out in the lamp's soft glow made her shiver.

Leo was slowly removing Belle's blouse, peeling it off her shoulders, its progress marked by a flurry of tender kisses. Gathering her breasts up like blossoms he pressed first one and then the other to his lips, lapping at the puckered buds.

Belle arched back with pleasure, cradling his head in her hands as he worshipped her with his tongue and lips. Her expression was ecstatic – Leo looked like an acolyte praying at an ancient altar, both figures golden, like a medieval icon celebrating physical pleasure.

Laura was trembling, but quite unable to take her eyes off the scenario.

Gently, Leo guided Belle back onto the desk. His eyes

192

were full of love and tenderness as he unfastened her skirt, his tongue slowing working down the valley between her breasts, over her belly, a dedicated pilgrim on the mystical journey towards their mutual salvation. As his lips closed on the mount of Venus Belle let out a low moan, the vibrations so earthy and ancient that they made the hairs on Laura's neck rise.

She could imagine the brush of each kiss, the intense heat of every tiny heady sensation.

Belle lifted her hips up towards Leo, her body mirroring the path of his kisses. He pulled away, grinning like a Cheshire cat, his lips slick with her juices.

'Missed you too,' he murmured.

Belle laughed. The sound was throaty, full of humour and real pleasure.

'You bastard, don't stop now,' she purred and then reached up and pulled him into her.

He kissed her fiercely, hungrily while his hands guided her legs up around his waist. With his lips still firmly fixed to hers, he slipped his cock deep into her. Belle gasped, her whole body tensing as he breached her.

Laura closed her eyes, imagining the sensations. The idea made her mouth water; she knew exactly what she was missing.

In the office the lovers began to move in earnest, Belle lifting herself up to brush her sex against Leo's belly, lifting again and again to draw him into her. Leo threw back his head, his face contorted with sheer delight as he thrust into her, moaning with pleasure. Laura focused on the tense sinews in his throat as he strained forward.

'Oh, my God that feels so good,' he murmured, driving harder.

Laura was stunned – all earlier thoughts of confession and Danny vanishing as her mind was swept along in the journey of the two lovers, every thrust, every touch, echoing deep inside her.

She could feel her own pleasure building alongside theirs. Unconsciously her fingers had moved down to stroke her sex – it was so tempting to bring herself to the edge of the abyss – but, the veranda outside Belle's office was hardly the place.

Laura remembered the vibrator Eva had given her was still in her washbag. Without looking back she hurried towards the cabin, the need glowing in the pit of her sex like a beacon fire.

Rushing along the board walk Laura was surprised when an Asian man suddenly stepped into her path. She was so wrapped up in her own thoughts she didn't see him until she almost fell over him.

'I'm sorry,' she said automatically and only then looked up into his face. To her horror she instantly recognised the features – it was the Asian businessman she had last seen in the lift at the Piermont when she had been going down to the basement with Danny Collins.

The images replayed in her mind like the frames of a film: The lift doors had opened silently to reveal a couple of Asian businessmen. As they stepped out, one looked Laura up and down, taking note of the fact that Danny's hand was locked firmly around her arm and then smiled at the tour guide.

'You okay?'

Danny had nodded as they passed. 'Sure thing, Nabim, just test driving one of Belle O'Malley's latest acquisitions.'

The man had laughed. 'Nice work if you can get it.'

Nabim – the name lit up in Laura mind. Now, standing in front of her, he smiled warmly and extended his hand.

'Hello, I was hoping I would find you here,' he said.

Laura backed away, mind racing, and fled towards the safety of her cabin.

In the hotel office, Belle gasped as Leo's finger traced the rise of her clitoris one more time. He was standing up, looking down at her nakedness, eyes suffused with desire, his cock buried to the hilt in her molten quim.

Their gaze was locked as they played out their own particular game of chicken – each of them was so close to the edge that one more caress, one more nibbling pulse of the muscles deep inside her might be just the thing to topple the other over the edge.

Leo grinned as she contracted her muscles around him, sweat lifting on his top lip as he strained to retain control.

'You're a real bitch, O'Malley,' he snorted.

Belle nodded. 'I know,' she murmured, running her hand down over her belly so that her fingers unseated his. It was enough. Leo dragged in a final ragged breath and then conceded defeat, crying out as the flood tide of lust and desire closed over them, both driving away all reason.

Chapter 17

Next morning Laura was one of the first down to breakfast – and was surprised to find Leo waiting for her at the table.

'Do you want to tell me what happened to you two in Cairns?' he asked, pouring them both a cup of coffee.

Laura looked up. 'Sorry?' She could read the concern in Leo's expression.

'Belle was upset last night when you got back, and it's not like her at all. Was there a problem while you were away?'

At that moment Nabim and his Asian companion took their places at a table on the far side of the dining room. Laura noticed him looking in her direction and quickly looked away – but not before Leo noticed her interest.

'You know our friend, the Asian exporter?' he said in surprise.

Laura reddened. 'No, not really, not personally, but I do know Danny Collins.'

Leo looked puzzled, so Laura continued, 'We ran into Danny while we were in the city – he made a lot of mileage out of the fact that Belle doesn't know about what I've been doing.' She reddened, thinking about the incident in the basement and then with the American in the lift at the casino. 'Yesterday he was at the hotel again – I don't think he was following us but he made things awkward.' Laura's colour deepened.

Leo nodded; comprehension dawning. 'Right – and then there's the fact that you're not supposed to know about Belle either. No wonder Belle said she felt vulnerable.'

From the table on the far side of the dining room Nabim lifted his hand and beckoned towards Leo.

'Any idea what our little friend over there might want?'

Laura shook her head. 'None at all, but I'd imagine it's got something to do with me. He saw me and Danny while we were in Cairns. He thinks I'm one of Belle's new girls.'

'You're a real loose cannon,' Leo said, with a grin and headed over to Nabim's table, just as Belle arrived.

'Morning,' she said with a broad smile. 'Sleep well?'

Laura had to admit that, despite everything, she had – like a baby, once she had satisfied her frustrations with the help of Eva's vibrator.

Remarkably O'Malley's had, in a matter of days, come to feel like home. It was a real relief to be back amongst people and places she recognised. Out on the sun deck Joe Blanco was sipping juice, a weather eye working slowly over the other hotel guests. When his apparently casual gaze reached hers he waved and smiled a good morning.

Down amongst the palms trees Laura could just see the roofs of the staff cabins – she guessed Eva would be there – and amongst the sprinkling of guests having an early breakfast were several faces she recognised both from Leo's late night tour and her trip out onto the reef. How odd that they should feel like part of an extended family.

Belle stretched and then helped herself to a bowl full of tropical fruit. 'Have you got any plans for today?'

Laura shook her head. 'Not really. I thought maybe I'd go for a walk or a swim, and then take a long lazy siesta.'

Since she'd woken up Laura had been toying with the idea of giving Gabriel, the pirate artist from the Reef Rider, a ring. Maybe he would like to share her siesta.

Belle laughed. 'Sounds like an excellent idea.'

Leo rejoined them, kissing Belle good morning with unselfconscious familiarity.

'Everything okay?' Belle asked as he took a place at the table.

He nodded. 'Yes, no worries. Nabim just wanted some information on one of our special excursions.' As he spoke, Laura noticed that his eyes were firmly fixed on her. She felt a tiny flutter of anticipation.

After breakfast Laura changed into her swimming costume,

tied on a sarong and wandered down to the beach. The sun was already warm, the wind whipping the sea into glittering peaks. In a secluded spot she sat down to watch the sea. Part of her had been half expecting Joe Blanco to pop up at any moment to renew his acquaintance; so she was surprised when it was Leo who appeared from between the trees.

'Aren't you supposed to be at work?' she said, lifting her sunglasses.

'Probably.' He settled himself down on the sand beside her. 'I've got an interesting little commission for you, if you want it.'

She stretched, arching her back, aware as she did so that Leo's eyes followed every movement.

Leo grinned. 'You know, if I'd got the time I'd fuck you now. You look gorgeous sitting there.'

Laura laughed. 'Shame you didn't mention it over breakfast – I've just rung Gabriel.'

Leo snorted. 'Nothing like a convert. Make sure he gives you a staff discount. You know, you really ought to think about staying permanently. Belle could do with a hand to run the business and you fit in here so well.'

Laura laughed. 'The thought has crossed my mind once or twice but it's impossible. For a start I'd definitely have to tell Belle about my conversion to the pleasures of the flesh.'

Leo nodded. 'While we're on the subject, it seems that you really whetted the appetite of our friend, Nabim. He's very keen to get to know you better.' Leo stroked a finger along the sole of her foot.

Laura wriggled away from him. 'That was the special excursion you were talking about this morning?'

'The very same. You learn fast. He's got a favourite scenario that he likes to act out whenever he gets the chance.' Leo grinned. 'He says he likes your English Rose complexion. And he's certain you will understand exactly what he wants – he told me it's a cultural thing.'

Laura pulled a face. 'I'm not with you.'

'Don't worry. You will be. I've asked Eva to give you a hand. Nabim is a regular here – very generous when it comes to tipping the girls too.'

Laura looked him up and down. 'So what is it he wants exactly?'

Leo grinned. 'Eva's going to meet you at your cabin. She'll tell you all about it.'

'A little S & M,' Eva said breathlessly as she dropped a large cardboard carton down on the end of Laura's bed, and then, smiling, embraced her warmly. 'Great to have you back. Did you enjoy your trip?'

Laura giggled as the blonde, arms still locked around her waist, licked the curve of her neck.

'Yes and no. It sounds weird. I missed being here. It was good to have some time alone with Belle, but it was really nice to get back. It's beginning to feel like home.'

Eva laughed. 'Sounds like you're getting hooked – and Nabim asked for you personally? My God, you're getting your own regulars already.'

'I met him in the Piermont while we were away. What is it he wants?'

Eva undid the top of the carton. 'Nothing you can't manage. Here, take a look at these.'

Laura moved closer and gasped in astonishment as Eva began to unpack the box; out of it came a black leather body suit, matching thigh boots, a studded leather mask and a vicious looking riding crop.

Eva grinned. 'Our friend Mr Nabim prefers a little pain with his pleasure or vice versa – apparently he told Leo being English you'd understand perfectly.' She took out a small tin and prised it open. 'Here we are, handcuffs, nipple clamps, cock cuff,' she continued casually as if reading out the ingredients of a cake.

Laura blushed scarlet.

Eva brushed aside her embarrassment. 'You don't have to worry, I'll get him ready for you – you're in charge of this.' She picked up the crop and gave it a few test strokes; it cut through the morning air with a malevolent hiss.

Laura swallowed hard, remembering only too well the sensation of the unforgiving leather biting into her flesh. It was a symbol of submission – its pain, its bite, an adjunct to the electrifying prospect of handing your body over to another. She took the crop from Eva, shivering as her fingers closed around the heavily bound shaft.

Eva smiled at her. 'Remember how good it feels to let go?' she asked as if reading Laura's thoughts. 'Beating Nabim may not turn you on, but maybe, if you're good, afterwards you and I could get together and finish the job off?' The blonde smiled, eyes alight with mischief. 'You know, I've really missed you, you and my little friend.'

Laura blushed. 'I've rung Gabriel at the Gallery – he's going to come and pick me up for lunch.' She pulled his card out her handbag. 'Do you know him?'

Eva fingered the card and grinned. 'Is there anyone who doesn't? Would you like to make it a threesome?'

Laura nodded. 'Why not?'

Eva handed her the leather suit. 'Great, in that case you'd better try this for size. I had to guess. Oh, and I brought you a pair of fishnets over too – I didn't think they were the sort of thing you'd take on holiday.'

Laura lifted an eyebrow. 'But you would?'

Eva laughed. 'Never go anywhere without them. You'll need a hand with the straps.'

A few minutes later Laura stared in disbelief at her reflection; the body suit was cut from the softest and most supple black leather, a studded flap coming up between her legs covering her sex, while bones in the side seams constricted her waist and pressed her breasts up and out, creating an impressive cleavage.

Along the boning on each side of her torso were a row of straps and buckles which, with Eva's help, she fastened tight. The effect was to pull the suit taut across her ribs, breasts, belly until it fitted her like a second skin. Worn over the fishnets with the long black boots the effect was absolutely stunning.

While Laura had been dressing, Eva had wriggled into a similar outfit and was cradling a whip. Eva handed her a long, towelling robe.

'I think we're just about ready to go and see Nabim,' she said.

'He's expecting us?'

Eva grinned. 'Of course, that's part of the game. He expects to be summoned by the ladies of correction at any time of the night or day – and he has to come when we call, that's part of the pleasure.' She took a small black box out of her handbag and pressed the button on the front.

'Nabim's pager,' she said in answer to Laura's unasked question. 'Follow me.'

Laura glanced around the cabin. 'What if Gabriel shows up while we're out?'

Eva took a sheet of paper from the dressing table. 'We'll leave him a note. Have you got a pen?'

A few minutes later they headed off through the grounds of the hotel to meet Nabim. They went by a circuitous route to avoid being seen. Down through the gardens, out along the beach and then up through a stand of palm trees, Laura kept pace with Eva.

At the back door of a large secluded cabin, Eva lifted a finger to her lips and pulled on her mask; Laura followed suit.

Eva grinned. 'You look fantastic,' she whispered. 'Just don't forget who is the boss. Nabim expects to be dominated, that's what he's paying for. Take your lead from me.'

Before she opened the door, Eva reached into her handbag and pulled out a scarlet lipstick. 'Pucker up,' she whispered to Laura. 'He likes his women to have big red lips.' Laura opened her mouth and let the blonde draw in a thick scarlet line. Eva smiled and handed Laura the stick. 'Now me – after all we are the stuff of which fantasies are made.'

Eva was right, she was stunning. Well over six foot tall in her high, spiked boots, her fantastic body chiselled into an erotic sculpture by the black body suit. The dark leather emphasised every contour, every plane. Laura felt an unexpected ripple of desire in her veins. From behind her mask Eva winked and then unlocked the cabin door.

Laura hadn't considered what she expected to find inside. To her surprise the room was set out like an ordinary sitting room – a rattan sofa and chairs, a low table, drinks cooler, a heavy gilt framed mirror – but Nabim was nowhere in sight. But before she could say anything, the front door of the little cabin flew open and the Asian businessman, breathless and red faced, stumbled inside.

'I'm very sorry,' he began.

Eva brought the handle of her whip down on the table with a mind numbing crack. 'Sorry? What do you mean sorry? How dare you be late. When we call you come – you know the rules. You should have been here waiting for us.'

Nabim nodded, lowering his head so that he appeared submissive and contrite – but Laura had already seen the flash of excitement in his eyes.

Eva poked him with the whip, insinuating the end between the buttons of his expensive, monogrammed silk shirt. 'And still dressed too; you really disappoint me, Nabim. I had told my friend how good you were, and now you've shown me up. I shall have to punish you.' Her voice was crisp and authoritative, her manner certainly inviting no contradiction.

Nabim began to unbutton his shirt.

'Faster!' Eva snapped. Her tone was so sharp that it made Laura jump.

He undressed quickly, carelessly discarding his clothes on the floor. Eva glowered at him. 'How dare you be so untidy,' she roared. The little Asian, naked now except for his boxer shorts, frantically gathered the clothes up, folding them with trembling fingers into a neat pile.

Laura looked on in amazement; Eva stood with her legs apart, arms crossed under her ample breasts, long fingers cradling the whip. When he had finished tidying Nabim fell to his knees and pressed his lips to the toe of her boot. 'Is that better, madam?' he purred.

Eva turned away sharply, leaving him crouched on the bare floor in his underpants.

'No,' she hissed, poking at the waist band of his shorts with the whip. 'Get those off too.'

His tiny hands fluttered to the scrap of paisley cotton and pushed the underpants down. Underneath he was wearing a tight black leather pouch, and even huddled as he was, Laura could see it held his cock tight up against his body. He was already hard and she wondered at the sense of restriction. Eva turned to her.

'I think my slave is ready for you now.'

Laura nodded nervously. 'Stand up,' she said. Her voice was uneven and far from confident.

Eva shot her an encouraging smile. 'You heard what madam said, Nabim. Her boys are obviously far better trained than you – she doesn't even need to raise her voice to get total obedience. I have a long way to go with you. That's why I asked her to join us.'

Nabim clambered to his feet and Laura looked him over, beginning to understand the power of the intricate charade. The man was well built, with a hint of thickening around his waist, his skin was the colour of milky coffee. He was trembling. She could feel his excitement building as her gaze moved over his naked body.

She stroked his chest with the crop, lingering on his nipples and the sparse triangle of hair that lay between them. She sighed, allowing herself to be drawn into the game.

'My boys are so much better trained,' she murmured. Her voice was stronger now and she could see Eva nodding her approval. 'They are always ready and waiting for me, naked, ready to do exactly whatever I command – this specimen is a total disgrace.'

She circled him, letting the tip of the crop record her journey. 'We have a lot of work to do here.' She looked Nabim in the eye, and although he looked away quickly she had seen the flare of desire.

Eva smiled. 'What do you suggest, madam?'

Laura nodded towards the handcuffs that Eva had dropped onto the side table. Nabim had seen the tiny gesture and she knew it had lifted him to another level of expectation.

The Asian fell onto his knees, begging the two women for mercy as Eva snapped the cuffs in place. Laura stared down at the man, remembering how wanton she felt the first day, undressing for Joe Blanco on the beach, how liberating, how glorious it had felt to follow not the course of logic but the path of instinct.

She stepped up in front of Nabim. 'I think you can leave him to me,' she whispered in a throaty voice that she barely recognised as her own.

Nabim looked up at her. She could see the hunger and expectation in his eyes – a polarity of her own. She let the head of the crop trace a path over his cheek and then stepped closer still.

Masked, totally anonymous she was free to take whatever she needed. Her demands, her orders, would be Nabim's stony, pain-filled path to release. He leant forward and pressed his lips to the smooth leather that cradled her sex – an act both of worship and submission. He was hers to command.

Even through the thin hide she could feel the heat of his lips, his mouth breathing life into her. She locked her hands in his hair and jerked him forward so that his face was held flat against her belly and then, just as she felt him begin to relax, she pushed him away again. He looked up at her, eyes as bright as jewels. She got hold of the end of the crop and flexed it into a sprung arc. She was ready to give Nabim exactly what it was he wanted. On the cabin floor the little Asian was trembling.

Belle glanced at the list of the bookings on her desk. Ominously there was a blank space beside Nabim's name.

'Did you tell Eva that Nabim had booked her for eleven o'clock?'

Leo looked blank. 'I thought you said you were going to tell her. I saw him heading over towards the cottage about ten minutes ago.'

Belle groaned. 'Did I? I don't remember.' She looked up at the clock. 'Damn, it's nearly half past. I'd better go over there and tell him. Can you ring Eva and get her over there asap.'

Leo nodded. 'Sure thing – oh and I saw Joe Blanco heading that way too.'

Belle looked heavenwards. 'If we're lucky maybe Joe took a pack of cards with him.'

As she approached the isolated cabin Belle glanced back

205

over her shoulder, hoping she would catch a glimpse of Eva *en route.*

Nabim was a good customer; not only was he easy to please, but he was so delighted to have found somewhere to indulge his fantasies that he frequently recommended O'Malley's to his friends and business contacts.

Joe Blanco was sitting out on the deck, staring into the cabin. Belle stepped up beside him and was about to open the door when something stopped her an instant before her hand fell on the latch. She stared in through the carefully arranged fly screens.

Inside the cabin there were not one but two girls. Nabim was bent over a small table, his wrists secured round one of the table legs. Belle immediately recognised Eva from her stature – but it was a small dark-haired girl in a mask laying on the whip.

The little Asian grunted as another blow exploded across his plump buttocks. His pale golden flesh was criss-crossed with the marks of previous blows. He was panting hard, sweat dripping off his face and chest as he struggled to retain some kind of control.

The slim girl gritted her teeth, diamonds of perspiration had lifted between her breasts – small pert breasts which were barely contained by the leather body suit. Belle stared at her, trying hard to work out which of her girls it was.

Beside Belle, Joe Blanco grinned. 'She's very good, eh? A natural.'

Belle nodded, not wanting to reveal that she had no idea who was servicing Nabim.

In the cabin Eva held out a hand – it seemed they intended to swop over.

The two girls met a few feet from Nabim. He lifted his head straining to watch them. Eva caught hold of her brown-haired companion's jaw and pulled her closer, kissing her full on the mouth. The girl groaned but didn't resist as Eva ran a hand down over her belly, slipping it gently between her legs. Her painted mouth left smears of scarlet in their wake as Eva worked the kiss down over the dark haired girl's shoulders. She pushed the thin leather cups down that supported the girl's breasts and kissed each of her nipples in turn, drawing them deep into her mouth. The lipstick left scarlet petals to frame the pale pink centres.

Nabim groaned in frustration. Eva pulled away and ran her whip over his arched back.

'Silence,' she snapped.

The girl took the whip out of Eva's hand.

'It's all right, I'll finish this, I understand exactly what he wants,' she purred and rounded on Nabim.

An instant later the Asian shrieked out in a mixture of pleasure and pain as the whip exploded across his flesh.

Outside Belle took a step back, mind reeling – she had recognised the voice instantly. There was no doubt about the identity of Nabim's dark-haired dominatrix.

'Laura,' she whispered in complete astonishment.

Joe Blanco looked up, eyes alight with pleasure. 'She is quite superb, isn't she?'

Belle turned away, struggling to make sense of the images and the ideas that flooded her head. Without looking back she hurried through the trees towards the office, her mind in complete turmoil.

Inside the cabin Laura sensed that Nabim was a split second away from release. She had seen and understood the tension building and building in the man's tied body, and now she drew back the whip for one last blow, bringing to a crescendo the passion and pain that would free him.

As it bit into his skin the Asian screamed out and thrust forward, his face contorting as the waves of orgasm careered through him.

Laura closed her eyes, feeling the throbbing pulse echo deep in her own belly.

Chapter 18

Belle flung the office door open and glared at Leo. He didn't move a muscle.

'You little bastard, you knew,' she snapped, reaching deep inside to find words to express the jumble of emotions that threatened to engulf her. 'You knew. You told her. After all I said. How could you?' Tears of pure frustration bubbled up in her eyes. She felt totally betrayed and yet at the same time could hardly believe it would be Leo who had betrayed her.

Still he didn't move or speak. Finally he got to his feet, his expression impassive and neutral.

'I didn't tell her, Belle. You ought to know me better than that by now. Laura found out for herself, almost as soon as she arrived. While we were worrying about keeping O'Malley's business under wraps she was out at Home Cove turning tricks with Danny Collins.'

Belle felt her mouth drop open. 'Danny? Are you serious?'

He nodded. 'Absolutely. She went over to Home Cove with your three-girl takeaway, with Joe Blanco riding shot gun. She met Danny in the bar while Eva and the other girls were upstairs with the clients.' He paused. 'You didn't realise it but Danny had you both over a barrel when you met him in Cairns. He threatened her too.'

Belle shook her head in disbelief. 'My God.'

In the matter of a few minutes her entire life seemed to have shifted.

Leo poured them both a brandy. 'I think it's high time you talked to Laura.'

Belle downed the drink in one. 'You're right.'

In the cabin down by the beach, Eva handed Laura a glass of wine and then settled herself on the rattan sofa. Nabim had left a few minutes earlier, leaving them both a handsome tip. Eva peeled off her leather mask and dropped it to the floor.

'What time did Gabriel say he'd be picking you up?'

Laura's body ached for satisfaction. The intense memories of Nabim's pleasure were fixed in her mind. She felt as if she had been taken out to the very brink of release and then cheated of her prize. The idea of an afternoon in bed with Eva and Gabriel was an electrifying prospect. Eva rolled over and ran a finger down across her belly.

'You know you look great dressed like that – almost good enough to eat. I'm really going to miss you when you go home.' She paused and ran a sugar pink tongue around her lips. 'You could always stay you know. Why don't you come over here with me and let me take that ache away?'

Laura shivered. 'I ought to go up my cabin and see if Gabriel's arrived yet – I told him to drive up along the beach so that he didn't go past Belle's office.'

Eva looked heavenward. 'I left him a note, remember? He'll find us.'

Laura grinned. 'I know, but I'm getting desperate,' she said, surprised that it was so easy to put her hunger into words.

Eva's eyes darkened. 'Don't be desperate. Why don't you let me help?' She reached out and pressed a kiss to Laura's stomach, making her flesh tingle with expectation. It was tempting to surrender to the blonde's invitation.

'Are you sure you two really need me?' said a dark brown voice. Laura looked up at Gabriel, who was making his way in through the back door carrying a picnic hamper over one arm.

He grinned at Eva. 'Trust you, isn't there some sort of unwritten rule about poaching clients?'

Eva giggled. 'Nice to see you too, Gabe. And with lunch as well – God, that girl's got you well trained.'

Despite the banter, Laura felt need bubbling up inside her as raw as a new burn. Nabim's excitement had fired hers. As Gabriel's gaze settled on her she knew he could sense her desire. Without prelude he stepped forward and kissed her hard.

'I'm really glad you called. You look fantastic,' he said in a low purr, running his hands down over the taut black leather bodysuit. Too hungry to reply Laura pulled him closer, tugging at the buttons on his shirt, and was delighted when Eva got up to help her. He grinned and held up his hands in a surrender.

They were like two lionesses who had brought down their prey. Caught up in a feeding frenzy Laura practically ripped the shirt off his back. Gabriel, flattered by their desire, was only too happy to play along as the girls stripped him naked.

He was just as beautiful as Laura remembered him – his body looked as if it had been carved from dark driftwood. She ran her hands over his torso, relishing the sensation of his heat and masculinity under her fingertips. Without a word the two women pulled him down onto the floor, caught up in their compelling need.

Gabriel's magnificent cock was already hard, a dark wraith reaching up towards the sky, the ring that pierced his foreskin a lost jewel. Without hesitation Laura unbuttoned the leather flap that covered her sex. The fishnet was pressed tight against her skin like the bars of a cage. Eva smiled and, reaching forward with her carmine-tipped fingers, ripped the netting away.

The mesh bit into her skin. Laura gasped as the woman's fingers slipped past the shreds and eased inside her. She was already wet, moisture clinging in crystal droplets to the dark hair around her sex. Eva's touch was tantalising, but all too brief, and an instant later she withdrew her finger and outlined the contours of Gabriel lips with it, trailing Laura's fragrant juices on his waiting tongue.

The dark man groaned with pleasure and without a second's hesitation Laura lowered herself onto his shaft. Straddling his slim hips she guided him deep inside her brimming sex, crying out with sheer relief as he pressed home.

The sensation was almost more than she could bear. From

the instant he began to move she could feel the waves of orgasm building up inside her. She ground her hips into him, oblivious to everything except the furious need that demanded to be met.

Anxious not to be left out Eva clambered across Gabriel's chest, facing Laura, and then gently lifted herself up onto her knees so that her sex was over his waiting lips. She undid the fastening at her crotch, her fingers teasing his tongue.

Laura felt as if every sense was alive. Eva kissed her hard, while Laura's hands sought out Eva's breasts, rolling her nipples between her fingertips until they were as hard and ripe as cherry pits.

Deep inside she could feel the cool kiss of Gabriel's cockring pressing against her most secret places. It seemed to take no more than seconds before Laura was at the point of no return. She had never demanded satisfaction more voraciously – and Gabriel's beautiful body answered the call.

On and on the waves rolled through her until she was giddy with pleasure. In the distance she could feel the others following close behind, nipping at her heels, racing towards their own oblivion, gasping to catch her. She felt Gabriel buck, forcing himself deeper and deeper, and then Eva roared with delight, grinding her quim into his face. Finally, there was just stillness, and a warm, satisfied glow in Laura's belly.

Rolling away from Gabriel and Eva, Laura struggled to her feet. Picking up a robe she headed for the door and a breath of air – and wasn't all together surprised to find Joe Blanco sitting outside, sunning himself on the deck.

He smiled and mimed a round of applause. From inside, through the open doors Eva bowed theatrically.

'We aim to please,' Laura said, aware that her pulse was still racing.

'You do, you do! By the way, Belle was down here looking for you a little while ago,' Joe said casually.

Laura stared at him, hardly able to believe what he had said. 'Belle? She was here?'

Joe nodded. 'That's right, she came down when you and Eva were with Nabim. I think she went back to the office – she seemed to be in a real hurry.'

Laura felt her stomach contract and before either Eva, Gabriel or Joe could say anything she ran towards the hotel.

She took the steps up to the office two at a time.

Inside Belle was sitting at the desk and Leo was standing beside the filing cabinet. They looked as if they were caught inside a photograph – both were cradling a drink, both had turned towards the door at the sound of her approach. There was split second when nobody spoke and then Leo lifted his empty glass, 'Would you like a brandy?'

Laura shook her head. She had no idea what she wanted to say.

Belle and Laura's gaze met.

'So how did it go with Nabim?' Belle asked in low even voice.

Laura took a deep breath, struggling to regain her composure. 'Fine – just fine,' she said haltingly.

The tension in the room was stretched between them like a spider web.

It was Belle who broke the deadlock and looked away first. She shook her head, lifting her hands in a gesture of appeal.

'I just don't believe this – it's no good. I don't know what to say to you. I've been breaking my neck to try and keep my business quiet and you knew all the time. Why in God's name didn't you say something sooner? We could have saved ourselves an awful lot of aggravation.'

Laura reddened. 'I didn't know where to start . . . and then when we met Danny Collins in Cairns . . .' she stopped, her voice fading.

The tension between them was gradually ebbing away like smoke blowing on a high wind.

'I'm really sorry,' Laura said in a small voice.

Belle shook her head, a smile playing across her generous mouth. 'Me too – if all this had been out in the open we could have told Danny Collins to go to hell and stayed in Cairns for a few more days.' Suddenly she laughed aloud.

'Little bastard – just wait till I see him. I'm going to wring his scrawny little neck.'

Leo picked up a message pad from the top of the filing cabinet.

'By the way I meant to tell you earlier, Laura. Two messages for you. Gareth rang from England. He wants you to ring him about the interview he's set up.' Leo pulled a face. 'Something to do with data processing? He left his office number in case you hadn't got it with you.' Leo glanced down at the note. 'He said he thought you really ought to buy a new outfit – maybe you could find something while you were on holiday, preferably black.'

Face impassive, Laura let her robe fall open, underneath she was wearing the tight leather suit that she had worn to whip Nabim.

To her relief, Belle threw back her head and roared with laughter.

Leo looked heavenwards and then continued. 'And Gabriel rang to say he might be a little late for lunch.'

Belle stared at Laura. 'Sweet Jesus. You know Gabriel too?'

Laura nodded.

'But he said he'll bring a picnic,' Leo concluded.

Laura couldn't bring herself to tell them that she had already seen Gabriel.

Belle shook her head again. 'The odd thing is that when I first saw you I knew and tried to ignore what my instincts told me.' She paused and glanced around the office. 'As you're part of the family firm now maybe I'll take you up on the offer of sorting out the office. Leo, why don't you go over to the bar and get us a bottle of champagne.'

When he had gone Belle got to her feet and embraced Laura gently. 'I wish we could have found a way to talk about this sooner. I hated lying to you. I really wanted to tell you about O'Malley's – in some ways you remind me so much of myself.' She paused. 'And I wanted to ask you something. I know it's a big step, but would you consider staying here with me? In Australia? O'Malley's really could do with another pair of hands. And I've always thought I could use a good business manager.'

Laura stared at her. 'Are you serious?'

Belle nodded. 'Absolutely. I've been thinking about how perfect it would be to have you here from the minute I laid eyes on you. I was just too uptight to say anything. I didn't know how to start.'

Laura glanced down at the note Leo had given her, eyes moving over Gareth's orders, neatly transcribed alongside the telephone number. She was surprised by Belle's offer, and yet in an instant she saw the alternative with perfect clarity – a life with Gareth or a man like him, a cold unfulfilling existence built on propriety and a sensible business suit, pensions and pay rises.

Laura blinked back the tears, wondering if the girl who had been carried along with Gareth's plans had ever really existed. What *was* certain was that she wasn't that girl now.

She looked up at Belle and then screwed the note into a tight ball.

'I'd love to,' she said, dropping the paper into the bin.

SEVEN DAYS

Adult Fiction for Lovers

J J Duke

Erica's arms were spread apart and she pulled against the silk bonds – not because she wanted to escape but to savour the experience. As the silk bit into her wrists, a surge of pure pleasure shot through her, so intense that the darkness behind the blindfold turned crimson . . .

Erica is not exactly an innocent abroad. On the other hand, she's never been in New York before. This trip could make or break her career in the fashion business. It could also free her from the inhibitions that prevent her exploring her sensual needs.

She has a week for her work commitments – and a week to take her pleasure in the world's wildest city. Now's her chance to make her most daring dreams come true. She's on a voyage of erotic discovery and she doesn't care if things get a little crazy. After all, it can only last seven days . . .

0 7472 5094 4

More Erotic Fiction from Headline Liaison

VOLUPTUOUS VOYAGE

Lacey Carlyle

The stranger came up behind her and slid a hand round her waist while the other glided over her breasts. Lucy stared out into the darkness as he fondled her. She knew she should be outraged but somehow she wasn't . . .

Fleeing from her American fiancé, the bloodless Boyd, after discovering he's more interested in her bank account than her body, Lucy meets an enigmatic stranger on the train to New York. Their brief sensual encounter leaves her wanting more, so with her passions on fire Lucy embarks for England accompanied by her schoolfriend, Faye.

They sail on a luxurious ocean liner, the *SS Aphrodite*, whose passenger list includes some of the most glamorous socialites of the 1930s. Among them are the exiled White Russians, Count Andrei and Princess Sonya, and the two friends are soon drawn into a dark and decadent world of bizarre eroticism . . .

0 7472 5145 2

If you enjoyed this book here is a selection of other bestselling Adult Fiction titles from Headline Liaison